WHEN HEROES FLEW

WHERE THE DAWN COMES UP LIKE THUNDER

H.W. "BUZZ" BERNARD

SEVERN RIVER

PUBLISHING

Severn River Publishing
www.SevernRiverBooks.com

ISBN: 978-1-64875-611-5 (Paperback)

ALSO BY H.W. "BUZZ" BERNARD

The When Heroes Flew Series

When Heroes Flew

The Shangri-La Raiders

The Roof of the World

Down a Dark Road

Where the Dawn Comes Up Like Thunder

Black Thursday

Standalone Books

Eyewall

Plague

Supercell

Blizzard

Cascadia

To find out more about H.W. "Buzz" Bernard and his books, visit

severnriverbooks.com

In memory of my brother, John Rodger Bernard

An' the dawn comes up like thunder outer China 'crost the Bay!

—from "Mandalay" by Rudyard Kipling

1

100th Station Hospital
New Delhi, India
May 9, 1944

I decided if I stopped believing in love, I'd stop believing in life.

So I clung to the conviction that Eve still loved me. That her abrupt departure—without a word of notice to me—from the hospital where she'd been assigned as an army nurse was due to a military exigency and not meant as a metaphoric Dear John letter.

"She didn't leave me a note, a message, anything?" I asked the duty nurse, a round little army lieutenant with round eyeglasses and a mouth that seemed to curve into a perfectly round "O" whenever she stopped speaking.

"I'm sorry, Major Shepherd, no. She left quite suddenly. She said she'd received orders from Eastern Air Command to report immediately to their headquarters, but to not mention it to anyone."

"Except you?"

She lowered her head. "No, sir," she mumbled. "She shouldn't even have told me. But we'd become good friends." She lifted her head and looked directly at me. "She told me what you two had been through. You know, in Burma." She paused. A flicker of compassion appeared in her gaze. "That must have been . . . horrible."

No, horrible would have been okay. What happened to Eve Johannsen and me six months ago in a Naga village perched on a remote mountaintop in the northern Burma rainforest was worse than horrible. An attack on the village by a Jap patrol had come close to costing both of us our lives. If it had, I suppose our reward might have been a free pass to heaven. Instead, we walked away with military awards—Purple Hearts and Silver Stars. Well, I limped away. But that's another story.

I nodded at the tiny, plump nurse, said thank you, and stepped back outside into the pre-monsoonal, blast-furnace heat of New Delhi. The weather officer in me told me it had to be at least a hundred degrees, but it could well have been a hundred and ten. What's ten degrees among friends when you're a pig on a spit?

I stood in the loggia of the barracks-like, stucco-walled hospital building and reined in my emotions. I swiped a forearm across my face and brushed away freshets of perspiration. And I had a chance to witness that old saw about mad dogs and Englishmen come to life. Groups of military personnel trudged beneath the midday sun: US Army servicemen, Indian Army troops—including Brits, Indians, and Gurkhas—Royal Air Force pilots, and a few Aussies and Kiwis in their wide-brimmed slouch hats.

Outside the stone-walled gate of the hospital, also known as the "American hospital," a couple of India's "sacred" cows strolled past, leaving turd-shaped calling cards in the middle of the street. The street itself seemed a Mixmaster of rickshaws, bicycles, ox-drawn carts, and British army lorries.

Gradually, the overpowering odors of life in New Delhi drifted into the hospital area. The more pleasant smells of baking naan, bubbling curry, and roasting chicken mingled with the gag-inducing stench of decaying garbage, open sewers, and human waste to produce an aroma unique to India. Not one that would have been mistaken as wafting from an American breakfast of fresh-brewed coffee, buttermilk flapjacks, and scrambled eggs.

Right now, though, I didn't give a damn about overpowering stinks, revered cows, or broiling heat. I needed to get to Calcutta and Eastern Air Command. Ironically, Calcutta was where I'd just come from after a long rehabilitation following an airmail special delivery from a Jap mortar in Burma—a blast that punched a hole in the back of my skull and managed to blow away enough bone in my right leg to make it, after extensive surgery, a tad shorter than the left one. The doc told me I'd walk the rest of my life with a "list and a limp." And that I would never fly again.

You see, I'm not only a weather officer assigned to the 10th Weather Squadron, I also fly—well, flew—C-47s, Gooney Birds, and C-46s, Ol' Dumbos, between India and China over the Hump, the Himalayas. My last flight didn't go well. Eve and I had to bail out of the Gooney I was piloting on a special medevac mission over Burma, and things went downhill from there. You know, all the usual—Japs, headhunters, snakes, leeches, tigers, incessant rain, and on and on.

Plus, at the time, Eve and I really didn't like each other. We didn't necessarily hate one another, but pretty damn close. To be honest, it wasn't all her fault . . . nor totally mine. Among the guys, she had the reputation of being "distant," and in one of our early encounters, I referred to her—probably with the help of some South African brandy—as the Ice Queen.

"What?" she had snapped, pinning me in a steely glare.

"Gosh," I replied, "you know, we hit it off so well, maybe we should grab a drink together sometime."

"Yeah, right after the war ends."

"You'll be last on my list."

"Fine. You keep your hands in your pockets and your pecker in your pants and we'll get along famously."

Such an exchange did not augur well for true romance.

At that point, I recall thinking I'd never met such a woman . . . one with a Rita Hayworth body and a Lizzie Borden personality.

Yet, despite our history of acerbic verbal exchanges, in the Burmese jungle things changed. We discovered we each bore badly damaged souls and that respect and care can heal even the deepest of wounds. I told her I'd lost my wife, Trish, to leukemia. That I had held Trish's hand in Letterman General Hospital in San Francisco as she took her last breath. And that after that, I had gone off to war.

Eve revealed to me she had lost her fiancé in the attack on Pearl Harbor. And that she, too, had grasped her loved one's hand as he passed. She also told me that following her loss, a senior US Army officer had offered her "comfort" by forcing himself on her—raping her—then telling her it's what she needed and that she would be forever grateful. He also reminded her if she ever accused him of "anything," it would be his word against hers, and that a field grade officer would always win that battle against a second lieutenant, which she was at the time.

So there we were, two guardian angels with broken wings trying to care for one another.

And we fell in love.

She reconfirmed our bond when she came to visit me during my rehab at the hospital in Calcutta.

"You still wanna be my gal?" I had said.

"If you want one with holes in her chest," she responded. In the same mortar attack that had sliced and diced me, she'd taken a load of shrapnel that a cardiothoracic surgeon in New Delhi had had to deal with.

"Well," I said, "it looks like the essential equipment was spared. Now you have to decide if you want a guy with a hole in his head . . . and a gimpy gait."

Her answer had been quick, simple, and sincere. "I do."

Following that meeting, we continued our recoveries, me in Calcutta, she in New Delhi. After she became well enough to work again, she returned to active duty. She sent me a letter telling me she'd been assigned to the same hospital where she'd carried out her rehab. And that I'd better get my butt there as soon as humanly possible . . . post-recovery.

So I knew without a doubt her sudden departure from that facility had not been an attempt to fire an arrow through my heart. It had been driven by something else, and I sure as hell was going to find out what and why, and where she was.

The commander of the 10th Weather Squadron, Colonel Dick Ellsworth, had procured a waiver for me to continue on active duty, too, despite my injuries—serving as squadron operations officer.

Ellsworth said he understood I wanted to see Eve again, but that he wanted me back at the unit's headquarters ASAP. That would work out just fine because of the squadron's location.

The weather shop, along with Eastern Air Command, had just relocated from New Delhi to Hastings Mill, a short distance north of Calcutta. That meant I could simultaneously resume my duties *and* spend some time harassing folks at EAC to find out where Eve had gone.

Thus, I decided my next order of business would be to contact Colonel Ellsworth and request that *Betsy*, his C-47, make a trip to New Delhi and pick up his squadron ops officer, me. I'd first met Ellsworth, *Betsy*, and her pilot, Major Tex Albaugh, the previous summer at Dum Dum Airport in Calcutta. There, they'd picked me up and spirited me off to far northeast India, known as Assam, where I began my adventures flying over the Hump.

At any rate, no more flying for me now, at least as a pilot, but I knew my work for the Tenth, despite it being a noncombat unit, would be far beyond a Three Stooges schtick, which was what some senior officers thought of weather support. I'd witnessed certain flag officers, specifically Major General Claire Chennault of Flying Tigers fame, refer to us derisively as "balloon blowers," despite the fact we carried a battleship-load of responsibilities.

We supported three different air commands—the Tenth and Fourteenth Air Forces plus the Air Transport Command's India-China Wing—and provided weather services for a vast region of the globe, twelve million square miles to be precise.

Our reach covered lands and countries most of us in the squadron had only read about, let alone known anything of their meteorology. We staked claims as far west as India's borders with Afghanistan and Persia, as far east as the East China Sea, as far north as the borders of Outer Mongolia, and as far south as the Cocos Islands in the Indian Ocean . . . in the southern hemisphere.

Not only did we have to deal with attitudes such as General Chennault's in China, but with those of Colonel Thomas Hardin, who headed the Hump operations for the India-China Wing. I came to think of Hardin—with whom I'd had a personal run-in—as Colonel Hard-On, especially after he wired the Wing commander that "the weather service in this sector is the only thing worse than communications." He later gave us the middle-finger salute when he proclaimed "there is no weather on the Hump."

Meaning American aviators would tackle the India-China route regardless of meteorological conditions.

Well, let *him* try to provide weather support for an area largely devoid of data and blanketed by vast deserts, thousands of square miles of ocean, and saber-toothed mountains that jutted into stratosphere. Yeah, there *is* weather on the Hump, and it had killed a lot of good men. That's why the flight route over the Himalayas had been dubbed the Aluminum Trail.

And that's where my best buddy, Captain Pete Zimmerman—I called him Zim—rests in eternity. We'd bonded at an air base called Chabua in Assam. He took me on my first flight over the Hump. It turned out we'd both grown up in the Pacific Northwest, I in the Idaho Panhandle, he in Oregon's Willamette Valley. We'd both graduated from the University of Washington in Seattle, and we both loved fishing. We agreed that after the war we'd spend our idle time, as much as we could whittle out, fishing for steelhead and salmon in the twisting rivers that plied the rugged Coast Range of Oregon. But for Zim, there would be no "after the war."

Zim had also fostered a love of poetry in me, teaching me about Rudyard Kipling and "Mandalay," and William Blake and "The Tyger." Tragically, Zim had flown off into a land where "the dawn comes up like thunder"—Kipling—and not returned.

Damn the people who said there was no weather on the Hump. Though I understood such sentiments focused on the mission, not the men. Still . . .

I stared at the kanju trees outside the hospital grounds. Their leaves wiggled in a hot breeze, and I thought of the losses I'd already absorbed in my brief life: Trish, Zim, a Colonel Willis—the medevac patient I'd had to sacrifice when I lost my C-47 over Burma—and now Eve. Well, Eve probably wasn't lost, but she was gone. And I would not stop believing she loved me. And I would not stop looking for her.

I felt a flurry of tears trace damp trails through the patina of dust that coated my face. Unmanly, I know. But, damn, I'd earned the right.

2

Hastings Mill, India
May 12, 1944

Tex Albaugh, after piloting *Betsy* through stacks of puffy cumulus that made for a rollercoaster-like ride—no extra charge—delivered me to Dum Dum Airport in Calcutta by early afternoon. From Dum Dum, Tex and I caught a ride in a jeep to the sprawling Hastings Air Base about seven miles northwest of the city on the west bank of the Hooghly River.

The Hooghly, I found out later, is a distributary of the mighty Ganges River. The Hooghly flows south from the Ganges in far eastern India and empties into the Bay of Bengal just south of Calcutta.

After we arrived at the Hastings complex, I decided to make a quick visit to Tenth Weather Squadron headquarters—which sat immediately adjacent to Hastings—and let Colonel Ellsworth know I'd arrived. To say I was impressed by the headquarters, at least the structure, would have been a bit like Emperor Hirohito telling Jimmy Doolittle after the 1942 bombing raid on Tokyo, "Ya caught us a bit off guard there, partner."

The Tenth's new home sat in a palatial white house on a shaded spread of land of generous size. The house, I guessed, must have belonged to a high-caste Indian family before the war. I mounted a flight of wide steps to the main floor. There, a bearded and turbaned Sikh—the ranking servant of the quarters, I presumed—greeted me with a broad smile and subtle bow. He stooped, dusted off my shoes with a white towel, then slung it over his left shoulder.

"May I prepare you a drink, good sir?" he said in excellent English with a British accent.

He walked to a well-stocked bar, pulled a glass off a shelf, and proceeded to wipe it down . . . with the same towel he'd just used to remove the grime from my shoes.

"Perhaps later," I said. "But thank you. I'm here to see Colonel Ellsworth."

"Ah, yes, very good, sir." Again the big smile. "Please, follow me."

I limped after him as he led me through a huge, high-ceilinged main room where there appeared to be closed-off apartment-like structures in each corner.

"Officers' quarters," the Sikh explained.

I followed him down a long hall lined with offices. The doors of the building were all louvered, and overhead ceiling fans, rotating at leisurely paces, kept the place reasonably comfortable even in the sweltering heat.

The Sikh servant reached a door at the end of the hall, knocked, and announced, "Colonel, sir, a distinguished guest to see you."

"Yes, yes, Santokh," Ellsworth said, "please, send him in."

I entered. Colonel Ellsworth stepped from behind his desk and greeted me with a hearty handshake and slap on the back. "Rod, it's great to see you again. I've been counting the days. You look well."

"There's a little gimp in my gait, sir. But I feel fine." Not entirely true, but I thought it better not to go into my personal feelings with my boss. At least initially.

"Have a seat."

"Thank you, Colonel—"

"Come on," Ellsworth interrupted, "it's Dick, remember?"

"Yes, sir." I seated myself in a comfortable leather-covered armchair. "Quite a place you've got here."

He smiled with his trademark easy grin. Sporting a lanky build and thick, dark hair, he looked ten years younger than his true thirty-three. "As soon as I heard General Stratemeyer, commander of the Army Air Forces in this theater, was moving the headquarters from New Delhi to Calcutta, Tex and I hightailed it over here and found this place. It's a former general officer's quarters. We're sitting on about two acres of land. The main base, next door, covers about forty." He paused and called for Santokh, then said to me, "How about some afternoon tea?"

I nodded. "In cups cleaned by—"

The colonel cut me off with a laugh. "We're still trying to teach Santokh and his minions a few things, but I can assure you the cups will not have been cleansed with a shoe rag."

"Then, yes, I'd like some afternoon tea."

"Back to Hastings while we wait. It's a former jute mill. Was the largest under one roof in the world. Tons of machinery had to be removed and relocated, and now, along with the mill and its ancillary buildings, Hastings is probably the most modern Army Air Forces headquarters there is. It's home to six thousand military personnel and probably another four thousand civilians, mainly Indians who do clerical and domestic work."

I whistled softly.

"And when you get over there, you'll see it has an outdoor theater, all kinds of sports fields, a dispensary, an officers' club, an enlisted men's club, a couple of open-air dance pavilions along the banks of the Hooghly, and a PX stocked as well as any in the States."

"Sounds swell. I think I'll be happy spending my time here rather than in a Burmese jungle." I smiled. Ellsworth didn't. That should have been a warning to me, but it didn't register at the time.

The tea arrived. While we sipped from the steaming cups—hadn't they heard of iced tea in India?—I told Ellsworth, at his request, about my lengthy recovery and rehab at the hospital in Calcutta. I finished up by letting him know I got around pretty well now without the use of a cane, that the blackouts I'd suffered in the immediate aftermath of my head wound had virtually ceased, and though I still got slammed by throbbing headaches once in a while, a couple of APCs—pills with aspirin, phenacetin, and caffeine—would usually handle them.

He nodded. "And how about your friend, the nurse? I'm sorry, I don't recall her name."

"Eve," I said softly. "Captain Genevieve Johannsen." I'd hoped he wouldn't ask me about her, but that was the colonel. He knew Eve and I had a "thing." And he really did care about his men and their families and loved ones. Besides, I knew I might need his help if I were to make any inroads in my inquiries about her at Eastern Air Command. So I told him how she'd suddenly dropped off my personal radar.

Ellsworth sat with his elbows on his desk and his hands steepled in front of him as he listened. After I'd finished, he picked up the handset of a telephone that sat on his desk.

"Eastern Air Command," he said into it. He waited a bit until someone on the other end answered. A brief conversation ensued. After it ended, Ellsworth spoke to me.

"I spoke to Brigadier General Leonard Stone's aide and arranged a meeting for you with Stone at seventeen hundred hours today. He's kind of unofficially in charge, at least temporarily, of personnel movements within the command. There's a lot going on in-theater now, a lot of bodies being shuffled around, especially since a new bomber command is being stood up."

"Oh?"

"It's called the Twentieth Bomber Command, based at Kharagpur about seventy miles west-southwest of here. B-29s."

"B-29s. Wow." I'd never seen one, only heard about them. They were supposed to be the most technologically advanced aircraft ever produced. They were called Superfortresses, the follow-on to the legendary B-17 Flying Fortresses. The Superfort was rumored to be able to fly at over thirty thousand feet—it was fully pressurized—have a range of over three thousand miles, and carry a massive bombload.

"They're going after the Japs in China, I assume." I meant it as more of a question than a statement.

Ellsworth remained silent for a moment, then shook his head. "This is just between you and me. You need to know, because the Tenth will be providing weather support for them. They're going after the Japs on mainland Japan."

"Japan? From India? Wow." Japan hadn't been touched by American bombs since Doolittle's visit in early '42, over two years ago.

"Not directly from India. The bombers will stage out of India but launch from a complex of bases we're building in China around a place called Chengtu. It's in western China, out of reach—we hope—of the Japs in occupied eastern China."

"Not to be a naysayer, sir, but you mean we're gonna have to provide forecasts from China across the Yellow Sea into Japan when we already struggle to do that for flights over the Hump?"

"Don't you just love challenges?" Ellsworth said with a straight face. But I knew a grin hid behind it.

"Of course, Dick. That's why I signed up for this chickenshit outfit."

Ellsworth laughed. "You need some rest. I've got you set up in the quarters in the southeast corner of this building. You may have noticed the billets when you came in. Santokh will show you the way to yours. Get settled. Go see General Stone. Then meet me back here tomorrow morning, and we'll go over your next assignment . . . in this chickenshit outfit."

"My next assignment? I won't be staying here?" I was puzzled.

"Your experience is invaluable."

Whatever that meant.

After I got settled in my quarters—quite a step, or three, up from the thatch-roofed *basha* with woven bamboo walls I'd subsisted in when flying out of Chabua—I headed over to Hastings Air Base and the headquarters of Eastern Air Command.

The base proved impressive. The old jute mill structures had been converted into military buildings that now sat—along with a sprawl of tents —amidst scattered stands of tropical trees and tall, skinny palms. Hastings seemed to have all the bustle of a small American town. It reminded me of home. At least the ambience did, not the weather.

While Calcutta proved almost as toasty as New Delhi as both cities waited for the return of the monsoon rains, the fact Calcutta sat adjacent to the Bay of Bengal allowed shirt-drenching humidity—even during this so-called dry season—to permeate everything. By the time I reached Eastern Air Command headquarters, I felt like a rag doll that had been left outside in a rainstorm.

A large-lettered sign above an arched entrance, one of many, to what looked like an old mill building constructed of concrete, let me know I'd arrived at the right place.

Headquarters
ARMY AIR FORCES
India Burma Theater
&

EASTERN AIR COMMAND

The interior of the headquarters contained a vast sea of desks at which dozens of personnel sat laboring diligently at whatever a headquarters' staff needed to do to support a major air command. A corporal sitting at a desk near the entrance popped to attention when he saw me and asked how he could assist. I told him, and he pointed to a far end of the building along which a hallway ran.

Offices set against the exterior wall of the building lined the hallway. Signs at the entrance to each office identified the occupant or function to be found within. At the end of the hallway in a corner office I found General Stone's lair. His aide, a Lieutenant Breckenridge, beckoned me in. He knocked on another door in the office, stuck his head in, said something, then spoke to me.

"The general says he'll be with you in just a few moments. Please, sir, have a seat." He gestured at a wooden chair outfitted with colorful cushions displaying images of Indian elephants woven into them. Semi-comfortable. The wait, as the general promised, proved to be short.

I entered his office, stood at attention, and identified myself. "Major Rodger Shepherd, US Army Air Forces. Thank you for seeing me, sir."

The general studied me. The name plaque on his desk announced: BRIGADIER GENERAL LEONARD STONE, JCS, XX BOMBER COMMAND LIASON. Holy cow, the guy was from the Joint Chiefs of Staff. As he held me in his gaze, I managed my own once-over of him. I had to admit, even from my male standpoint, he seemed a handsome guy—square-jawed, tanned, close-cropped silver hair. On his uniform he wore both aviator and paratrooper wings. He appeared approachable, but his inspection of me seemed stern and not necessarily friendly.

Finally, he spoke. "As you were. Army, you say, not navy?"

"Sir?"

"You're standing with a slight list to starboard. Not exactly what we expect of army field grade officers."

The bastard didn't crack a smile. He wasn't kidding around with me.

"Sorry, sir," I replied. "War wound."

"I see. Maybe you shouldn't be in the service at all. Cripples aren't necessarily going to help us."

"I've got a waiver, sir," I said through a clenched jaw.

He leaned back in his desk chair. He didn't ask me to sit. "All right, Major Shepherd-with-a-waiver, why are you here? I hope it's a matter I can deal with quickly. As you can see, I've got a few other things on my plate." He swept his arm back and forth in front of him, gesturing at stacks of paperwork that rose like the Himalayas from his desk and two adjacent tables. I had a feeling my request wasn't going to go well.

"I'm looking for a nurse."

"Christ on a crutch, you and ten thousand other GIs. Does it look like I'm running a dating service here, Major?"

Wow. Was this guy a piece of work. I grit my teeth, told myself to tread softly and try to avoid stepping on my own poncho. "It's not like that, General. We served in Burma together, were both wounded in a Jap attack, went through rehab in India, then she suddenly disappeared. We'd become . . . well, good friends, so I was surprised when she dropped out of sight without telling me. I heard she'd been told to report here, to Eastern Air Command, and that you were, at least for the moment, in charge of over-seeing personnel movements within the command."

Stone issued a long sigh, as if he were bored or put out that I'd come to him with my dilemma. "Do you have any idea how much is going on in this theater, Major, how many personnel we're shifting around, how many new troops we're greeting every day? Hundreds. We're standing up a new command, we're increasing the number of flights over the Hump, and we've got Generals Stilwell and Merrill and their men trying to take back northern Burma while the Limeys punch into central Burma. And you're asking me about an individual nurse?"

I hoped it was a rhetorical question and elected to keep my mouth shut.

The general continued pontificating. "I sign dozens of orders every day. I certainly wouldn't remember doing so for a nurse, or even a group of nurses. But I tell you what, in deference to your Purple Heart, I'll take a quick look for you, Major. Give me her name and rank and about when you think her orders were issued."

"It would have been around the first of May for a Captain Genevieve Johannsen."

"Okay, hang tight. Smoke 'em if you got 'em while I make a quick search." He scraped his chair back, grumbling, and stalked out of the room, presumably to scour a records storage area.

I wondered why he didn't have his aide look, but maybe he wasn't a delegator. I didn't have any cigarettes, so just remained standing and surveyed the office while I waited. It appeared pretty stark. No family pictures. Just official photos—award and promotion ceremonies, and him with other flag officers—and a dozen or so plaques and framed memorabilia. Also a world map with pushpins jammed in it, I suppose indicating all the locations he'd visited. A number of bases in the States, Alaska, Hawaii, Canada, North Africa, Crete, Great Britain, Bermuda, Australia, and, of course, China, Burma, and India. He'd been around.

Twenty minutes elapsed before he returned and seated himself while I remained standing. "Sorry, Major," he said, "no joy. I went through our files starting with late April up until now. I could find no orders with Captain Johannsen's name. Nothing ordering her here or elsewhere in the theater."

Damn. I felt gut punched. "Sorry I wasted your time, sir," I mumbled.

"If I may be frank, Major, you wouldn't be the first guy an army nurse wanted to disappear on. Get my drift? Look, why don't you head over to the O-Club. We've got more than our share of WACs and nurses and even a few civilian teachers on this base."

"Yes, sir. Terrific idea." *What an asshole.* "Thank you for your time."

He nodded, then said, "Good luck, Major Shepherd . . . and stay away from Jap mortars in the future."

I beat a hasty exit. And followed the general's advice. I headed toward the officers' club. I knew exactly how to handle my setbacks and disappointments. Same way I did in Assam when I got blitzed in Chabua one night, fired a flare gun down the length of my *basha*, and set it on fire. I hoped the Hastings Club would be well stocked with Jim Beam. The hell with nurses and WACs.

3

Hastings Air Base
Near Calcutta, India
May 12, 1944

The club turned out to be jumping. Not what I wanted . . . but should have expected. Friday night. Nickel drinks, lots of gals—WACs and Red Cross dollies—and a dance band called The Monswooners. Playing at an outdoor pavilion, they were actually pretty good, belting out numbers like "Don't Sit Under the Apple Tree," "Down South Camp Meetin'," and "At Last."

But I didn't give a damn about dancing. Dinner? Maybe. The dining room looked inviting. Indian waiters decked out in fancy turbans and long, white jackets bound with colorful sashes rushed about serving steaks—I wondered if the sacred cow population around the base had dropped—and mashed potatoes and just about anything else American you could think of. No, what I really wanted was a drink. Several.

So, succumbing to my baser instincts, I made my way through the Friday-night throng of officers to a bamboo bar backed by a zebra-striped wall festooned with pinups. I secured a Jim Beam, then, beneath a thin stratus of cigarette smoke, went in search of a quiet—relative term—corner of the club. I found a vinyl-cushioned chrome lounge chair resting against a wall opposite the bar and plopped into it. My intent had been to savor the initial round of getting reacquainted with Jim, but that lasted only about a minute. I signaled one of the Indian waiters who stood nearby and requested a refill. "Two," I said, and held up two fingers so there would be no mistake.

I slowed my intake of the two follow-ons. The swirl of the boisterous conversations around me and the echoes of the swing music from the pavilion gave way to a soothing buzz within my head as the straight bourbon whiskey did its thing. My thoughts, which remained initially coherent, drifted back to my encounter with General Leonard Stone.

I resented his implication that Eve and I had somehow just had a fling. *"If I may be frank, Major, you wouldn't be the first guy an army nurse wanted to disappear on. Get my drift?"* What Eve and I had had—still had, I believed—was hardly a typical wartime affair. In fact, looking back on it, our coming together had been anything but classically romantic. In a jungle filled with bugs and animals intent on eating us, Japs determined to kill us, and natives casting covetous glances at our heads, we'd come to genuinely care and look out for one another.

We'd been scratched and bloodied, covered in insect bites, outfitted in tattered and muddied uniforms, and smelled like barnyard animals, yet we'd fallen in love. Because our souls had reached out to each other's. But now Eve was gone, and I wanted to find out why and where. No, what I wanted to find was Eve herself.

"Rod?"

I looked up. Colonel Ellsworth stood next to me. I started to get up.

"No," he said, and gestured with his hand for me to remain seated. "You look comfy. Everything okay?"

"Never better, sir."

"Was General Stone able to shed any light on what might have happened to Captain Johannsen?"

"No, sir. Dead end."

"Well, I'm sorry. Care to join me and a couple of the fellas for dinner?"

"Thank you for the invitation . . . Dick. But I think I'll just hang out here. Got some thinking to do."

"Very good. I'll see you in the morning." He started to walk away, but stopped and turned and eyed my drink . . . drinks. "Pace yourself, Rod."

I nodded. I knew I was good at that. I lifted my glass in a unilateral toast. "To a good evening, Colonel." Then I signaled the waiter for two more.

While I waited for my refueling, I dwelt further on my meeting with the general. A couple of questions bubbled into my rapidly clouding mind, questions for which I had no answers and that made me pretty damn circumspect of ol' Lenny. Why had he, himself, gone to see if he could find any orders with Eve's name on them instead of dispatching his aide? And how did he know I'd been hit by a mortar? I'd never mentioned that to him.

My replacement drinks arrived, and I went to work on them, pacing myself as Colonel Ellsworth had suggested. By late evening, I figured I'd had enough. Five. I found myself lost in an alcoholic haze. Exactly where I wanted to be. No worries. No concerns. No sorrows.

I wove my way back to my quarters, amazed I was able to acquire my target VFR. I mounted the steps to the Tenth's headquarters, but the effort proved taxing. The steps seemed to undulate as if ocean swells rippled through them. Weird. I stumbled once or twice but made it to the entrance.

Inside, the Sikh servant, Santokh, and his twin brother greeted me. I didn't recall him having a twin. I ran a zigzag course to my room and pushed through the double doors . . . I didn't recall double doors, either. I think Santokh yelled something at me, but wasn't sure.

I crash-landed on my bed. I felt a body squirm and jerk beneath mine and whisper something in my ear. My God, Eve. I'd found Eve.

Sure I had.

Headquarters Tenth Weather Squadron
Hastings Air Base
May 13, 1944

I awoke the next morning, late, with a bushel of cotton in my mouth, a bass drum thundering in my head, and a blue-black bruise blemishing my left cheek. I quickly shed the uniform I'd slept in—it looked as though it had been trampled by a water buffalo—pulled on a fresh one, and beat feet for Colonel Ellsworth's office.

He looked up when I entered and gestured for me to sit. "Nice job pacing yourself," he said, unsmiling.

"Sorry, sir."

"You entered Captain Reilly's billets and dive-bombed him in bed. Got a right hook to your cheek in retaliation. Then the captain and Santokh wrangled you into your own quarters, tossed you into bed, and left you to sleep it off."

"I'm sorry—"

"You said that already. Free pass this time. One-time good deal. Now tell me what happened with General Stone."

I did. Ellsworth listened intently. After I'd finished, he said, "I understand the reason for your bender now. But again, no more. I'm sorry I can't allow you additional time to search for Eve, but we're still fighting a war, and I've got an assignment for you."

I nodded, even though nodding hurt my head.

Ellsworth stood and walked to a map behind his desk. "We're going to insert some weather observation teams into the Naga Hills." He pointed at northern Burma and the mountainous rainforest where Eve and I had almost lost our lives a little over six months ago.

"Really?" I mumbled, my hangover-fogged brain unable to come up with a more astute response.

"We need all the data we can gather out of that region to support what are known as Long-Range Penetration Groups—guerrilla teams— operating in the area. There's the outfit known as Merrill's Marauders, Americans led by General Frank Merrill, and the Chindits, British and Gurkha troops that were trained and led by a Brigadier Orde Wingate. Unfortunately, Wingate was killed in a plane crash a couple of months ago."

I struggled to focus. "So these guerrilla groups, I assume, are supporting Allied efforts to recapture occupied Burma?"

"Yes. And the only supplies and reinforcements they're getting are via airdrops. Colonel Philip Cochran's Air Commandos are taking care of that.

So, you can see why it's absolutely essential we know what the weather is doing in northern Burma."

Ellsworth returned to his desk chair and looked directly at me. "I want you to accompany the weather teams' initial deployment into the Naga Hills."

That statement cleared the fog in my brain pretty fast. "Really, Dick? You know I damn near lost my life there."

"But you managed to come out alive. That's the kind of experience I need to help get our weather guys set up there."

This, I decided, would require a return trip to the bamboo bar tonight.

"Don't even think about it," Ellsworth said, a smile creeping across his face.

The guy's a mind reader, too? I stared out a window of the office at the Hooghly River. A variety of small craft, many rickety and appearing barely seaworthy, plowed up and down the sluggish waterway. Most were unmotorized, but a few—coal powered, perhaps—belched black smoke from small vertical stacks. A shallow-draft, open-air boat, the Hastings-Bengal-Wellington ferry, maneuvered into a pier at the base and disgorged about a half dozen GIs. I wondered if I could sneak aboard one of the junks, or whatever the Indians called them, and drift off into the Bay of Bengal, where I could get eaten by sharks . . . or meet some other more merciful fate rather than being dumped into the Burmese jungle again.

"You aren't going to have to stay with them," Ellsworth said, breaking my foolish musing and referring, I assume, to the weather teams. "I just need you to introduce them to the Nagas, hopefully the same guys you were with when we yanked you out of there last October. We've got the coordinates of the village, so you should be able to find your way back."

"The Nagas might not be real happy to see me again, since my last visit there unleashed an Armageddon on their home."

"You gotta remember, Rod, the Japs weren't after you, they were after the Nagas . . . who hate the Japs. You, and the guys toting Brens in Blackie's C-47, probably saved their bacon."

Blackie, Captain John Porter, headed an unofficial rescue unit for downed pilots that staged out of an air base in Assam. Blackie flew a Gooney Bird and always made certain his crew carried British Brens, considered by many the best light machine guns in the world. Blackie and his gang had opened up on the Japs attacking the village Eve and I had been holed up in, and pretty much made mincemeat out of them. But not before Eve and I came pretty close to ending up like Bonnie and Clyde.

"Good ol' Blackie," I said.

Ellsworth pinched his lips together and flashed me a sad-eyed look. "He's gone, you know."

"Gone?"

"Last December. He was flying a B-25 on a rescue mission when Jap fighters jumped him."

"Oh." *Well, shit. Ain't war wonderful.*

"But back to the business at hand," Ellsworth said, "we'd like to get the teams into Burma before the southwest monsoon hits, so we've got less than a month."

The southwest monsoon would bring clouds and incessant rains, so I understood the urgency. "Yeah, I don't want to be jumping out of an airplane in conditions where I can't see the ground."

"Well, here's the good news. You don't have to jump this time. You can drive in."

"Say again."

"You ever hear of the Ledo Road?"

"No, sir."

Ellsworth stood and strode back to the map. He used his finger to point to Assam and the air base at Chabua from where I'd flown my missions over the Hump. Then he moved his finger southeast from Chabua.

"There's a village called Ledo about thirty, thirty-five miles southeast of Chabua. Ledo is a railhead that sits less than twenty-five miles from the Burmese border. At General Joseph Stilwell's behest, a road is being hacked out through northern Burma that will eventually link up with the old Burma Road. As the Allies clear the Japs out of the region, the road-building follows."

"The Burma Road," I said, "that's the one we used to use to get supplies from India into China before the Japs snatched it."

"And after the Japs took it, that's when we began the airlift over the Hump."

I thought about the topography and terrain in northern Burma. Thick rainforest, steep mountains, swift rivers. Rocks, boulders, mud, mosquitoes, leeches. "I dunno, sir, road-building in that country sounds damn near impossible."

"I don't know how they're doing it, but they're doing it. I've heard there are maybe ten thousand GIs working on it, and probably three times that many locals. Believe it or not, over one hundred miles of usable road have already been constructed. And scuttlebutt has it the lead bulldozers are at work eighty miles ahead of that."

"Well, all that's going to slow down when the monsoon rains hit."

"And that's why I want to get the weather teams in there within the next few weeks, before the hard rains come." The colonel returned to his seat. "How's some tea sound?"

Not good. "Thanks, but I'll take a pass, sir."

He frowned. "I understand. I'd offer you some hair of the dog, but I don't have any."

"Cold turkey, then. So tell me about the teams." I drew a deep breath, hoping a fresh supply of oxygen would mount a counterattack against the little hangover guys beating on my head with hammers and punching me in the stomach with boxing gloves.

"Three teams," Ellsworth said, "two men each. Mostly staff sergeants, a couple of corporals. They'll have handheld anemometers, psychrometers, barometers, radios . . . and weapons, of course."

"And my duties?"

"See if you can get them set up with your old buddies in the village there. Ideally, the Nagas will help out as guides, porters, coolies, whatever, and maybe even introduce them to other tribes."

"Right. As long as the tribes aren't trying to harvest each other's heads."

I thought about my last visit to the jungle and the Nagas. Not pleasant memories. "Tell you what, for one thing, I could use all the six-two-two the squadron can round up."

Six-two-two was insect repellent, six parts of some kind of chemical, two parts of some other kind, and two parts of a third kind. It worked pretty well, but it probably tasted like Budweiser to the leeches. At least on this next trip into the rainforest I'd be wearing a fresh, full uniform—long pants and long sleeves—and not something that looked like it had been caught in a threshing machine.

"Oh," I added, "and let's round up all the trinkets we can lay our hands on. You know, bottle caps, shiny buttons, silverware, military insignia, coins, maybe even some flight caps. To the Nagas, all those things are great treasures and status symbols. We can use them as incentives and rewards. You know, things to bargain with."

Ellsworth nodded and scribbled notes on a piece of paper. "Okay," he said, looking up from the paper, "I'll contact Tex and get him to fly you and the teams up to Chabua next week. You can take it from there."

We finished our meeting, and with my head still feeling like a gymnasium punching bag, I headed to the dispensary to see if I could beg, borrow, or steal some APCs.

Stacks of cumulus, like scoops of vanilla ice cream ladled into teetering towers, speckled the hazy blue sky. Once the southwest monsoon reached us, the stacks would billow into thunderstorms almost daily. But not today, not yet. The leading edge of the monsoon winds remained to our south, biding their time over the southern reaches of the Bay of Bengal, but at the same time creeping relentlessly toward Calcutta. The weatherman in me guessed their ETA would be early June.

At the moment, however, I remained more interested in my ETA at the dispensary. It turned out the facility stood at the opposite end of the air base from Tenth Weather headquarters. Needless to say, by the time I'd hiked the length of the base, I'd pretty much sweated through my uniform, and it clung to me like a damp sponge.

The dispensary itself proved large and austere, but busy. I guessed it had probably been a warehouse in the old jute mill days. At the entrance desk, I found a spot beneath a ceiling fan and waited for the chief orderly.

When he addressed me, I explained the tropical sun had gotten to me and I needed some APCs to combat the resultant headaches. I felt it unnecessary to mention my old pal Jim might have factored into things. Not that the guy couldn't have figured that out after a quick glance at me. The walking dead.

"Yes, sir," the orderly, a freckle-faced Technician 4th Class, said. "I think we can fix you right up." I could have sworn he flashed me a knowing grin, but maybe my guilty conscience colored my perception. Anyhow, he seemed nice enough, so I ventured a further question.

"You got any nurses here?"

"Only three, sir." He cast me a suspicious look.

I tried to issue a disarming smile. "No, I'm not looking for a date, if that's what you're thinking. I'm looking for a Captain Genevieve Johannsen. We served in Assam together."

"No, sir. No captains here. Only shavetails."

Meaning newly minted second lieutenants. So my search for Eve would continue, but it would not be a full-time effort. It would be catch-as-catch-can. I had to deliver some guys into the Burmese jungle first.

4

Chabua, Assam, India
US Army Air Forces Base
May 22, 1944

The air base in Assam really hadn't changed much in the half year since I'd last been there. It sat on the broad floodplain of the headwaters of the Brahmaputra River, a waterway that eventually emptied into the Bay of Bengal east of Calcutta . . . where I'd just come from.

Base ops remained primitive, a wooden-and-stucco structure with a thatched roof. The adjacent control tower, similar. Gently terraced green fields—tea plantations—shared the flatlands around the base with stands of tall grass and tropical trees. Dark-skinned Indian workers and foul-tempered assertive monkeys, Assam macaques, roamed the dirt streets of the base.

I well remembered the warning about monkeys the major in charge of operations had given me on my visit to Chabua. "Don't ever let 'em inside. They'll rip things apart looking for food. And don't try to make friends with them. With the teeth they have, they'd just as soon tear into your arm as a banana."

I also recalled that my initial trip to the base had been when I'd first met Eve. We'd both been passengers on *Betsy* inbound from Calcutta. Eve had been silent, sullen, and withdrawn. I'd tried to strike up a conversation with her, but it had been like trying to be chatty with a turnip. After that, I resolved to keep my distance from her. Which I did until a chance encounter at the base hospital one evening. That was the one that had led to her infamous "hands in your pockets, pecker in your pants" line. We weren't exactly a match made in heaven. It would take Burma to do heaven's work. But now, that had all come undone. Eve had disappeared, and I was getting ready to trek back into Burma.

I decided to pay a courtesy visit to whoever was running flying operations at the base. Major Vinnie Hatcher had been in charge of things when I'd initially arrived. He'd given me the warning about the monkeys, and we'd gotten along well. But he'd been dismissed after Colonel Hardin took charge of the India-China Wing. Hardin replaced Hatcher with a Lieutenant Colonel Shaver with whom I locked horns almost immediately. After Shaver spotted me wearing reading glasses one day, he informed me he didn't want any damn "four-eyes" flying his airplanes and removed me from flying status. So I hoped he no longer ran the place.

I found the ops officer's door and knocked. The sign on the door said Lieutenant Colonel Wayne Riley, USAAF, so I guessed I'd be safe. New occupant.

"Come," a voice said.

I entered and introduced myself.

A jut-chinned lieutenant colonel with close-cropped brown hair seated behind a government-issue metal desk stood. "Wayne Riley, Rod. Glad to meet you. Sit your butt down." He gestured at a chair in front of the desk.

I thanked him and sat. A quick glance around the office revealed the same moldy, rusty metal bookcases that had been there on my first visit. An electric fan on the colonel's desk rotated spastically but managed to provide a modicum of relief to the clutching heat and humidity.

"I've heard about you, Rod," Riley said. "Quite an adventure you had in Burma. You've become a bit of a legend with the guys flying the Hump, you know."

I didn't know, but nodded my head in acknowledgment. "If I am, it was accidental. It's all about just trying to stay alive, you know."

"I imagine. But you did it."

A sound—a mix of a squeal and a grunt—snapped my attention to the room's open window, where a rosy-cheeked macaque squatted. Metal bars had been installed on the window, and the monkey gripped them with his hands like a jailed prisoner and stared into the office.

I laughed. "Looks like you finally figured out how to handle Chabua's mascots, I see."

"Yeah, little bastards are all over the place. A couple of them got into the building a few months back and tore the place apart looking for food. Did more damage than the Japs might have."

"Speaking of which, how's the airlift doing?"

Riley pursed his lips and shook his head. "Not as well as everyone would like. We've got more birds in the air now and we're getting a lot more shit into China than we were a year ago, but we've been unable to increase our tonnage significantly over the last six months."

"Why?"

"We're limited by the capacity of our aircraft, the weather, and the fact we still have to fly the northern route."

He meant the route over the high Himalayas. The route to the south traversed lower mountains—meaning planes could carry less fuel and heavier loads—but the Japs still ruled the airways there, so flying that track remained a nonstarter.

"And I suppose we continue to lose aircraft left and right?"

"Sadly," Riley growled. He brushed a hand over the stubble on his head. "You know, in the first two months of this year, almost fifty birds went down."

"Jesus. So that's one, what, every couple hundred flights?"

"Every two hundred and eighteen, to be exact. That's why a lotta the guys here say they'd rather be flying bombing missions over Germany. Higher probability of survival."

"We're pushing them too hard."

"Probably. And you may be wondering, since I understand you're in the weather business, how many of the crashes are due to weather. Not all, by any means. A lot are the result of mechanical failure and pilot error."

A sharp rap sounded on Riley's door.

"Come," he said again.

A small corporal entered. "They said this was important." He handed the colonel a sheet of yellow teletype paper, then pivoted and left the room.

Riley read the message printed on the paper. A smile crept across his face. "Well, well, well. This is good news." He looked up at me. "You've heard of Merrill's Marauders?"

"Yes, sir. The American guerrilla group that's running out ahead of the main Allied force trying to recapture Burma."

"Seems they've taken the airfield at Myitkyina."

That sent a positive jolt through me. I sat even more upright in my chair. "That takes Jap fighter aircraft off the board in this part of Burma, then."

Riley smacked his desk with the palm of his hand. "Yes!" The fan wobbled to a stop. "And that means we'll be able to start flying the southern route over the Hump again."

"That should increase the tonnage we're getting into China."

"You bet. And here's the kicker. We've got a new transport called the C-54 coming into the theater."

"I've heard of it. Called the Skymaster."

"The military version of the DC-4 airliner. Big mother. Can stuff almost twice the tonnage into her as we can Ol' Dumbo. Bottom line, with the C-54 coming on-line and the southern track opening up, we oughta have General Chennault and Chiang Kai-shek and the rest of the Chinks peeing in their pants with joy in a few months."

The monkey at the window bared his fangs at us and tried to shake the bars. Riley threw a pencil at him, and he scampered off into the street. "Little bastard," he muttered.

"Back to Merrill's Marauders for a moment," I said.

"Sure."

"They're the reason I'm back at Chabua. We need reliable weather obs out of northern Burma so we can better support the Long-Range Penetration Groups like Merrill's. With that in mind, I've been tasked to lead some observation teams back into the Naga Hills."

"My, aren't you a glutton for punishment."

"Not my idea, sir."

"No doubt. Well, if getting some teams in there will help you weather guessers, I'm all for it. What can I do to help?"

"I understand I don't have to jump out of an airplane this time. I hear there's something called the Ledo Road."

"You bet. I can arrange to get you and your guys to the village of Ledo, and from there you ought to be able to hitch a ride on a two-and-a-half-ton six-wheeler to wherever you want. There's a constant stream of traffic from Ledo to wherever work has progressed to on the road. As a matter of fact, I've got some contacts with the engineers at Ledo, so I'll see if I can get your bunch some tickets on one of those big-mother trucks."

I thanked the colonel. We made small talk for a while longer, then I departed for the base hospital where Eve had worked prior to our Burma adventure.

The hospital building hadn't changed since I'd last seen it, but the sign over the main entrance had. It now read IIIth STATION HOSPITAL instead of 95th STATION HOSPITAL. I recalled that the Ninety-Fifth—and Eve—had been in the process of relocating from Chabua to Kunming, China, just before Eve's and my Burmese "excursion." Even though a different unit occupied the hospital now, I hoped that someone there might have heard something about Eve. Grasping at straws, I knew.

The building brought back a flood of memories other than those of Eve. It's where my good buddy Zim, after my inaugural mission over the Hump, had brought me for my first taste of post-mission "combat whiskey"—in truth, South African brandy doled out by the dispensary.

God, how I missed Zim. I suppose it's foolish in wartime to make post-war plans, but, as close friends will, we ignored the possibility that we might not survive combat and made them anyhow. We talked about the things we'd do together—fish the great rivers of the Pacific Northwest where we'd both grown up, tell stories to our kids and grandkids about our wartime adventures—that we knew would grow wilder and more exaggerated as we aged—and perhaps even hold semi-sober discussions about Kipling and Blake.

We would not, of course. Captain Pete Zimmerman, flying C-46 tail number 8806 had been swallowed whole by the weather gods and mountain devils who rule the Himalayas. He never even got off a distress message before his epitaph was written in twisted metal along the Aluminum Trail in September 1943.

At the main nurse's station I found a matronly-looking captain who'd obviously been around for a while. Maybe she'd even worked with or met Eve at some point.

"May I help you, Major?" she said, forcing a smile.

I told her my story. She frowned as I wrapped it up, and looked askance at me, as though she didn't quite believe it.

"First, I don't know of the captain—Johannsen, you said her name was?"

I nodded.

"Johannsen. Never run across her. But then there are lots of nurses in the service I don't know. What really puzzles me, though, is that you said she was ordered by Eastern Air Command to report to their headquarters in Calcutta."

"Yes, ma'am. That's what I was told at the hospital in New Delhi."

"That would be very unusual. To my knowledge—and I've gained a little bit over my years in the service—orders for nurses are cut by the Medical Corps chain of command, not by any other outfit. Understand, we are organic to the Medical Corps, not Eastern Air Command. I suppose anything is possible, especially in wartime, but I've never heard of orders for medical personnel being issued by any other organization than the Corps."

She gave me a hard stare, like she expected me to 'fess up I was feeding her a tall tale, yanking her chain. I didn't, of course. But somebody was sure yanking my chain. I thanked the nurse and departed, more confused than ever. And more frustrated than ever. I wanted to play Dick Tracy and get to the bottom of this mystery, but I had a little side trip to Burma to make first.

I headed back to my *basha* to change out of my sweat-saturated uniform so I'd look—and smell—at least semi-presentable at the officers' mess for dinner. The *basha* I was billeted in quickly reinforced the initial notion of the Chabua lodging I'd gotten back in August. It looked like something constructed, shoddily, by one of the Three Little Pigs—bamboo frame, woven bamboo walls, and a thatched roof. One huff or puff by a Big Bad Wolf and the resident piggies would have been part of a BLT. Or, as I found out—accidentally, you understand—one round fired from a flare gun through the dwelling and you'd have a daylight roof. Reeds and straw burn easily, even in rainy climates.

Later, at dinner, Lieutenant Colonel Riley, the ops guy, found me. "Here's your contact in Assam for the Ledo Road business," he said. He dropped a piece of paper with a name scribbled on it on my table.

On the paper: *Captain Wendell Washington, commander, Company B, 1883rd Engineer Aviation Battalion.*

Riley went on. "I've scheduled, through the captain, you and your teams a ride out of Ledo day after tomorrow at noon. We'll truck you over there tomorrow."

"Yeah, might as well get it over with," I mumbled—unenthusiastically —between bites of something billed on the mess menu as Salisbury steak. I guessed it might have been ground monkey rather than hamburger.

"By the way, you'll find Washington an interesting guy," Riley said.

"Oh?"

Riley chuckled. "Yeah. He makes Man Mountain Dean look like a toddler, and possesses a bass-baritone voice that would put Paul Robeson's to shame."

I must have given the colonel a blank stare.

"Paul Robeson. He sang 'Ol' Man River' in *Show Boat*."

I got it. "Yeah. Oh, to be on the Mighty Mississippi and not in the goddamned Burmese jungle."

"Send me a postcard."

5

The village of Ledo
Assam, India
May 24, 1944

Colonel Riley had understated the appearance and audio qualities of Captain Wendell Washington. He stood well over six feet tall and looked as though he'd been chiseled from the trunk of an ebony tree. If there'd been a seismograph nearby, his voice would have registered on it.

"Welcome to the Ledo Road," he rumbled as he strode toward me and saluted.

I returned his greeting, but perhaps my stare, which I held a bit too long, gave away my surprise.

He flashed me a broad grin. "Because I'm the size of a road grader or because I'm colored?" he asked.

"I suppose either reason would be unacceptable," I muttered.

"Forget it, Major. I'm used to it. And I'll tell you up front you'll quickly discover that more than half the engineer battalions working on this road are Negro."

I nodded. "Well, Captain Washington, I'm pleased to make your acquaintance. Thank you for offering me and my men a lift into the Naga Hills."

He surveyed the weather observation teams that accompanied me, and some of the guys, I'm sure, gawked at the size and dark skin of the man who stood before them.

"I see you've got them well prepared," Washington said, "based on your experience, I presume. I understand you've visited Burma before."

"Nothing I signed up for."

Washington laughed. "Me either."

"The last time I vacationed in Burma," I said, "all I had was my forty-five, a machete, and a uniform so shredded it looked like it had been used for bayonet practice. *I* didn't look much better. Happens when you jump out of an airplane and land in a jungle."

"I imagine the leeches and mosquitoes ate you alive."

"They feasted."

"So I'm glad to see you've got your men geared up in long pants, long sleeves, and slouch hats. Nice to see the rifles, too."

"Much need for the weaponry?"

Washington shook his head. "Not for Japs anymore. They've pretty much skedaddled out of the part of Burma we're headed for. Can't speak for the tigers and snakes, though."

Thunder rumbled out of the gray clouds cloaking the low range of mountains east of Ledo. It reminded me that although daily showers had become the norm over the past week, the full, soaking force of the wet monsoon was yet to attack. When it did, daily drenchings, rather than showers, would become commonplace. Monthly rainfalls would be tallied in feet as opposed to inches. I didn't envy the people who had to build roads in such conditions.

Captain Washington glanced eastward at the darkening skies. "Let's get mounted up and get rolling. The frog-stranglers ain't gonna hold off forever." He pointed at a Deuce and a Half that idled nearby. "Usually I let a private or corporal push these things around, but I'll be your driver today, Major. I like to get out and check the road and visit the crews whenever I can, so this is an excellent excuse to do that *and* get you and your men to wherever you'd like to go."

The three weather observation teams clambered up into the canvas-covered rear of the truck—a two-and-a-half-ton six-by-six—and I stepped up onto the running board of the beast and slid into the passenger's seat. Once we all got settled, Washington eased the six-by-six onto the Ledo Road in a bellow of black smoke accompanied by the mechanical roar of a GMC straight-six engine. He proved adept at shifting gears, but stayed mostly in second and third as he herded the beast along the graveled track.

"How far have you been able to push the road into Burma?" I asked. I marveled at the quality of the construction as we labored up steep grades, negotiated hairpin turns, and rolled past sheer drop-offs that had me squeezing my eyes shut. All of this roadwork sliced through teak forests that towered a hundred, maybe two hundred, feet above us, stands of bamboo so thick they looked like solid walls, and jungle plants with leaves the size of pup tents.

He answered in voice whose resonance matched that of the GMC motor. "We've got the road metalled—that means reinforced, graded, and covered in crushed gavel—all the way to a place called Shingbwlyang. That's a little over a hundred miles southeast of Ledo. We've completed final grading of the roadbed about fifty miles beyond that. And the lead bulldozer is another thirty-fives miles ahead of that work. From there, oh, maybe another one hundred and ninety miles will bring us to a spur of the old Burma Road. And once that connection is completed, voilà, a land route from India to China will again be open for business."

"You know, it's beyond remarkable what you boys have accomplished."

Washington stared at me as if I'd said something wrong.

"If I may, sir," he said after holding me in his gaze a few moments, "we'd prefer to be called men. And it hasn't been just us. Lots of Indian laborers and even some Burmese natives and Chinese coolies."

"I stand corrected, Captain. Men it is."

Large raindrops slammed against the windshield, splattering like bugs on a summer afternoon.

"Well, here it comes," rumbled Washington. "This, you know, has been our biggest enemy. The weather. Not Japs. The downpours and violent electrical storms. Constant in the rainy season. We get bridge and culvert washouts, landslides, flash floods. I've seen the water in creeks come up ten feet in a matter of minutes and take out our bridges with tons of debris—logs, rocks, root balls."

He switched on the windshield wipers and slowed the six-by-six. The green jungle around us morphed into a glistening grayness as the rain thundered down, almost drowning out conversation.

A convoy of road rollers, graders, and rock crushers crawled toward us from the direction of the road head. Washington pulled to the side of the graveled track and stopped, even though the road appeared wide enough to accommodate traffic in both directions. "Better safe than sorry in these conditions."

"Where are they headed?" I asked.

"Back to Ledo for maintenance. One of our biggest problems out here is spare parts. Lord, sometimes we have to manufacture our own."

"So, the weather, spare parts . . . what other challenges?"

Washington laughed. "Bugs and disease. Lack of land surveys." He paused, then rumbled, "And no hush puppies or chitlins."

"You're from the South?"

"Hard to hide that. 'Bama."

"You don't sound like you're from Dixie. So I'm betting you didn't get an engineering degree in the South."

The convoy passed. Washington eased the truck forward through the blinding cloudburst.

"Purdue University," he said. "I took advantage of something called the ESMWT program. Engineering, Science, Management War Training. I didn't earn a degree, but I got a hell of a good education."

"But you got a head start someplace along the way."

"My mother and father worked as domestics for a well-to-do family in the Wiregrass country of southern Alabama, near a place called Dothan. We actually were treated pretty well . . . just so long as we remembered 'our place.' The family raised horses and grew peanuts—"

"Not cotton?"

"Nah. The boll weevil took care of that in the '20s. Good ol' boll weevil. Kept me and my brothers and sisters outta the fields from sunup to sundown. Instead, since the family had an extensive library, I picked books instead of cotton. Even though I was just a toddler."

"You could read as a youngster?"

Washington laughed and downshifted as the six-by-six ground through a series of switchbacks snaking up the side of a steep, heavily forested ridge. "No, I couldn't read, but I loved the pictures some of the books had. I must have asked Ma a million questions about them. I probably drove her nuts because she made sure I got my schooling and learned how to read and write. And I still love books. I guess that's what helped me get into Purdue. How about you, sir, where'd you go to school?"

"A long way from Alabama. I was born in northern Idaho—Coeur d'Alene—and got my degree in atmospheric science at the University of Washington in Seattle, then a master's degree from Cal Tech. Then the army grabbed me, taught me to fly C-47s and C-46s, and shipped me off to Guadalcanal, where I flew for what was known as the Cactus Air Force. I ended up flying the Hump here in the CBI Theater. But that was before I had to bail out over northern Burma, and before the Japs used me for mortar target practice. I don't fly anymore." I omitted from the story the time I'd spent with my late wife, Trish, as she passed away from cancer.

"I'd heard the Burma story. You're kind of a legend around here, you know."

"Nothing I'd aspired to."

"There was a nurse, too, a very attractive blonde, the story goes. If I'm not trampling on decorum, may I ask—"

"You may. She got ripped by mortar fragments, too, but made it out. Yeah, she was a real looker, if I do say so myself. She spent some time in a hospital in New Delhi and recovered. But . . ." I decided I'd said enough.

"Sir?" That single word reverberated with something akin to genuine curiosity, perhaps tinged with empathy. Or maybe I just wanted it to sound that way. Anyway, I decided to tell him.

"Well, you see, Captain, the nurse has kind of gone MIA. The army claims they have no record of her or of any assignment after New Delhi. God, I don't know if she's still in-theater or back in the States or well or sick or what." My voice trailed off. I felt semi-embarrassed I'd slapped my heart onto my sleeve. I had no doubt Washington sensed there was more between me and the nurse—me and Eve—than typical combat camaraderie.

He remained silent for a bit before he spoke. When he did, his voice washed over me like a warm, soothing ocean current. "You know, sir, there's lots of secret stuff going on these days. New units standing up, new bases being built, personnel being shifted around on the QT. Look, there isn't much I can do to help. But we've got a lot of coolie work crews shifting back and forth between here and China. I can ask around if anyone has ever seen, like you said, a nurse who's a real looker. I speak just enough Mandarin to get by."

I mumbled my self-conscious thanks. But I knew for now I had to concentrate on the mission at hand.

The truck reached the crest of the ridge and began to lumber down the eastern side. The rain slackened, and bursts of sunshine lit the jungle surrounding us in a shimmering aquamarine glow. Ahead on the road, Washington spotted a group of native laborers working on a broken culvert. He brought the six-by-six to a stop, jumped down, splashed through muddy puddles dotting the road, and approached the workers.

I watched as the captain carried out a brief, animated conversation with the leader of the group using lots of arm waving and hand gestures. Lots of grins, too. It clearly wasn't an adversarial exchange.

Washington climbed back into the truck. "Just wanted to make sure everything was okay and they had all the tools they needed."

"Good grief, Captain. Don't tell me you speak Hindi, too?"

"No, sir, I don't. But that's not the common language in this part of India. It's Assamese. I don't know that, either, but I've learned a few words. So the conversations with the natives are a little bit of Assamese, a little bit of pidgin English, and a whole lot of sign language."

"Seems to work."

"I want to make sure the workers—both Indians and GIs—are taken care of and have all the stuff they need. That's the best way of getting this job done. And speaking of that, you've got a job, too, Major. Any idea where you and your men should be dropped off?"

"I can come up with a good guess. I'd like to get somewhere near the village I was wounded in. I'm hoping I've still got some friends there. In particular, there was a Naga kid, a young boy named Tommy—I think he got that name from the Brits he'd worked with before the Americans arrived—who spoke a little English. He became my right-hand man and a decent translator. I'd love to find him again. As for the coordinates of the place, the rescue plane pilot said I was picked up near twenty-seven north and ninety-six east, or about thirty-five or forty miles east of the Assam border."

"There's a map in the rucksack on the floorboard by your feet. Pull it out, and let's take a look at it."

I fished a damp paper map out of the mildewed pack and spread it out in front of us.

"Okay," Washington said, "twenty-seven north would put us about here, at the seventy-mile marker, just north of Tagap Ga." He tapped the map with a meaty forefinger.

I slipped on my reading glasses and studied the map. "Right. Then it looks like twenty, twenty-five miles east would get us to our destination."

"As the crow flies," Washington noted.

"And we sure as hell can't hike through this rugged terrain 'as the crow flies.' So I'm thinking it'll be a good two-day slog."

"You're gonna have to ford the Chindwin River, too. But it's fairly narrow in many spots."

"Then after that, it looks like we gotta trek through some mountains before we reach a relatively level upland here." I pointed at the topographic isolines on the map.

"And by that point, you should be only about fifteen miles or so from where you wanna be."

"As the crow flies."

Washington laughed. It sounded like a landslide. "Twenty-five miles for an inebriated crow."

I slid the spectacles back into my tunic pocket. "I'm hoping we'll run into some Nagas before that. If we're lucky, ones from the village I was in before."

"No more headhunters out there, I guess? We've all heard stories, you know."

"Actually . . ." My voice trailed off, remembering.

"Actually what?" Washington stared wide-eyed at me.

"Your head's safe as long as you aren't a Jap."

"Oh, Jesus." The captain jammed the truck into gear, and we rolled southward. Steam rose from the drenched rainforest crowding the road as sunshine sliced through billowing cumulus and cooked the land below.

We jounced along the graveled road for another forty-five minutes, after which Washington brought the vehicle to a halt along a short straight stretch. "This is about as close as I can get you to the twenty-seventh parallel. Head due east from here, as best you can, and that should bring you, eventually, to the village you're looking for. For starters, I believe there's a footpath near here that will lead you to the river."

"I'll find it," I said. "Listen, my longer-range plan is, if I can get the teams set up with the natives, I aim on being back here in about four or five days. If you could alert your guys, the ones who drive this route, to be on the lookout for me, I'd love to hitch a ride back to Ledo."

"I'll do better than that, Major Shepherd. I'll patrol this section myself around the time you expect to be back here."

"Thank you, Captain. I appreciate your courtesy."

We shook hands, and Captain Washington wished me Godspeed, his voice resonating like the rumble of distant thunder. The weather observation teams unloaded their gear from the rear of the truck while I took compass bearings to set our course. In short order, we were ready to move out. Washington gave us a wave and pulled the truck away, leaving only the stink of gasoline and a thin, black trail of exhaust suspended in the air.

After the truck disappeared, all that lingered was the steaming humidity and the cacophonous symphony of the rainforest—the howls of monkeys, the screech of birds, the peeps and squeals of tiny animals, and the occasional snorts and roars of things larger.

Master Sergeant Ed Coleman—curly, red hair, and a ruddy complexion—the senior NCO of the group, strode over to stand beside me on the edge of the road.

"Welcome to the jungle, Sarge," I said.

"I've always wanted a tropical vacation, sir."

"You may want your money back by the time this is over. Let's get going."

We moved along the road for a short distance until I spotted a semi-overgrown footpath leading into the jungle and hopefully toward the river.

I stepped off down the trail, hacking at vines and overhanging branches with my machete, as the men squished along behind me in single file.

I knew we were in trouble before we ever reached the water. I could hear it, thundering and crashing like a mountain waterfall as it rushed downstream, filled with debris from the recent cloudburst.

We reached the banks of the swollen river. "Not gonna be crossing today," Sergeant Coleman observed.

As narrow as the river appeared, its flooded fury made it obvious that anyone who attempted to ford it would be swept away on a turbulent and deadly journey—an eight-hundred-mile trip first into the Irrawaddy River and finally into the Andaman Sea. Of course, by that time, what remained of anyone's carcass would have been finished off by saltwater crocodiles.

So, barely had our trek begun when it became stalled. We strung up our jungle hammocks and prepared to spend the night waiting for the river to recede. The hammocks proved less than comfortable, but at least they kept us off the boggy ground and prevented spiders and snakes from snuggling in with us. A zipper-opening mosquito net attached to a rainproof canopy offered additional protection from unwanted bedmates.

Gradually, the roar of the water gave way to the night symphony of the jungle. I slept fitfully and dreamed of Eve and the brutal nights we had spent together in the rainforest—no hammocks, no mosquito nets, no jungle clothing. I desperately wanted to resume my search for her but had to accept the fact that wasn't going to happen soon.

Instead, here I sat, camped beside a flooded jungle river waiting for it to go down so I could cross and plunge ever deeper into the rainforest in search of the small, brown people who called this part of Burma home.

6

The Naga Hills
Northern Burma
May 25, 1944

The following day dawned dry but with a fuzzy, gray cloak of low-hanging stratus draped over the jungle canopy. The usual chitter, yowls, and warbles of monkeys and birds greeted us as we arose.

The high water in the river had receded, and we were able to wade across the stream getting no more than our boots and the bottom of our pants wet. After crossing the Chindwin, we made good progress along a variety of footpaths, game trails, and even some overgrown, muddy roads likely carved out by the Brits earlier in the war. The density of the trees, vines, and bushes through which we pushed, in combination with the thick overcast, spread a dusk-like dimness over the rainforest. In many places, visibility appeared limited to just a few yards. Once, we rounded a bend in a narrow path to discover a snake the size of a fire hose slithering across the trail.

One of the young enlisted guys immediately behind me yelped, "Boa constrictor!" and shouldered his rifle.

"Don't," I said, and pushed the barrel of his gun up. "It's not a boa, it's a python. Boas live in South America."

"What's the difference? Don't they both eat you?"

"Only if you piss them off. I suggest letting him go his way, and we'll go ours."

"You're sure, sir?"

I decided to have a little fun with the poor kid. "Pretty much. But sometimes they travel in packs and hang out in trees. They'll suspend themselves from a branch, drop down like a hawk, snatch you up, and *pfft*, you're wrapped up and down his gullet before anyone realizes you're gone." Total bullshit, of course, but I needed a little comic relief, maybe to relieve my own tension.

After that, the poor kid's head was on a swivel and going up and down as if being yanked by puppet strings. I kept an eye on him for about half an hour, then decided I'd better tell him the truth or he'd end up with muscle spasms in his neck so severe we'd have to medevac him. He laughed when I told him, but I don't think he thought it was particularly funny.

We actually made decent time through the rainforest, crested several ridges, and reached the relatively level upland I'd identified earlier on the topo map. It turned out to be more rolling than level but still provided a welcome relief from the rollercoaster paths we'd been following.

Sergeant Coleman moved up beside me. "Sir, I don't mean to be a Nervous Nelly or nuthin', but I have the feeling we're being watched, like someone is stalking us."

I chuckled silently. "You're not being a Nervous Nelly, Sarge. Someone *is* watching us."

He cocked his head at me. "You've seen 'em?"

"No. But remember, I've been here before. I know how these little folks operate. We're strangers that have pushed into their backyard. They live here, they're good at it. They'll check us out for a day or two and decide if we're Good Guys or Bad Guys. If we pass muster, they'll send the Welcome Wagon."

Coleman stared at me.

"Figuratively speaking," I said.

"What if they decide we're black-hat people?"

They wouldn't, of course, but I couldn't resist having a little fun with the sergeant, too, maybe just to cut the tension further and provide another bit of comic relief for everyone.

"They're headhunters, remember?"

"Oh, dear God. You don't mean . . ." His voice trailed off to incomprehensible mutterings.

I made a show out of giving him a good once-over. "Actually, with that red mop of yours, you might be a real prize for them. Not many redheads around here. That might save the rest of us."

Coleman cut loose with a long, burbly fart—the flatulence of fear.

I stepped away from him. "Of course, even you might survive if you're gonna defend yourself with poison gas."

I couldn't contain my deceit any longer and burst out laughing.

The younger enlisted men, who had gathered near us, cut loose with guffaws, too. Coleman realized our little byplay had relaxed everyone, and smiled, but didn't join in the tee-heeing. Instead he warned, "Just remember, guys, always toe the line with me, 'cuz we didn't pack any gas masks." More chuckles followed, and I think everyone pressed on carrying a little less apprehension than they previously had.

And truthfully, any apprehension proved to be unnecessary. After an uneventful overnight bivouac, we encountered the native "Welcome Wagon" the following day. As we moved uphill along a muddy track, we rounded a bend and came face-to-face with three Naga warriors standing side by side in the trail, blocking our way. Someone behind me said, "Oh, shit," just as three more natives stepped into the path at the rear of our column.

"It's okay, guys," I said. "They aren't going to jump us."

"Jesus, how do you know, boss?" someone asked. A kid with a shaky voice.

"Because their spears are stuck pointy-end down in the ground. And besides, if they were going to attack, we wouldn't be standing here wondering if they were going to attack. We'd be splayed out on the jungle floor looking like life-sized pincushions." No one found that comment humorous.

The Naga tribesmen in front of us wore expressions that looked neither hostile nor friendly. Curious, perhaps. They appeared as I remembered them—small, brown, and naked except for loincloths. Lithe and muscular, they sported piles of black hair stacked on their heads. One had a small bone, probably from an animal, stuck through his earlobe. Another wore a tiny skull, perhaps an infant monkey's, suspended from a hemp cord around his neck. I assumed he might be the group's leader.

For a moment, no one spoke. Only the screech of birds and the occasional howl of a macaque reverberated through the rainforest. From deeper in the jungle came the rushing drumbeat of rain as a cloudburst hammered down on another part of the lush greenery.

I tried to recall some of the words the Nagas had used on my previous jungle adventure. I approached, slowly, the guy I assumed to be the Nagas' commander. He appeared to be too young to be a chief, but I guessed he was probably good buddies with whoever the tribe's muckety-muck was.

I tapped my chest with my right hand and said, "*Ahmoodicum*," as I walked toward the Naga warrior. I recalled that was the word the Nagas had used for *American*. The two natives on either side of the guy stepped forward to prevent me from coming any closer. They didn't threaten me, just stopped me.

"*Ahmoodicum?*" the presumed leader said.

I nodded.

He babbled something in Naga, and his two henchmen stepped back.

I decided to ask for the "king" of the tribe I'd worked with closely on my prior Burmese odyssey. I had thought of him as King Kally, but that was my personal nickname for him. His real name was Kalakeya.

"My name Rod," I said, and thumped my chest again. "I look for King Kalakeya."

No reaction.

I tried again. "I look for King Kalakeya."

Nothing.

Third time. "I look for King Kalakeya." I spoke slowly and deliberately, perhaps raising my voice a little too much, as if the natives were hard of hearing, not speakers of a different language.

At that point, the warriors leaned their heads together and babbled to each other in Nagamese for several minutes. Finished, the leader motioned for me and my men to follow him and his sidekicks. They set off at an Olympic pace and soon left us far behind. With my gimpy leg, which began to hurt like hell, I—we—stood no chance of keeping up with them.

They eventually stopped and waited for us. When we caught up with them, they seemed to be grumbling to each other, probably about our snail's pace, and likely making snide remarks about our long pants, long-sleeved shirts, heavy boots, stuffed backpacks, and a leader who stumbled along like the ancient of ancients. My body, not surprisingly, had become lathered in sweat. If I'd had some soap, I probably could have bathed. Probably needed to, too.

Once we overtook the headhunters, they took off again, but at a slower clip.

"How much farther?" Coleman asked me after a while.

"I have no way of knowing, Sarge, since I don't even know where we are." We'd been snaking through the jungle for several hours—up mountainsides, down steep slopes, and splashing through rushing streams.

Shortly before sunset, and totally exhausted, we staggered to a halt. The Naga leader, the guy with the tiny skull suspended from his neck, indicated we should sit. We did, but not before I told the guys to check for leeches. We pulled a few off of each other, but nothing like the blood feast we would have provided the little suckers if we hadn't been in protective clothing. As we waited, we drank from our canteens, shared cigarettes, and listened to the jungle serenade. Meanwhile, the warriors' boss man and two of his buddies had taken off again, leaving the other Nagas with us.

As twilight settled in and the symphony of the rainforest grew louder and more cacophonous, the native warriors returned, this time with a guest, my old friend Tommy. The young Naga, whose age I pegged at twelve or thirteen, burst into a grin and a sprint when he spotted me. I arose and limped toward him.

He pulled up short when we neared each other, snapped to attention, and gave me an opened-palm British-style salute. "GI Rod," he exclaimed, "you come back."

"Yes, Tommy, I come back."

"But you walk crooked. You hurt?"

"Yes. Remember, we have fight with Japs in your village?"

He nodded.

"Japs hurt my leg. Now one leg shorter than other." I accompanied my explanation with hand gestures.

Tommy seemed to understand and said, "Okay, we walk slow now. Take you and GIs to village."

"King Kalakeya?"

"Yes. King be happy see you."

That I doubted, since on my previous visit I'd left his village riddled with bullet holes, dotted with mortar craters, and a few of the villagers critically and possibly even fatally wounded.

Tommy ran his gaze over the men behind me, likely studying their equipment and weapons. Even though it had been only six months or so since I'd last seen him, he appeared significantly older. He appeared noticeably taller, more muscular, and even displayed a few wispy hairs on his upper lip. I noticed an M3 trench knife tucked into the folds of his loincloth. To me, he still seemed like a kid. But I knew that jungle life and the conflict with the Japs had likely molded him into a fierce warrior.

He finished his once-over of the men who accompanied me, then locked me in his gaze. "Sunshine woman, she no come back with you?"

"Sunshine woman" referred to Eve and her blond hair—hair like sunshine, the Nagas called it. A blonde, for obvious reasons, was held in awe by people who knew only black hair. Tommy had been instrumental in helping me extricate Eve from a difficult situation when we'd been here before. She'd been "gifted" to a rival tribe to establish peace between King Kally's bunch and the other Naga village. It had taken some dicey finagling to get her back, but with Tommy's help, we'd managed it. And now I had no idea where she was or what had become of her. I sure as shit couldn't tell Tommy that.

"She resting at home, Tommy. No come back."

"Ah, I glad she okay. You like her. I know." He grinned at me.

Clever little bastard. But I loved him.

Because it had grown dark, I decided we should call it a day. Tommy said he would return at sunrise. We dined on K rations—tiny beef and pork loaves, canned cheese, hard biscuits, and chocolate bars that even ants wouldn't go near—then the men strung up their hammocks, and we spent a third night sleeping in the jungle. Just us, millions of bugs, thousands of birds, and hundreds of animals. I had a feeling there were a few Nagas out there, too, keeping an eye on us.

As promised, Tommy returned when the sun came up, though it was hard to tell exactly when it did. A thick, gray mist hung in the rainforest canopy, hiding the sun and turning the day into a humid, monochrome rendering.

Accompanied by the sounds of an awakening jungle—the chatter of monkeys and squawking of birds—we hiked for about an hour until we reached Tommy's mountaintop home. It appeared as I remembered it, though I had no reason to suspect it should have changed. I doubted it had changed for a hundred years, maybe a thousand.

But I wondered what it would be like in another hundred years, now that "civilization" had reached the Naga culture. Civilization in the form of men killing each other with machines that flew and spit fire and dropped metal bottles that exploded, with weapons that sounded like thunderclaps and tore bodies asunder, with a hatred that enveloped the land like a septic cocoon.

Civilization. Would Tommy's culture survive that? Or would the tides of war and so-called modernization merely flow around the tiny Naga hamlets, leaving them untouched like boulders anchored in the swift current of a river? After another century, could one return here and see the same bucolic scene that unfolded around my men and me as Tommy, strutting like a drum major, led us into his home?

Young children, totally naked—laughing and giggling—scurried alongside us. Women, with multicolored skirts wrapped around their hips and material similar to the men's loincloths covering the upper portions of their bodies, took a break from their cooking duties to examine us. They stood next to large pots suspended above fire pits and boiling whatever Nagas dined on. On my previous visit, I'd seen a severed Jap head tossed into one of the pots, so I shied away from eating anything but rice and whatever looked like veggies. Soup was off my menu. But I had to admit, I loved the meaty aroma now wafting from the pots.

The village men, the warriors, stood by silently as we paraded into their settlement. They didn't appear threatening, and I guessed they were probably waiting for their headman, the king, to greet us.

As we tramped over the muddy grounds of the hamlet, a couple of huge, black water buffalo snorted and gave way to us. Some other creatures that looked like big, ugly pigs wallowed in mudholes, and clucking chickens darted to and fro, probably trying to keep their distance from the women with the cooking pots. Mangy dogs trotted along with the kids, probably wondering if we were dinner or dinner guests.

The bamboo thatched-roof huts the Nagas lived in sat on slender log pilings about ten feet tall. Notches slashed into larger logs formed stairways into the homes. As I recalled, the elevation of the huts kept them dry and made it difficult for enemies to attack them.

At Tommy's signal, we stopped near the center of the village. "I go get King Kalakeya," he said. "You wait." He darted off toward the biggest hut in the settlement.

The guy I'd come to think of as "King Kally" in my earlier visit showed up about ten minutes later. Short and muscular with a head of thick, wooly hair, he approached me with a big smile on his weathered face. With half his teeth missing, however, I couldn't classify it as a toothy smile. He extended his hand, Western style, in greeting.

"*Ahmoodicum Rood*," he said. American Rod.

I took his hand and shook it. "Thank you for again welcoming *Ahmoodicums* into your village," I said. Tommy translated for me.

The king released my hand, stepped back, and launched into a long speech in the Naga language. It seemed to be directed as much to his subjects—who smiled and occasionally laughed as he rambled on—as to me and my men.

As he continued to rattle on, I had a chance to study him more closely. I noticed three feathers still protruded from his jumble of tar-colored hair. They, I presumed, signaled his status as tribal king. But the primitive necklace I recalled him wearing months ago seemed different. I remembered it being festooned with the tiny, carved wooden heads, both animal and human. Now, shiny pieces of twisted metal adorned it. I stared, wondering what they were, where they had come from. Then I realized they were legacies of the attack on his village that Eve and I had almost died in. Pieces of shrapnel from Jap mortar shells.

The king finished his rambling monologue, and Tommy translated for me, summarizing, I assume, what he'd said.

"King Kalakeya say Americans welcome here. Drive Jap dwarfs away. But he said, as always, Americans lost, stumbling around in jungle, lost like baby water buffalo, and Nagas must save them."

I figured that had been the king's line that had drawn the most laughs. Total bullshit, of course, but I decided not to dispute it. Better to let it stand and boost the Nagas' egos.

"Thank King Kalakeya for rescuing us and for allowing us to share the hospitality and bounty of his village."

Tommy stared at me.

"Oh . . . for allowing us to share the friendliness and . . . uh, food of the people here."

Tommy nodded and translated.

"And tell him we need his help again," I added.

Tommy looked puzzled, but passed my request to the king. Kally glanced at me, nodded, then spoke to Tommy.

As I waited for their conversation to conclude, I noticed the morning had grown darker. In fact, using landmarks I had identified on my previous visit here to mark the cardinal compass points, I realized the sky to the southwest had turned midnight black.

The natives saw it, too, and began moving their cooking tools and children into huts. Tommy returned and motioned for me and my men to hurry to a shelter constructed of bamboo poles lashed together with thick vines. The poles supported a sloped roof of rainforest leaves the size of elephant ears. A minute or two after we gathered in the shelter, a downpour hit. No thunder, no wind. Just the roaring drumbeat of a cloudburst drenching the jungle, drowning out all other sounds, and turning the village grounds into a muddy landscape crisscrossed with rivulets and tiny creeks.

In thirty minutes, it was over. Shafts of sunlight speared through the clouds, and spirals of steam rose from the drenched earth as if from a boiling witches' brew. If one of the weather observation teams had been able to break out its sling psychrometer, I was certain we'd have found the relative humidity tickling one hundred percent.

As we waited for the rainwater to drain from the village grounds, I explained to Tommy—or hoped I did—what we wanted, what I wanted him to relay to King Kally. In addition to employing the limited English that Tommy understood, I resorted to sign language and etched crude drawings in the hard-packed soil beneath the shelter.

Tommy seemed to grasp what I was telling him. "You want take your men to mountaintops, toward where sun come up?"

"Yes." I held up two fingers. "Two men on first mountaintop. Then two more men on next mountaintop, maybe one day's walk in direction of where sun come up."

Tommy smiled. "Then two more on last mountain, one more day's walk?"

He got it. I wanted the observation teams on mountaintops—better for transmitting their observations on radio—and about twenty miles apart, roughly a day's trek through the jungle on trails the Nagas knew. I hoped the data the teams transmitted would reach back all the way to Chabua or other bases in Assam. If not Chabua, then at least as far as Fort Hertz, a British base in northern Burma that would probably be only thirty miles or so from our teams.

I explained to Tommy I'd like men from his village to keep an eye on my guys and make sure they always had plenty of water and food. I told him I'd pay for their attention. That's why I'd lugged along a couple of bags of trinkets as remuneration. The Nagas had no use for traditional money but always seemed more than eager to accept bottle caps, odd coins, and metallic military insignia as payment for their services.

"Yes, sir, GI Rod," Tommy said. "I make sure King Kalakeya understand. We do good. Okay?"

"Okay."

Tommy furrowed his brow and again studied me and my men. He seemed puzzled about something.

"You have question, Tommy?" I asked.

"Why you want men on mountains?" He swatted away some sort of ebony-colored beetle that had strolled into the shelter during the rainstorm. The thing had pincers bigger than its legs protruding from its head. I suspected if you tried to grab it, it would crush your fingers.

Tommy continued. "You want watch for enemies? For Japs? We do that."

"No. Not watch for enemies. Watch weather."

The furrow on his brow deepened. I'd just thrown him a Dizzy Dean curveball.

"Watch weather? Why for?"

"For men who fly in machines, the metal birds."

"Oooohhh," he responded, drawing out the word, perhaps not quite understanding the importance of weather to aviators. "How do that?"

"Well, we measure how warm it is, how fast wind blows, how many clouds in sky."

"But how you measure?" Curious kid, and pretty damn smart, too.

I spoke to Sergeant Coleman. "Sarge, I hear you guys got some hand-held anemometers."

Coleman grunted. "Three sets, courtesy of the German Kriegsmarine."

I stared, dumbfounded. "The US Army doesn't have its own?"

"Nothing operational yet. Apparently they're still in development."

"Where'd the ones you're packing come from?"

"Captured German U-boats."

"Thank you, Karl Dönitz," I muttered under my breath.

"Who?" Coleman asked.

"The commander of the German U-boat fleet. Look, pull out an anemometer. I wanna show the kid how we measure wind speeds."

Coleman grumbled but went to work fishing through a backpack until he found an anemometer. He handed the instrument to me. "I'll let you demonstrate, sir."

In the wake of the rainstorm, a light breeze had sprung to life, wafting in the smells of the jungle mixed with the odor of fresh mud and the more pleasant aromas of whatever the Nagas had resumed cooking. A flock of naked children had gathered around the shelter to see what was going on, to see what these strange men with white skin and head-to-toe clothing were up to.

"Tommy, this thing is what we use to measure how fast wind blowing." I held up the small, four-cup anemometer. I walked out from beneath the shelter into the open air and lifted the anemometer above my head to allow the cups to spin freely. Beneath the cups in a circular compartment, a gauge moved in proportion to how fast the cups spun, thus indicating the speed of the wind.

"Hey, Sarge, did you know our German friends measure wind speed in meters per second?"

"We've got conversion charts to knots and miles per hour."

The cups whirled vigorously, and the younger kids began jumping and pointing and laughing. They thought of the anemometer as a toy. I imagined for them it likely ignited the same sort of excitement that a Lionel electric train had for me as a preadolescent.

I checked the gauge. "Three meters per second," I said to Coleman.

He pulled out a conversion chart. "Just under six knots."

Tommy stood beside me, smiling. I pointed at the gauge. "This gives us a number that tells us how fast the wind is blowing." The concept of knots or miles per hour or meters per second would have been meaningless to him. I wasn't even sure he understood what the word "number" meant. He understood what "how many" meant, so I struggled to come up with an explanation of wind speed for him. I let him hold the anemometer briefly, much to the delight of the younger crowd, then motioned him back into the shelter, where we'd be out of the breeze.

The cups on the anemometer ceased spinning. "Blow on cups," I said. He did, and set them rotating again. He laughed. His eyes sparkled. I pointed at the dial that indicated wind speed. "See how strong." He nodded.

I took the anemometer from him, drew a deep breath, and blew with all my might on the cups. I sent them into a dizzying whirl and pointed at the speed indicator. It had rotated to a position almost twice as far as Tommy had gotten it. "More stronger," I said. "Big wind."

"Like storm," he said, and laughed.

"Like storm."

The children who had followed us to the edge of the shelter had worked themselves into a tizzy, pointing, screaming, and jumping up and down. Several reached for the instrument, wanting to play with it themselves. I shook my head. "Not toy," I said, trying to sound gruff. They, of course, didn't understand me.

Tommy took over, yelling at them in Nagamese. They quieted down and trudged away with their heads down, obviously disappointed they couldn't play with the greatest toy they'd ever seen.

"Hey, Major," Coleman said, smirking, "you wanna demonstrate the sling psychrometer to 'em?"

I shot the sergeant an evil eye. Seeing a grown man twirling a whirligig —side-by-side thermometers fastened to a stick and linked to a handle— would have, I was sure, sent the Naga kids into paroxysms of laughter.

"We'll leave well enough alone," I answered. I turned to Tommy. "So, will you tell King we need help from warriors? That we pay good?"

He snapped off another pretty decent replica of a British salute and darted off to King Kally's residence. He returned a short while later. "We help," he said. "We go when sun come up again." Tomorrow morning. I'd hoped for sooner, but decided I'd best be happy with what the Nagas offered.

May 28, 1944

The day dawned bright and humid with puffy white clouds dotting the ridges and hills and already beginning to bubble skyward, a sure sign they'd explode into massive cumulonimbus by afternoon. Then, in turn, these great stacks of roiling clouds would unleash earth-pounding down-pours accompanied by brilliant spears of lightning and rolling thunder.

Those certainly weren't the kinds of conditions I wanted to be thrashing through the jungle in, but it made me realize the southwest monsoon was upon us. A little early, perhaps, but not unexpected. Most days for the next five months would be similar.

Tommy and six Naga tribesmen showed up, ready to lead the observation teams eastward. I shook hands with my guys, patted them on the back, and wished each Godspeed and good luck.

Tommy grabbed my shirtsleeve. "You no go?"

"I go home, back to where I came from."

"I go with you."

I knew the young man had become attached to me, and probably looked upon me like a favorite uncle, but I really needed him to accompany the warriors to act as a translator between them and the weather folks. I rested my hand on his shoulder and stared him in the eye.

"Tommy, you very important. You must go with warriors since you speak good English and understand Naga words. You must help Americans that way. Understand?"

He hung his head. Disappointment. "I understand. But how *you* find way home?"

"Maybe you get warrior to show me way." I meant the statement as a question.

"Okay, I do." He hesitated. "But you come back after many sunrises, yes? Like now, when you come back?"

There seemed a certain pleading in his words, in his eyes. I think he realized that I probably wouldn't be returning and that we were saying goodbye. To tell the truth, I hated thinking I'd never see him again, either. If it hadn't been for this little guy who had a minimal grasp of English, I'd hate to think what would have happened to me and Eve when we'd bailed out of that shot-to-pieces plane six months ago and plunged into the jungles of Burma.

"Tommy, I tell you truth. I probably not come back. We in war. Many things to do. Many places to go. You have become great man. And I mean *man*. But when you become man, life get more hard. Must make hard choices, do hard things. Sometimes must say goodbye even to good people. Like I say to you now."

I saw tears welling in his eyes, but I knew he wouldn't cry. That, I knew, was not in the Naga tradition. At least not in this tribe's tradition.

"We shake hands," I said. "Like men. Say goodbye." I extended my hand to him. But he did a surprising thing. He ignored my hand and stepped forward and hugged me. I'd never witnessed such a thing among his tribe. His bushy hair, redolent with woodsmoke and cooking odors, pushed into my face. He pulled away rapidly and turned to dash off. I suspected his quick movements were so I wouldn't see a tear or two that I guessed might be tracking down his cheeks.

As he sprinted away, he yelled, "I find you good warrior to take you home, GI Rod."

He did find me a good warrior, an unusually tall Naga, a lean, sinewy young man who carried a spear with a rusty metal tip. He didn't smile or say much—not that we could have carried on a conversation—but he seemed aware of my physical limitations. He kept up a good pace once we got moving, but didn't push it. He knew the trails and shortcuts, and we made much better time heading back toward the Ledo Road than I and my men had coming in. Though my leg hurt, I gimped along gamely and managed to keep up with him.

As I'd feared, the cotton-ball clouds of morning morphed into billowing black bruisers as the day wore on. The atmosphere grew still and heavy. It felt as if I could have taken a spoon and scooped sips of water from the air. By late afternoon, thunder, like distant artillery, grumbled through the valleys and reverberated off the hills. I'd hoped to make the Chindwin River before the rain hit, but that seemed unlikely now.

I guessed we'd managed to get within a mile or two of the river when Jerry—that's what I'd decided to call my Naga escort—signaled for a stop. He went to work fashioning a shelter out of giant jungle leaves, then, when finished, motioned me in. I fished a tarp out of my backpack and spread it on the ground. We shared some sort of jerky—monkey meat, I suppose— he'd fished out of a pouch as we waited for the rain.

We didn't have to wait long. It came with a rush and a soft roar. Huge drops hammered through the canopy of the rainforest and pummeled the earth below, turning it into a river delta with dozens of tiny streams channeling through the mud, seeking lower ground, and snaking around rocks and deadfall and decaying underbrush.

The lightning and thunder relented as the storm unloaded its water on us. The racket of the cascading rain took over, drowning out every other sound as the cloudburst went on and on. But in our leafy shelter, we remained amazingly dry, with only a few stray drops weaseling their way into our temporary abode.

Gradually, the intensity of the precipitation eased and settled into a monotonous, almost comforting, rhythm. I glanced over at Jerry. He'd actually dozed off. He remained in a sitting position with his chin nestled into his chest and snored softly.

I finally found my way to the land of Wynken, Blynken, and Nod, too. I awoke in the humid darkness, curled up on the tarpaulin. The rain had ended. Jerry still slept, still in a sitting position. I had no idea what time it was. I thrashed around for a bit and managed to wake up Jerry.

He said something in Nagamese, one of the few times he'd said much of anything, and instantly fell back asleep. I interpreted what he'd said as meaning we had a few more hours until dawn, although I really had no idea. For all I knew, he might have said, "Jeepers, don't be such an eager beaver, GI. Grab some more shut-eye." So I did.

May 29, 1944

Sunlight creeping into the shelter awakened me for good. Jerry had already arisen and seemed anxious to hit the trail. He picked a few leeches off me, then motioned for me to follow as he headed westward.

In short order, we reached the Chindwin. Jerry, who'd been stoic throughout our trek, actually cracked a smile, pounded his chest with his fist, and took off, heading back into the jungle. I guess he figured he'd done his job.

And I guess he had. He'd gotten me back to the river. Now all I had to do was cross it and hike back up to the Ledo Road. The trouble was, yesterday's downpour had the river running high and fast again. I knew if I tried to ford it, my next stop would be the Andaman Sea, eight hundred miles south. So I plopped down on the bank and waited. I hoped by midday it might be low and slow enough for me to make it to the other side.

I ached all over from yesterday's hike. That plus the sunlight and warmth of the morning eased me into siestaville, where I tumbled down a rabbit hole and daydreamed about Eve. I felt her warmth and her touch and her lips on mine. I heard her voice saying with conviction—okay, with *love*—on the grounds of a hospital yard in Calcutta that she wanted to be my gal.

So what happened? Where had she gone? And why in the hell did she have to disappear in a theater of war that was home to almost half the world's population? Or was I even correct in assuming she was still here? Could she have been sent back to the States? Or even to Europe?

I snapped out of my reverie and came to with a start, wondering why life had to be so complex. Why couldn't it be simple, like just worrying about dying in an airplane crash, being blown up by Japs, or getting consumed by cholera? *Eve, Eve, Eve. Where are you?*

I realized that the sound of turbulent water had disappeared and that the Chindwin now ran at acceptable levels. I'd get soaked to my waist, but I wanted to get back to the road so I wouldn't miss Captain Washington. I shouldered my pack, slung my .45 and its holster around my neck, lifted my MI carbine above my head, and stepped into the swiftly flowing stream.

I made it across without incident. Once on the other side, I kept moving. I had no idea when Washington might be passing by, but he said he'd be patrolling this section of the road during the timeframe I'd told him I hoped to be back.

I reached the packed-gravel road in short order and stepped onto the shoulder. No traffic appeared, and I could hear none in the distance. I set my gear on the ground and strapped the .45 back on my hip. And waited. I paced back and forth along the edge of the road and listened to the warble and screech of the birds and the squeaks and squeals of the monkeys. A jungle musical, although it would never make it as a Busby Berkeley film.

But I grew uneasy. Perhaps I'd spent enough time in the rainforest that I'd become a little more native-like in my senses. I had the gnawing feeling that something or someone was watching me. I stopped walking and listened, trying to sort the usual jungle sounds from any noise that didn't belong. I couldn't. But the feeling persisted.

Perhaps Jerry had returned, forded the river, and decided to keep an eye on me. Funny he wouldn't have announced himself, though. A Jap? Couldn't be. They'd been cleared out of northern Burma. A tiger? Doubted it. As far as I knew, they didn't stalk humans. Still . . .

"Hey, someone out there?" I called out. Not that I expected an answer. At least the hollering made me feel proactive. Naturally, I got no response to my yelling. I rested my hand on the butt of my Colt. But the figurative hairs on the back of my neck continued to stand at attention. With my eyes,

I searched the tangle of trees and vines on both sides of the road. But I saw no movement or anything that looked out of place.

I took a few more steps along the side of the road, listening carefully. But only the notes of the birds and hubbub from the monkeys reached my ears. I moved back toward the spot where I'd left my equipment. But then I heard something that made me halt again. The whine of a distant engine—from a jeep or truck—moving along the road. A long way off, however. All the same, comforting. I took the final few strides toward my backpack and M1.

That's when the Jap stood up from behind a leafy shrub a few yards from where my stuff lay. He aimed his rifle at my heart.

7

On the Ledo Road
Northern Burma
May 29, 1944

I swallowed hard. My heart hammered as if it were trying to beat its way out of my chest cavity. I made an instantaneous decision *not* to draw my pistol.

The Jap yelled at me. But I had no idea what he said. My best guess was he wanted me to raise my hands, so I did. I wondered if he'd heard the distant engine noise. I hoped he hadn't.

"Okay, okay," I said, trying to give my voice a soothing edge. But the words came out sounding as if someone were trying to strangle me. I stared at the Jap, and he stared at me. I realized then he was just a kid, maybe sixteen or seventeen. He'd probably gotten separated from his unit when they'd retreated. He looked lost, confused, emaciated. His uniform hung on him like tattered pieces of cloth, and I'd bet he hadn't bathed in weeks. He might have been more frightened than I was. Though I doubted it.

He yelled again in Japanese. I shrugged my shoulders slowly, trying to indicate I had no idea what he wanted. My heart rate hadn't slowed, and I wondered if a guy could have a heart attack from just too much fear. I knew there was likely nothing more dangerous than a terrified kid with a gun. A Jap soldier to boot.

He bobbed his rifle up and down. Maybe he wanted me to kneel. I looked down at the ground, then back at him. He nodded. I knelt. I studied his weapon—scratched, battered, rusty. Maybe even a little mud around the muzzle. Would the thing even shoot? Maybe not, but I decided I didn't need to find out. At least not right away. I listened again for the sound of the motor I thought I'd heard earlier. It seemed to have faded. *Damn.* Could I have any worse luck?

The Jap babbled something more at me. I shook my head, trying to indicate I didn't understand him. I hoped he didn't think I was refusing to do something. A thought came to me. "Hungry?" I asked, and slowly moved my hand toward my mouth.

Something flickered in his eyes. He didn't smile, merely held his gaze on me. I stared back. That's when I spotted something behind him, maybe a couple of kilometers up the road—the silhouette of a vehicle—a jeep, I guessed—parked on the crest of a small rise. A figure strode down the road in our direction. I tried not to fix my gaze on the shape, but instead attempted to keep the Jap kid engaged in what I had to say.

"Food?" I said. "Maybe some delicious chocolate bars, dried sausage, or hard biscuits? Yum, yum." I made chewing motions with my mouth, then ran my tongue over my lips. "I'll have you back to your fighting weight in no time." Probably a poor choice of a metaphor, but since he couldn't understand me, it didn't make any difference. The distant figure—a big soldier—walking along the road toward us grew nearer.

"You like eat?" I said to the kid, knowing pidgin English probably wouldn't work any better than standard English. Keeping his weapon pointed at my torso, he continued to stare at me. I nodded at my pack. "Food, yes?"

He looked down at my pack, then back at me. Maybe I'd made a bad choice. Maybe now that the kid knew I had food, he'd just blow my brains out and snatch the pack.

"Don't get any wild ideas," I said, trying to hold his attention. My heart rate had slowed, but maybe my ol' ticker was just plain tuckered out.

That's when the soldier approaching us began to sing. Well, not so much sing as rumble. Captain Wendell Washington, 1883rd Engineer Aviation Battalion.

"Heigh-ho, heigh-ho,
It's home from work we go,
Heigh-ho, heigh-ho, heigh-ho."

On his shoulder, he carried a shovel like a rifle. *Jesus, aren't engineers issued weapons?*

The kid whipped a glance in the direction of the singing. Then snapped his gaze back at me, his eyes the size of the Rising Sun roundel on a Jap Zero. I didn't know if he'd ever seen a black man before, but I'd bet if he had, not one the size of Washington . . . who must have looked like one of the Biblical Nephilim striding toward him, a giant probably about to send him to a meeting with his ancestors.

Washington switched songs, breaking into "Whistle While You Work." He continued his determined stride, his bass-baritone voice reverberating through the humid midday air.

The little Jap's head swiveled back and forth between me and Washington. He could easily shoot us both, assuming his mud-encrusted rifle still functioned. But his arms began to tremble, and he appeared scared out of his wits.

Washington kept coming. He lifted the shovel from his shoulder and pointed it at the kid like a bayonet.

The kid lowered his gun, spun, and sprinted into the rainforest, kicking up a rooster tail of road gravel like a galloping gazelle. I looked down at the spot where he had stood. A puddle of pee glimmered in the sunshine.

Washington, his shovel now at port arms, reached me, grinning like he'd found the pot of gold at the end of the rainbow.

"What happened to your little brother in arms?" he rumbled.

"You scared the piss out of him. Literally."

"Probably never seen a colored man before."

"At least not one the size of a mature sequoia."

Washington laughed. "I know I can appear a bit intimidating at times."

"Think how you'd look with a Colt forty-five instead of a shovel. Cripes, don't you guys carry weapons?"

"I thought we'd cleared out the Japs from these parts. I had my pistol stowed in my pack. I just grabbed the shovel 'cuz it was handy."

"Well, you'd never pass for one of the Seven Dwarfs."

"Not even Grumpy?"

"Taken. How about Scary?" I picked up my gear and backpack. "But I suspect the dwarves have a height limitation. Anyhow, I'm ready to get out of there. How about you?"

"Your limo awaits, sir."

We trudged back up the gentle rise to where Washington had left his jeep.

In short order we were rolling back toward Assam, specifically Ledo. Washington seemed a tight, uncomfortable fit in the vehicle, with his knees almost touching what in an automobile would have been the dashboard. That aside, he hunched over the steering wheel and herded the jeep along the gravel highway in masterful fashion.

I, for the first time in days, was able to stretch out and enjoy riding—well, jouncing—through the jungle as opposed to slogging along on foot. My bum leg ached, but at least I remained in one piece—strike that—at least I remained alive, thanks to Captain Washington.

As we zigzagged through the hills climbing toward the Assam-Burma border, we encountered a convoy of Deuce and a Halfs rolling in the opposite direction. Washington pulled to the shoulder in a wide spot and allowed them to pass, giving the drivers occasional waves. Once they'd moved past, the afternoon fell silent.

"I've got a couple of messages for you," Washington said, before putting the jeep back in gear.

"Yes?"

"A Lieutenant Colonel Riley back at Chabua requests your presence ASAP."

"Did he say why?"

"Not specifically. Just something about a type of airplane they've been using that tends to crash and burn way too often."

"What's that got to do with me?"

Washington shrugged. "Beats me. I guess he thought you might be able to help figure out why that's happening."

"Sure, me. A pilot with a gimpy leg who's been stripped of his wings."

"I guess the colonel still thinks you must know your business."

"Dare I ask what the other message is?"

"It's kinda from me, sir."

"Kinda from you?"

"Remember how you told me about this blonde nurse you'd lost track of?"

I stared at Washington.

"Well," he said, "I caught wind that one of our Chinese laborers had spotted an American woman with 'yellow' hair at an air base in China where he was helping repair a runway."

Something akin to an electric shock rippled through my body. I jerked upright in the jeep's seat. "What base?"

"That's just it. He doesn't know. I spoke to him in sign language and what few words of Mandarin—"

"Jesus, Captain, how can he not know?"

"You have to understand, the Chinese herd these poor workers around like sheep. They load them into a truck, stuff them onto a train, or cram them into an airplane and carry them off to wherever they're needed. They don't tell them where they're going or, after they get there, where they are. They just put them to work, twelve or fourteen hours a day, then when they're finished, it's off to the next job."

"Yeah, yeah, I know." I understood that the coolies were just chattel for the Chinese government, but still . . . "Did the guy remember anything? Like the landscape, the weather? Palm trees, firs, hot, cold?"

Washington shook his head. "Not much. He worked there in the winter and recalls that it was cool and dry, maybe about ten or eleven hours of daylight. He said he happened to notice the woman because of her 'yellow' hair. She tended to injured workers two or three times."

"She must have been a nurse, then."

Washington nodded.

"But otherwise, cool and dry with ten or twelve hours of daylight doesn't help much. That would cover most Allied air bases in China in the wintertime."

"And last I heard," added Washington, "we've got over a dozen airfields there." He slipped the jeep into gear and moved it back onto the road.

I sat back in my seat and closed my eyes. While I'd learned nothing definitive, at least now I was able to believe there was a reasonably high probability that Eve—the label I'd stamped on the "yellow-haired" nurse the coolie had spotted—remained in-theater, in China. But if that was her, why didn't the army have any record of her? And why hadn't she attempted to contact me? I decided then and there I needed to get back to Hastings Air Base as quickly as I could and pay Brigadier General Leonard Stone another visit.

But I knew before I did that, I had to go see what Lieutenant Colonel Riley at the air base in Chabua wanted.

Chabua, Assam, India
US Army Air Forces Base
May 30, 1944

Lieutenant Colonel Riley, looking haggard and exasperated, sat behind his desk and motioned me into his office.

"Have a seat," he said.

The fan on his desk still rotated in a herky-jerky manner but seemed to do nothing more than distribute the oppressive humidity to all corners of the tiny room.

Riley brushed tiny beads of sweat from his forehead. "So, you survived another trip into the wilds of Burma, I see."

"Nothing too challenging this time," I responded. "Only a Jap straggler who seemed more frightened of Americans than I was of him." I told Riley the story.

He chuckled softly. "I can't imagine anything more terrifying than Captain Wendell Washington advancing on you with a weaponized shovel."

I glanced over at the barred window and noticed the absence of Riley's monkey mascot. "Where's your macaque friend?"

"Haven't seen him for a few days. If I'm lucky, maybe he got too close to the runway when that C-109 crashed and exploded last week."

"C-109, sir?" I hadn't heard of that type of aircraft.

"It's why I wanted you back here, Major. The C-109 is an emasculated version of the B-24 bomber. All of its weaponry has been stripped away, and it's been converted into a fuel-carrying transport. Trouble is, they've been crashing and burning with a greater frequency than any bird we've ever flown. The guys have begun calling it the C-One-Oh-Boom. The flying coffin."

"Well, that's encouraging." I shook my head. "But I don't understand what it has to do with me. I'm off flying status, and was never qualified on a B-24, anyhow. I'm a weather officer. And unless these crashes have something to do with the weather, I don't see how I could contribute anything."

Riley stood and began pacing back and forth behind his desk. "I'll tell you how. We've lost five C-109s in the past three weeks." His voice rose. "That's totally unacceptable. We've made some adjustments in how much fuel these birds can carry as cargo, but, damn it, they're still going down. I need someone smart, experienced, and objective to take a look at what we're doing and why we keep losing these airplanes."

"Not me, I hope," I stammered.

"Yeah, you, Major. Like it or not, wings or not, you've established yourself as one of the best, most resourceful, and most analytical pilots—former pilot—in the CBI Theater."

"What about my weather squadron duties?"

"I've already cleared your presence here with Colonel Ellsworth, so don't worry about rushing to get back to Hastings Mill."

Actually I was. But, of course, I couldn't tell Riley why, that I wanted to get back there so I could go toe-to-toe with a flag officer and find out why I was being fed a line of bullshit about Eve. Funny how this damn war and my military duties kept getting in the way of stuff I really wanted to do.

"Yes, sir," I responded to Riley, without a lot of enthusiasm. "Where would you like me to start?" I figured the sooner I could execute the assignment he'd laid on me, the sooner I could return to Hastings Mill.

Riley stopped pacing and sat back down. "I've arranged to have you meet with a Captain Otis McGinley first thing tomorrow morning. He's got a lot of time at the controls of a B-24, and has had the crap scared out of him more than once driving a C-109. He knows a lot about the aircraft and can offer you an excellent primer on each."

"What time and where?"

"Oh-eight-hundred in the main hangar. Now, get back to your *basha*, enjoy a hot . . . well, lukewarm shower, grab some grub, snatch some sack time, and hit the ground running tomorrow."

Limping, I thought. "Got it, sir. I'll do my damnedest to find out what's going on with your C-One-Oh-Booms. And I guess I should ask, before I get started, why the sudden need to convert bombers to tankers? Does it have something to do with that new bomber command?"

"The Twentieth?"

"Yes."

"You've heard about it, then?"

"The weather squadron is tasked with supporting the Twentieth."

Riley drummed his fingers on the desk. "Yeah, okay. Here's the deal— we need to get as much avgas as we can to a place called Chengtu, China, to support that new bomber the Twentieth will be flying, the B-29. The twenty-nines are based here in India but will stage out of Chengtu on raids. So that's where it'll be 'fill 'er up' time for those big babies."

"And then on to Japan?"

Riley nodded. "But not just Japan. I've heard they're going to hit targets in Thailand, Sumatra, and Manchuria, too."

May 31, 1944

The next morning, I skipped breakfast and sloshed my way through a drenching downpour to the main hangar. I found Captain McGinley waiting for me. He sported the body of a fifty-five-gallon fuel drum with arms and legs as thick as oak tree branches. I guessed he'd grown up on a farm.

"Captain Otis McGinley," he said, smiling. "But call me O-Mac.

Everyone does." We shook hands, and he nearly crushed mine with a vise-like grip.

"Rod Shepherd," I said. "Call me Gimpy. Everyone does." I just made that up, but I instantly liked the guy and wanted to call his attention to the fact that I was no longer an active flyer.

"Ha," he responded, "you may be Gimpy, but I heard you were a hell of a pilot before your safari in Burma."

I shrugged. "So I hear you've got some problems with the C-109. What can you tell me?"

"That it's a flying bomb."

"Right. Look, why don't you start with the plane itself. I know what a B-24 is, but not a C-109."

He pivoted and pointed at a huge four-engined, slab-sided aircraft with twin vertical stabilizers sitting in the hangar. "There's your C-109. It's fundamentally a B-24, you understand. It's not an airplane that was built from the ground up. It's a bomber with all of its gun turrets removed and fuel bladders crammed into its bomb bay instead of bombs."

I whistled softly.

"There are two flexible fiber tanks in the forward half of the bomb bay and two more in the rear. Sixteen hundred gallons in all."

I did some quick math in my head. The fuel as cargo would weigh just under ten thousand pounds.

"What's the max bombload for a twenty-four?"

"Eight thousand pounds. I know what you're thinking. The fuel as cargo is almost two thousand pounds more. But remember, the fifty-cals and ammo are gone. So that probably makes up for the extra cargo load."

"Okay," I said slowly. I could see O-Mac was about to add a few more details. "There's a 'but,' isn't there?"

"Yep. A hundred-gallon tank has been squeezed into what used to be the bombardier's compartment." He pointed at the lower part of the nose of the C-109. "And three more specially contoured metal tanks have been jammed into the space above the bomb bay. Those three tanks hold a total of three hundred thirty-four gallons."

Again, I did some quick mental math.

"So there goes the advantage of having the weaponry removed."

"Yes, sir. With a full load of fuel for flight and as cargo, the takeoff weight for the One-Oh-Boom would be several thousand pounds *over* the maximum. So needless to say, we cut the max fuel load—as cargo—by about forty percent." He paused and gazed for a moment at the immense plane squatting in the hangar.

Then he went on. "We learned a few other things the hard way. We found that if the bomb bay doors were not cracked open for ventilation, the birds would sometimes explode when the electric flaps were retracted after takeoff. Also, to help vent the buildup of fumes, we extended a hose from the bomb bay out through the fuselage." He turned to look directly at me. "But still, the accidents keep happening."

"I've heard the B-24 is a handful to fly," I said.

"It is, but I never had any problems with it."

"Looks like you've got the muscles to fly one even without hydraulics."

"I wouldn't want to try that, but I guess it helps to have been raised on an Oklahoma ranch toting bales of hay, roping calves, and bulldogging steers."

"Where do most of the accidents happen? On takeoff? Landing? In flight?"

"Mostly on takeoffs. Although I know from experience that landings can be a challenge, too. Especially on some of the shorter, higher-altitude runways in China. With a full load of fuel, the thing is as unstable as a drunken sailor, and about as nimble as a hippopotamus trying to dance in quicksand."

On the metal roof of the hangar, the rain continued to hammer down like an anvil chorus.

I stepped back from the C-109 to get a broader look at it. I tried to get a feel for where all the cargo fuel tanks sat in relation to the overall structure of the airplane. I studied the long, flat wings and the horizontal tail section with its twin vertical stabilizers.

"Where are the main fuel cells for flight located?" I asked.

"In the wings and in the upper part of the fuselage directly in line with the wings."

"Wow. No kidding? That must make a great target for the enemy."

"The Luftwaffe fighter pilots in Europe sure as hell knew where to aim.

Hit a wing root and a B-24 became a Roman candle on a downward trajectory."

I grunted a response. I didn't particularly like what I saw as I stared at the C-109. Much of the weight of the aircraft appeared concentrated in its forward half. But that in and of itself shouldn't make it crash on takeoffs. I began to mold a theory but decided I needed to learn a whole bunch more about how the One-Oh-Boom flew. But *how* I'd have to learn didn't appeal to me. Not one damn bit.

"You got a mission coming up soon, Captain?" I asked.

"Nope. I got a few days off. Why? What are you thinking?"

I snorted a laugh. "That sometimes to find out what the cannibals are up to, you gotta walk naked through their village."

8

Chabua, Assam, India
US Army Air Forces Base
May 31, 1944

By "walking naked through their village," I meant that sometimes you have to do things you'd absolutely rather not in order to find out what's really going on. That meant, in my case, taking a ride on one of those damned "flying coffins" to see if I could spot something that all too frequently led to them becoming funeral pyres. And hope to hell in the process I didn't become part of one.

O-Mac told me there was a C-One-Oh-Boom going out that afternoon headed for Chengtu. He got me a spot on the manifest as a "flight observer."

By early afternoon, the monsoonal cloudburst had abated, leaving leaden skies and suffocating humidity in its wake. I arrived on the flight line at thirteen hundred hours and watched as the hulking aircraft took on thousands of gallons of high-octane aviation fuel in its cargo tanks. I noticed that none of the workers deigned to smoke, even within a hundred yards of the tanker trucks and plane.

I found the pilot, a lithe, freckle-faced first lieutenant by the name of

Alan Goodman. I introduced myself and asked the question foremost in my mind, "You had much experience flying these things, Lieutenant?"

"Not much, sir. Just a couple of trips from here to Kunming with relatively light loads."

"How about the rest of the crew?"

"The copilot, David Shabensky, is just over from the States. The navigator is Captain Kevin Rains. He's been over the Hump quite a few times, so we aren't gonna get lost."

I wasn't worried about that. I was a lot more concerned about getting airborne.

"Who else is on the crew?"

"Sergeant Barney Oglethorpe is the flight engineer. He's been around. We aren't carrying a radio operator on this trip, so you'll be able to sit in his spot right behind the flight deck."

I explained to Lieutenant Goodman that I wasn't there to try to find fault with him or his crew, but that I hoped to uncover a clue, or clues, as to why C-109s crashed much too frequently on takeoffs. I knew the checklists he and his copilot would run through prior to takeoff were designed to make certain their bird got into the air safely, but for my own enlightenment, since I wasn't qualified in the C-109, I asked Goodman a lot of questions.

Despite his lack of mission experience, he snapped off the answers without hesitation. That gave me some comfort. I queried him about takeoff settings for the flaps, ailerons, rudders, and elevators. For the fuel mixture. For the turbo superchargers. Finally, I asked about takeoff speeds.

"Normally, about a hundred knots, sir. But with the load we're toting today, maybe one-oh-five. We're hauling about fourteen hundred gallons of avgas as cargo."

"You worried?"

He hesitated a long time before answering. "Yeah, to be honest. Nobody really likes flying these things. They've got a shitty track record. But we're gonna do everything right. I want to stay alive as much as anybody. So the checklists will be followed to the letter. Nothing missed. One tiny deviation, and we scrap the mission."

"I'm with you, Lieutenant." As a pilot—well, ex-pilot—I didn't like putting my life in the hands of another aviator, especially a "kid," but it seemed the only way I was likely to discover if there was a flaw in the system that could be overcome to make the C-109 a safer aircraft.

I had a theory as to why they might auger in more than they should, but I needed to see the process in action, witness it firsthand, in order to verify it. While I didn't have a background in aeronautical engineering, I sure as hell had enough experience as a pilot to sense when something might be off-kilter. Maybe what I was about to do wasn't the smartest way of finding out, but I didn't have time to oversee a long, drawn-out study. We were fighting a war. So making the C-109 into something other than a flying bomb was a time-sensitive issue.

"Major," Goodman said, "Lieutenant Shabensky and I are gonna do the walk-around now. Feel free to tag along." I did, but kept my distance and didn't say anything. I didn't notice anything amiss.

I followed the crew as they pulled themselves up into the bird through the bomb bay. In spite of the fact the bay had been vented as the cargo fuel was being pumped on board, the smell of avgas hung heavy in the air.

A narrow, corrugated steel catwalk spanned the length of the bomb bay. The crew sidled along it to their compartments in the front part of the aircraft. The navigator went to his position in the lower portion of the nose, forward of the cockpit. The pilot and copilot clambered up a long step onto the engineer's deck, then up a shorter step into the cockpit. I followed. The pilot wriggled into the left-hand seat, the copilot into the right one. I stood behind them.

As the ground crew outside disconnected the auxiliary power unit, called a "putt-putt" because of its chugging engine sound, Goodman and Shabensky ran through the engine pre-start checklist. I listened and watched closely. They proved deliberate and unhurried in the procedure.

The engine start process proceeded without a hitch. In sequence, each of the four big Pratt & Whitneys coughed to life, belching streamers of black smoke into the tropical air. The aircraft vibrated with the bass growl of the motors as they spun their three-bladed props into action.

"How much horsepower?" I yelled, to be heard over the throb of the engines.

"Twelve hundred each, so forty-eight hundred in all," Goodman hollered back.

Wow. And I'd thought my C-46 had carried a lot of oomph with its two Pratt & Whitneys cranking out forty-two hundred horses. But the C-109, the ex–heavy bomber, would be hauling a whole lot more lumber a whole lot higher and faster than the Commando ever did. I tried not to think of the big *if.* That, of course, being *if* we got airborne.

Goodman handed me a headset and throat mike, and I slipped them on.

The two lieutenants ran through their final checks and engine run-ups, then herded the huge aircraft, a waddling steel-and-aluminum beast, onto the taxiway. They waited for clearance from the tower, then guided the bird onto the runway into takeoff position. I took a quick glance behind me. The bomb bay doors, as I'd heard was wise, had been cracked open. Ventilation. Still, fumes of hydraulic fluid, gasoline, oil, and exhaust sifted through the cockpit.

Goodman held the brakes with the toes of his boots. He made a final scan of the instruments. He turned to his copilot. "Good?"

"Roger. Good."

I remained standing behind the two pilots. Coming up was the most critical part of the entire mission, getting airborne. And I had to witness the process. What bothered me, really bothered me, was seeing crash trucks already lining up along the edge of the runway. What the hell? With over four tons of high-octane fuel on board, if we crashed, there wouldn't be anything left for the crash crews to rescue. Well, maybe they could keep the jungle from burning down.

"Ready?" Goodman turned his head to look at me.

I nodded. "I hope the cannibals had a good breakfast."

"Sir?"

"Good luck."

He released the brakes and shoved the throttles forward. Shabensky placed his hand beneath Goodman's on the throttles to make sure they wouldn't slip when Goodman took his hand off them to move the control wheel.

The four engines cut loose with a thunderous bellow, and the plane—

rattling, shaking, creaking—lumbered down the runway. It seemed to gain speed only slowly. Much too slowly, it seemed to me. But I was used to piloting a different kind of bird. Not an ex–heavy bomber.

Shabensky called out the ground speeds. Forty knots. Sixty knots. Eighty.

The end of the runway hove into view. A green tangle of tropical trees and dense underbrush grew larger and larger, beckoning us into a fiery hereafter.

"One hundred knots," Shabensky said. His voice sounded calm over the interphone.

We weren't lifting. I saw why. Goodman was pulling himself into the control column instead of pulling it back toward him. We weren't going to get off the ground that way.

"Jesus, no," I screamed.

"One hundred five," Shabensky yelled.

The wheels of the plane remained pinned to the runway as we hurtled toward our green, and likely explosive, destiny.

"Pull it back," I bellowed. I leaned over Goodman's shoulder and grabbed the control column. Together, we yanked it back. Shabensky did the same with his.

The bird thundered over the end of the runway, wheels off the ground, but barreling toward the rainforest.

We had a second or two to live. My vision tunneled, focused on a tall cluster of bamboo. Dead ahead. Waiting to turn us into a fireball. I squeezed my eyes shut. No need to witness my own execution.

It didn't happen. Bellowing like a primordial beast, the C-109 raked through the bamboo canopy. Snapping, cracking, and pinging noises resonated through the interior of the bird. Yet it stayed airborne. Wobbling.

"Gear up," Shabensky said into the interphone, his voice calm and steady. As if the takeoff had been routine.

Goodman failed to respond.

I tapped him on the shoulder. "Gear up," I repeated.

As if in a trance—maybe he was—he nodded and raised the gear.

Shabensky ran through the remainder of the post-takeoff checklist. Goodman responded like a robot. But at least he responded.

The C-109 continued to climb, lifting over the India-Burma border and soaring above the emerald jungles below us.

Drained of energy and emotion, weakness and lightheadedness overwhelmed me. A post-adrenalin-rush reaction, I suppose. I sank into a canvas cushion on the floor of the engineer's flight deck.

After maybe half an hour, I felt recovered enough to stand and move back into the cockpit. As we'd continued to gain elevation, I'd donned an oxygen mask. I stood behind and between the two pilots. Goodman appeared to have recuperated from the terror of the takeoff. He glanced over his shoulder at me.

"So what the hell happened back there?" he asked. "We'd reached rotation speed but weren't lifting."

I drew a deep breath. "A theory," I said. "I have a theory, but it's only that."

"More than I have," Goodman responded.

"I think with the way a C-109 is loaded, with the bulk of the weight forward, and especially with over six hundred pounds of cargo fuel in the nose, you've got a nose-heavy bird. And with the big horizontal stabilizer on its tail, that means the faster you go—which would normally help lift the plane—the more the nose is shoved down. The landing gear gets glued to the runway.

"When you're bearing as much weight as we were, you gotta make sure you pull back on the control column—hard—when rotation speed is reached. You were letting the airplane fly you, not the other way around."

Goodman sighed. "I guess that's the end of my flying career."

"I wasn't tasked with pilot evaluation. I was asked to figure out why crashing and burning seems endemic to these birds. I think I just did that. And if one pilot ever had firsthand experience in knowing what *not* to do, that would be you."

"Hear, hear," Shabensky said, turning toward Goodman. "I'll fly anywhere with you from here on out."

"The first thing I'm going to recommend," I said, following up on my thoughts, "is to get rid of that goddamned nose tank in these birds. You don't need a sea anchor on an airplane."

We settled into a cruise altitude near twenty-seven thousand feet.

"The terrain must look familiar to you, Major," Goodman said.

"Not really. I always flew a more southern route. The C-46 doesn't have the service ceiling this baby does. The mountains on this northern track are a heck of a lot higher than I ever had to worry about. I rarely got over twenty thousand feet in Ol' Dumbo, and the Gooney Birds couldn't get that high."

"But the rivers are the same ones, aren't they?"

"Yes." Far below us, silver ribbons—the N'Mai River, the Salween, the Mekong—slithered through lush, emerald valleys between saber-toothed mountain ranges. Gray-and-white blankets of clouds wrapped themselves around the snow-capped peaks of the towering giants as if wanting to hide them from the prying eyes of outsiders.

The rivers themselves, I knew, would flow relentlessly southward for hundreds of miles, winding through China, Burma, Thailand, and French Indochina. At the end of their journeys, they'd disgorge snowmelt from the Himalayas and runoff from tropical cloudbursts into the Andaman and South China Seas.

I continued to stand in the cockpit, mesmerized by the remote vastness of the land below us. I thought we were over Yunnan Province headed toward Sichuan, but wasn't certain I recalled the names correctly.

"Hey, guys, nav here," came a voice over the interphone. "Coming up in about fifteen minutes, we'll be over Li-Chiang. Take a gander off the port wing. There should be two massive peaks. The aeronautical charts label them as twenty-three thousand feet, plus or minus. You'll be looking into Tibet."

Captain Rains, the navigator, wasn't kidding. A mountain range that jutted toward the stratosphere towered majestically above and to the north of Li-Chiang, a small Chinese city. We soared over Li-Chiang, then banked northeastward toward Chengtu, our destination.

As we neared Chengtu, Goodman spoke to me. "There are four Allied bases around Chengtu. We'll be landing at one called Kiunglai. It's about forty miles west-southwest of the city. The others are closer."

"Which one is the main base?"

"Hsinching. About fifteen miles southwest of Chengtu. It's been designated as Twentieth Bomber Command's forward headquarters."

Their main headquarters, I knew, remained in India. These bases in China would be the ones from which the B-29 bombers would launch their attacks. I hadn't been privy to when the first raids would be launched, but guessed that at the rate the Army Air Forces were delivering fuel to China, it would be soon.

The big engines on our bird sounded fine, virile and loud, as we let down through a deck of scattered cumulus to begin our approach to Kiunglai. The stench of avgas still hung in the cockpit, courtesy of the overload of fuel we bore for the B-29s.

Below us spread a boundless green plain of cultivated rice paddies stretching from horizon to horizon. It offered a stunning change from the rugged topography over which we'd flown for the past few hours. I knew from studying maps that what lay below us was the Chengtu Plain, where waterways eventually drained into the mighty Yangtze River on its almost four-thousand-mile journey from the Tibetan Plateau to the East China Sea. It was virtually impossible for me to grasp the vastness of this part of Asia.

I watched Goodman and Shabensky struggle with the controls of the plane as they flew the base leg and final approach into the airfield. The C-109, designed to carry bombs, not gasoline, rolled from side to side like a fishing trawler in heavy seas.

"Gawd," Goodman exclaimed, sweat beading his forehead as he wrestled to keep the wings level, "this is like trying to get a three-hundred-pound hog to dance like Odette in *Swan Lake*."

I wondered how Goodman knew about ballet, but decided not to ask. He seemed a little busy.

He managed to set the aircraft down on the pierced steel planking runway, but hammered it home hard, blowing a tire in the process. The usual cadre of crash trucks and ambulances followed us down the runway, goslings trailing a mother goose . . . not that they could have done much if two thousand gallons of cargo fuel had detonated, vaporizing everything within a hundred yards of it. I decided then and there I would never fly another mission aboard a fully loaded C-One-Oh-Boom. But I sure as hell had to salute the guys who did.

Kiunglai, Sichuan, China
US Army Air Forces Base

We rolled to a stop at the end of the runway, then turned and taxied to where the fuel would be off-loaded—hand-pumped into waiting tanker trucks. Once the engines had been cut, the brakes set, and the wheels chocked, I was the first guy out of the bird. I walked a short distance from the plane and drew a deep breath. The air, cooler and less humid than that which strangled Chabua, still stank of petroleum, but at least seemed less malodorous than the fumes that had made the trip over the Hump with us.

As I waited for Goodman, Shabensky, and the rest to deplane, one of the ground crew, a bearded sergeant, ambled over to me.

"Sir, do you realize there are bamboo shoots entangled in the landing gear?"

Maybe I'd faced death often enough now I was able to laugh at it, poke a finger in its eye. "We were on a strafing run," I said. "Got a little too low, I guess."

"Sir?" He looked askance at me. "I didn't know these birds were equipped to do that."

"Just hold a Sten gun out the cockpit window and let 'er rip."

"Japs?"

"Monkeys."

The sergeant took a step back from me. "Monkeys?"

"Mean little bastards. Think they own the air base at Chabua." I thought about the evil, sharp-fanged macaques that liked to hang around base ops.

"Uh, yes, sir. Okay. We'll dredge out the shoots and replace the blown tire. And try to stay a little higher on your next, uh, strafing run." The NCO backed away from me, probably convinced I was several bags short of a full load.

Lieutenant Goodman walked up to me. "Sorry about the sloppy takeoff and rough landing, Major."

"What's life without a little spice? You got us here, didn't you? We didn't end up as hamburger aerosol."

He smiled weakly. "I promise a smoother ride home."

"No avgas cargo?"

"Deadheading back to Chabua."

"I'll join you, then. Time?"

"Wheels up at oh-seven-hundred tomorrow."

"Okay. Grab some food, then some quality rack time. I'm gonna see if I can hitch a ride over to—what did you say the name of the base is that's the Twentieth's forward headquarters?"

"Hsinching. Business?" He cocked his head.

I could sense the wheels turning in his brain. He probably thought I was hell-bent on writing him up. "Personal business, Lieutenant. You'll still have your wings in the morning."

"Yes, sir. Thank you, sir."

I trooped over to the operations building. My personal business focused on continuing my search for Eve, though I didn't have a damn thing to go on. Nothing but shots in the dark. I decided Kiunglai, as a satellite base to Hsinching, probably didn't have a dispensary or a hospital, but Hsinching, as the bomber command's headquarters, might.

I asked the duty NCO—a grizzled old first sergeant who, it turned out, spoke a little Mandarin—in the ops office if there was a medical facility on base. As I suspected, he said there wasn't, but that there was a field hospital at Hsinching. I asked about transportation to Hsinching. He shook his head. "Nothing official. There's not much action around here right now. But maybe I could scare up a local to get you there."

"And back?"

"I'll see what I can do." He disappeared, then returned about fifteen minutes later. "I found a coolie who said he'd take you there and back in his wagon. He's not keen on being on the road after dark, but I think if you drop a few silver coins—dimes, quarters, fifty-cent pieces—in his hand, he'll be happy."

"What happens after dark?"

"Not much, really. Every once in a while the Japs like to fly over and rattle our cage. You know, drop a few bombs. But the raids are ineffective.

And besides, the countryside is blacked out at night. Oh, and there are bandits, too. But they're mostly in the counties southwest of here, so they're not a big problem around Chengtu. The Chinks, at least the coolies, they're just easily spooked, I guess."

I sighed. Faint heart never won fair lady.

I found the coolie, a wizened little guy with sinewy muscles who appeared about fifty but was likely only thirty, waiting for me near the main gate to the base. He wore a broad-brimmed straw hat with a flat, round crown; tattered khaki work clothes; and sandals of hemp that looked like they'd been chewed on by a water buffalo.

A muscular black ox yoked to a small bullock cart sporting two solid-wood wheels waited with him. The coolie, perched on a plank at the front of the weather-beaten cart, motioned me to climb in behind him. Debris from dirt and gravel littered the bed of the wagon, but it seemed more dusty than muddy, so I plopped my butt down and leaned back against the low wooden siding of my "taxi."

The coolie said giddy up, or something similar to that in Mandarin, flicked a bamboo stick at the rump of the ox, and with a lurch we wobbled off toward Hsinching. I hoped. My fate rested in the hands of a guy I couldn't communicate with and who I assumed knew the way to our destination. There were no road signs, of course, not that they would have helped me anyway, since I couldn't read Chinese. And it would soon be dark. The old first sergeant had told me the trip would be about five hours. It was currently about five in the afternoon, so we'd certainly finish our journey in darkness.

Once we were away from the base, we jounced along a narrow gravel road built above an endless sweep of rice paddies where hundreds of peasants labored. Occasional short columns of Chinese troops passed by, marching in the opposite direction of our travel. But what became most noticeable to me wasn't visible. It was audible. The grating squeal of the cart's axle. My God, it sounded like a choir of banshees wailing in a cavern.

After about an hour of the ear-piercing caterwauling, I placed my hands over my ears and lowered my head between my knees. I knew with absolute certainty I'd be severely hearing impaired by the end of the trip. The coolie seemed not to notice and appeared to be humming to himself. Or maybe he already was stone-deaf. Squeak, squeak, SQUEAL. Squeak, squeak, SQUEAL. Endless.

Finally, shortly after dark, the cart and the cacophony ceased. I lifted my hands from my ears and raised my head to peer over the side of the cart. We seemed to be in the middle of nowhere. The afternoon clouds had dissipated. Overhead, on a tapestry of black velvet, billions of stars streamed across the sky in rivers of fiery white brilliance. Never had I seen such a wondrous display, not even on clear, frigid nights in the Idaho Panhandle where I'd grown up.

It brought home to me my relative insignificance in an infinite universe, accentuated by my presence in the vastness of this foreign land in which I now found myself, and by the loneliness that had consumed me even as surrounded by billions of people. Insignificance. Yes. But maybe, just maybe, if I could ever find Eve, or discover what had happened to her, I wouldn't be insignificant to her.

In the starlit blackness, I could barely discern the form of the coolie standing at the edge of a rice paddy and urinating into it. Great, I thought, not only do they use human waste to fertilize the paddies, they must also use human pee to help irrigate them. In the future, I vowed to eat only incinerated rice. Not boiled. Not fried. Incinerated.

With the sudden quietude that now embraced us, I could hear the sounds of the night. A symphonic chorus of frogs and peepers and night birds . . . and the soft tinkling of a coolie taking a whiz into the national food supply of China.

Not a bad idea, I decided, and clambered down out of the cart to join him. As I stood relieving myself, the stench of the "naturally fertilized" paddy rose to greet me, along with the vague odors of distant cooking fires, cooking whatever Chinese cooked. I decided not to think about what that might be.

We resumed our journey and the ululating wail of the cart's axle. I re-assumed my position in the cart and decided if I made it to the end of our trip with not just my hearing intact but my sanity, I would be able to survive whatever torture the Japs might devise should they ever capture me.

Hsinching, Sichuan, China
US Army Air Forces Base

Finally, the agonizing trek came to an end. We wobbled to a stop at the entrance to what I presumed to be the air base at Hsinching. An MP standing at a guard shack lit by a kerosene lantern confirmed that it was.

"What is that thing you're riding in," he asked, "some sort of psychological warfare vehicle the Chinks are testing? The noise would wake the dead."

I stepped close to the MP, a young corporal. "Look, I can't order you to do this, but I would be eternally grateful if you could scare up someone with axle grease, lure the coolie away from the cart—maybe offer him some cigarettes—and give that damn axle a quick lube job. I gotta ride back to Kiunglai in that jalopy in a few hours, and I'm afraid I'm gonna need an ear trumpet by the time I get there if I have to listen to that squealing for another five hours."

The MP laughed and said he thought he could take care of it.

"Okay, thanks. Next request: Could you point me in the direction of the hospital?"

"Yes, sir. See that two-story structure about five hundred yards from us over there?" He pointed.

I could barely make out the silhouette of a building half-hidden behind some trees in the blackout conditions of the base. "Is it open now?"

"There's probably a nurse or orderly on duty."

"Many nurses here?"

"A few. There's one, some of the boys tell me, who's a real looker but a total cold fish. There's a rumor going around, total bull crap, of course, that she's Lana Turner incognito. Hiding out from someone."

My heartbeat skipped a stroke or two.

9

Hsinching, Sichuan, China
US Army Air Forces Base
May 31, 1944

I headed toward the hospital, guided only by its shadowy outline in the shimmering starlight. Only tiny slivers of light escaped from behind heavily curtained windows. I found a gravel path as I neared the building. My boots, crunching on the tiny stones of the walkway, provided a weak tympanic accompaniment to the music of the night critters.

I reached the front entrance and slipped into the structure. A bored, slightly overweight nurse reading an old *Life* magazine sat at the check-in desk. She removed the reading glasses she wore and stood.

"What can I do for you, Major?" she asked.

"I'm looking for a nurse."

She smiled broadly. "Well, here I am."

"A specific nurse."

"Oh." She appeared almost crestfallen, but then gave me a leering look. "Thought I had a live one for a moment." At least she had a sense of humor.

"I'm trying to track down a Captain Genevieve Johannsen," I said. My heart rate bumped up. Anticipation.

"Nope. No one by that name here."

"You're sure?" A smidgen of disappointment rippled through me.

"There are only three nurses here. Me and two others. I know both of them, and neither is named Johannsen." She paused. "I'm Lucy, by the way."

"Okay, I believe you, Lucy. So how about a good-looking blonde? Would that fit one of the other nurses?"

"Oh ... I ..."

"What?"

"Well, Darlene Ackerman. She's considered quite attractive. Keeps pretty much to herself, though. Hard to get to know."

"Blonde?"

Lucy nodded.

"Where might I find—is it *Captain* Ackerman?"

"She'd be in the women's barracks. But that's off-limits after twenty-two hundred."

"Look, Lucy, I'm not here on some nefarious mission. I have to get back to Kiunglai before sunup, so it's kind of imperative I check on Captain Ackerman now and see if she, well, might be the same person as Captain Johannsen."

"That sounds kind of weird, sir." She gave me a squinty-eyed once-over.

"Yeah, I know." I thought things over. How could I make things seem less weird? "So how about this? Here're my dog tags." I removed them from around my neck. "Hang on to them until I get back here. I won't take long, I promise. But I really need to visit Captain Ackerman." I handed Lucy the dog tags.

She sighed and took them. "All right, Major"—she looked at the tags—"Shepherd. You really don't seem like a weirdo. You'll find the nurses' billets just behind the hospital." She pointed down a long hallway. "Go out the back door, then about fifty yards straight back."

"Thank you, Lucy." I started down the hallway.

"Knock long and loud when you get there," she called after me. "You don't want to startle anybody."

I knocked long and loud when I got there. No one answered. Was everyone sleeping? I tried the doorknob. The door wasn't locked, so I stepped into the dimly lit billets. From halfway down the hall, I heard water running. Someone in a shower? I moved toward the sound.

I reached the doorway to a shower room. The water stopped. I rapped on the doorframe, hard, and called out, "It's Major Rod Shepherd, United States Army Air Forces. Anyone in there?" Of course there was, and I felt like a dunce for asking the question as soon as the words left my mouth. But there came no response.

"Hello?" I said.

"Jesus, why couldn't you be like any other Peeping Tom and just stick your nose over a windowsill?"

Eve Johannsen stood before me, a huge towel wrapped around her dripping wet—and very spectacular—body.

"Eve." I took a step toward her, my heart thumping like a Thompson submachine gun.

"Stay," she said, snapping off a command as if I were a dog.

I stopped, puzzled, stunned. It wasn't the kind of greeting I'd expected from the woman I'd fallen in love with. Been through hell and back with. Water drained off the golden strands of her hair plastered to the sides of her softly angular face. Her blue eyes flashed an icy warning at me: stay away.

"Eve, it's me, Rod." Hadn't she heard me when I'd knocked?

"Get out," she barked.

"Eve—"

"Get out or I'll call the MPs."

"What? What the hell, Eve? What's going on?"

"Nothing's going on, but I know you're going out."

"Eve, I thought—"

"Don't think, flyboy. It doesn't become you. Out!"

"Out? Eve, I've been looking for you for weeks."

"Oh my God, Major. Have you become Denny Dimwit? Can't you tell when a gal doesn't want to be found? Now I'm gonna start to count, and if you aren't out of here by the time I reach ten, MPs it is. One—"

"You sure you can count that high, nurse?" Just like the old days, she'd drawn out the worst in me. Somehow, someway, she'd found her way back to the sharp-tongued harpy she'd been before we'd survived a plane crash, a brush with headhunters, and a Jap mortar attack in the Burmese jungle. And before we'd clung to each other in a Calcutta hospital in the aftermath and pledged our love to one another.

"I can count that high, Major. And I can also admit when a wartime fling is DOA."

"Fling? You call what we had a fling?'

"Two."

"What happened, Eve? Tell me, please."

"Three."

I backed away. "It was way more than a fling, and you damn well know it."

"Four."

A female voice sounded from behind me. "Trouble in here, Captain Ackerman?" Another nurse.

"No," Eve said. "This officer was just leaving. He mistook me for someone else." She pivoted abruptly and disappeared into an anteroom. I thought I heard her stifle a sob, but I suppose it more likely fell into the category of the wishful imagination of a jilted lover.

I turned, nodded at the other nurse—in her PJs—and strode from the barracks. Once outside and back in the embrace of darkness, I stopped, leaned forward, placed my hands on my thighs, and fought to draw deep breaths. I felt as if someone had driven a dozen sledgehammer blows into my solar plexus.

After a few minutes, I stood erect and stumbled back through the darkness toward the rear entrance of the hospital. Inside, I found Lucy still engrossed in the *Life* magazine.

"Dog tags," I mumbled.

She looked up. "So, did you find Captain Ackerman? Was she the same person as—" Her voice trailed off. I suppose she saw the pained, crestfallen look on my face. She handed my dog tags to me.

"Thanks." I barely got the word out. I turned and shuffled toward the exit.

"If you ever need a friend . . . " Lucy called after me.

Once outside, I got my bearings and headed toward the main gate. A soft chorus of night peepers seemed to be mocking my misery as my boots scuffled along the gravel path. All I wanted now was to get away from this damned backwater base, back to Kiunglai, back to Chabua. Hell, back to the States, but I knew that wasn't in the cards.

What the hell had happened with Eve? Was it something I'd done? Hadn't done?

At the gate, I found the same MP on duty as when I'd arrived. He saluted me and said, "Sir, good news and bad." Like I needed more bad news.

"Good news first," I grunted.

"We gave the cart a good lube job. No more squeaky axle."

"Okay. Bad?"

"The coolie has disappeared."

"What do you mean?"

"I mean he skedaddled, left."

I shook my head. "Why? What's going on?"

The young MP hesitated, looked down at his feet.

"I'm guessing you won't find the answer down there, Corporal."

"Yes, sir. Well, one of the guys who greased the axle understands a little Chinese. He said the coolie was screaming at us that since we took the screech out of his axle, it wouldn't scare off his personal dragons anymore. So he just took off and left the cart."

"Good frigging grief," I muttered. I remembered now about how Chinese peasants believe they have invisible bad-luck dragons that constantly stalk them. The peasants build special alcoves into their homes just inside the front door so dragons can't sneak in. They build sharp turns into their footbridges believing that if their bad-luck reptile comes in hot pursuit, it won't be able to handle the zigzags and will fall into the drink and drown.

I'd had a personal encounter with a coolie trying to dust off his own bad-luck dragon in Kunming a year earlier. On my first takeoff in the CBI Theater at the controls of a C-46, a Chink who'd been part of a runway work crew darted out in front of my plane as it rocketed down the runway. The theory was that if the peasant could make it, his pursuing dragon wouldn't. Instead, it would get chopped to pieces by the props—instant mincemeat and no more bad luck for the Chinaman. Of course, if the coolie wasn't a great sprinter, the dragon would walk off with a gold medal.

Anyhow, here I stood, apparently the new caretaker of the coolie's bad-luck dragon. "Well, I need to get back to Kiunglai by sunrise," I said to the MP. "Any ideas?"

"There's a jeep that leaves here every morning for Kiunglai. It usually carries documents and a few med supplies and stuff, but usually doesn't depart until around sunup."

"That won't help. My flight is wheels up about then."

"Sorry, sir." The kid stared at his boots again.

Time to throw my weight—my rank—around, I decided. "Okay, Corporal, you know the jeep driver?"

"Yes, sir."

"Good. I want you to go find him, tell him he's got an emergency run tomorrow, and that he's going to be leaving at oh-four-thirty with an army major as his passenger. Got it?"

"I can't just leave my post, sir."

"I'll hold the fort. That's an order."

The MP took off at a trot, I stood guard at the gate, and the corporal returned about fifteen minutes later. Mission accomplished.

I sacked out in the abandoned oxcart. I maybe dozed off two or three times, but the ox kept snorting and farting and moving around, and I didn't really sleep. A gruff sergeant shook me fully awake a few hours later.

"You da major I'm drivin' to Kiunglai?" he growled. He obviously wasn't happy about being rousted out so early.

"That's me, Sarge."

"Let's go, den. You kin ride shotgun."

I patted the .45 holstered to my hip. "No problem."

"No. I mean wit a real shotgun." He handed me a short-barreled Winchester 12-gauge as we walked toward his jeep.

"You expecting trouble?"

"In da dark? Always."

"Japs?"

"I dunno, Major. I ain't never driven da route in da dark before. Maybe it's a milk run, like always. But I'm like a Boy Scout, always prepared."

I couldn't argue. I clambered into the jeep, and we launched down the road with a jolt, the taped-over headlights providing just enough illumination through a horizontal slot in the tape.

I tried to think of what unknown threats might be lurking for us. Japs? Probably not in this part of the country. Bandits? I'd heard they mainly hung out in the mountains west of Chengtu. Commies? I thought they pretended to be our buddies now since we both fought the Japs. Although I'd heard Mao Tse-tung's Communists and Chiang Kai-shek's Nationalists often struggled for possession of Allied supplies, since both factions wanted to take control of the country once the Japs had been banished.

The sarge—who never said his name—turned out to be not much of a conversationalist, so we bumped along in relative silence except for the growl of the jeep's engine. At least I didn't have to listen to the shriek of an oxcart axle holding bad-luck dragons at bay.

Behind us, the first sliver of brightness, the herald of a rising sun, tinted the eastern horizon.

"'Nudder five or ten minutes, we'll be der," Sergeant Silence said.

Not so, it turned out. Suddenly, ahead of us, out of the darkness, loomed a barrier of five or six men. The sergeant brought the jeep to a halt.

"Hell," he muttered.

Two men, one bearing an ancient-looking rifle and the other carrying something akin to a small machete, detached themselves from the group and approached us. They didn't look like Japs, but bore little resemblance to the Chinese I'd come to know. They appeared smaller and darker. Their faces displayed the same features as Mongolians I'd seen photographs of. Barefoot, they wore what looked like long wool or felt jackets over baggy pants, and had cloth turbans wrapped around their heads. Speaking a language I didn't recognize as Chinese—not that I had any great expertise in that field—they motioned us out of the jeep.

We exited. "Any idea who these guys are?" I whispered to the sergeant.

"Lolos, I tink, but I ain't never seen none before."

"Who?"

"Lolo people. I heard dey live in da mountains 'round here. Other Chinks call dem barbarians."

Of course. That made my list complete. A year ago I'd been waylaid by

Japs and headhunters. A few days ago, another Jap, and now a band of barbarians called Lolos. If I survived all this crap, I thought, I should probably write a book.

"Any idea what they want?"

"We'll find out quick, Major."

The guy I presumed to be the leader, the one with the rifle, babbled something at us, then pointed at the shotgun I carried and the .45 holstered on my hip. I handed over the Winchester. He nodded at my pistol. I shook my head. No way he was taking my sidearm. Quicker than I could blink, the bandit with the machete flicked it at my gun belt, sliced it in half, and sent the .45 splashing onto the muddy road.

"Okay, you can have that, too," I said.

The Lolos continued to chatter away. The rifleman pointed his weapon at the rear of the jeep and the canvas covering the crated supplies we carried.

"What do you think they're after?" I asked the sergeant.

He shrugged. "I heard dey mostly want opium."

"Think they'd settle for Lucky Strikes?"

"Doubt it."

"You got any opium stashed away?"

The sergeant glared at me.

One of the other Lolos from the group approached the jeep and peeked under the canvas. He shook his head and said something to his buddies. The man with the rifle stepped forward and rammed the gun's barrel against the sergeant's head.

"Hold on," I yelled, "you sure you guys wouldn't like some Lucky Strikes? Chesterfields? Philip Morrises?" I mimicked smoking.

All that got me was the rifle jammed against *my* head. Something like that tends to focus your thoughts.

"Sarge," I said, my voice a bit shaky, "you got any idea what we're carrying for supplies?"

"No, sir. Didn't check. Everyt'ing was preloaded."

I recalled what the MP corporal had told me. "Med supplies?"

"Maybe. Don't know."

I tried to give the bandit with the rifle barrel shoved against my skull a steady, confident glare, then slowly inclined my head toward the back of the jeep. "Okay?" I said.

He looked puzzled, but drew the rifle away and said, "Ouhway." Okay, I guess.

"Whaddaya doin'?" Sergeant Silence said.

"Trying to save us from becoming barbarian barbecue."

I moved slowly toward the rear of the jeep and peeled back the canvas cover. I saw what I hoped I might find, and what I'd bet my life the Lolos already knew about, though I had no idea how.

One of the crates bore the label:

UNITED STATES ARMY MEDICAL SUPPLIES
SOLUTION OF MORPHINE TARTRATE
48 count 6-pack 1.5 cc syrettes
E R SQUIBB & SONS NEW YORK

I turned to the rifleman. "Here ya go, buddy. Good ol' American-made opium. Better than that poppy-made junk you guys smoke in Lolo Land. There's enough here you fellas can sit around in a stupor for a month." I patted the case. "O-pee-um."

Rifle guy thumped the case with the barrel of his gun. "Ohh pum?"

"Right on. Ohh pum. Best in the world."

A couple more Lolos bounded up to the jeep, yanked the crate out, and pried it open with some sort of slender iron pole. One of them reached into the crate, extracted a package of syrettes, opened it, examined it, then held it aloft with a big grin on his Mongoloid face. "Ohh pum!"

I guess we'd made new best buddies. The leader of the bandits, the rifleman, patted the sergeant on the shoulder, then shook my hand, smiled, and relieved me of my wristwatch. Such is the price of eternal friendship, I suppose.

The Lolo bandits, carrying their loot, disappeared into the morning haze. Sarge and I completed our journey to Kiunglai . . . short a shotgun, a .45, a wristwatch, and a crate of morphine syrettes.

Oh, and to be brutally honest, me short an army nurse.

10

Chabua, Assam, India
US Army Air Forces Base
June 2, 1944

With Lieutenant Goodman at the controls of the C-109, we made it back to Chabua without incident. I wrote up my report, turned it over to Lieutenant Colonel Riley, then followed it up with a verbal summary of what I recommended based on my harrowing trip to Chengtu.

"The two points I want to emphasize most about the C-109," I concluded in my briefing to Riley, "are, one, get rid of the avgas transport tank in the bombardier's position, plus the three extra tanks crammed into the bomb bay. And two, tell the pilots to *fly* the bird off the ground, not wait for the plane to lift off on its own. Even if you get the extra weight out of the forward portion of the aircraft—by removing the fuel bladders—the thing is still going to be a handful to get into the air."

"The powers that be aren't going to be happy about getting less fuel into China," Riley said. He ran his hand over the brown stubble on his head. He continued to look harried and overworked.

"The powers that be aren't the ones getting incinerated in the C-109," I answered. Perhaps too cavalier a response. I wasn't the one who would have to deliver that message.

"No argument from me, Major. But too many of the big bosses at Twentieth Bomber Command are of the 'damn the torpedoes, full speed ahead' type. Hard chargers. So I may get the bum's rush when I suggest it might be prudent for C-109s to carry less fuel per sortie to Chengtu."

He rose from his seat and extended his hand to me. "Anyhow, you did your part, and I thank you heartily. I'll carry your findings on up the chain of command."

I took his hand. "Best of luck, sir. I don't envy your trip into the lion's den."

"Well, at least the guys I'll be facing aren't Japs or headhunters." He smiled knowingly at me. "So what's next for you?"

"Back to Hastings. There's a general there I'd like to pay a . . . well . . . social call on. And I need to find out what Colonel Ellsworth at squadron headquarters has lined up for me."

I caught a hop back to Hastings in a Gooney Bird the following day, arriving there in the late afternoon.

Hastings Air Base
June 3, 1944

My first stop after landing was to visit Colonel Ellsworth and let him know that I was "back in town." My exhaustion—and probably the gut punch I'd taken from Eve—was apparently obvious to him.

He locked his hands behind his head, leaned back in his chair, and ran an appraising gaze over me. "Looks like you need to kick back for a day or two, Rod. You can catch me up Monday on what you've been doing, and after that we'll go over your next assignment. But for now, please partake of a good meal at the club, then catch up on your sleep. Tomorrow, just take it easy."

Before heading to the club, I stopped by my quarters, showered, and changed uniforms. When I arrived at the club, my thoughts weren't on eating. As usual, my baser—or maybe more immature—instincts had taken over, and I wandered into the bamboo bar seeking my old buddy, Jim. As bad an idea as I knew it to be intellectually, emotionally I knew I could always lose myself in the nonjudgmental camaraderie of two or three shots of Jim Beam. Okay, maybe more. I'd have to see how the evening went.

I found a comfortable chair in the lounge next to a small cocktail table and settled into it. A blue-gray haze of cigarette smoke hovered near the ceiling while the Monswooners swung through a respectable version of "Stompin' at the Savoy." One of the turbaned Indian waiters strode over to me and bowed deferentially. "Sir?"

"Beam, neat. Two." I held up two fingers.

The band blew into its next piece, "Don't Be That Way," and I thought of Eve and wondered why she'd been "that way." A way that puzzled me. Hurt me. I began to consider the possibility that I'd been merely a rescue log, a chunk of stability for her to cling to in the rushing flood of her emotions after she'd opened up to me about what had happened at Pearl Harbor—the devastating loss she'd suffered, and the demeaning challenges she'd faced in the immediate wake of that horror. Now that the roiling waters of her soul had receded, perhaps she no longer needed—or wanted—a life preserver.

The waiter returned with my drinks and placed them on the table. "Will there be anything else, sir?"

"Don't be a stranger."

"Oh, I am no stranger, sir. I have worked here for—"

"I got it," I said. "I mean check back on me in a little bit to see if I need a refill."

He smiled, nodded, and left me alone with my thoughts. And the Beam. I stared at the two glasses and their amber nectar for a long while without reaching for one. I knew that once I started, it would set me up for a smooth slide into oblivion. I wasn't keen on waking the following morning with Thor taking batting practice in my head.

But what the hell. I grabbed one of the glasses. I lifted it toward the ceiling. "Here's to Eve." I downed half of it, set it back on the table.

"As I live and breathe, if it isn't Major Rod Shepherd, recovered from the wounds he suffered in the Battle of Burma."

I glanced up, startled. There stood a man from my past, Padre Dom—Dominic Rana—the army chaplain who'd befriended me at just about the lowest point in my life, when I lay in a Calcutta hospital bed recuperating after the Jap mortar attack in Burma. He was also the guy who'd found Eve and reunited the two of us after I thought she'd been killed in the same attack.

"Padre Dom. Damn. Oops. Well, anyhow, great to see you. Grab a chair and sit, if you'd like."

"No, no. Looks like you're anticipating a guest." His gaze fell on the two whiskey glasses. "I wouldn't want to intrude."

"No guests coming, Padre." I paused. "They're both mine."

"Well, maybe I will join you." He dragged a straight-backed chair next to me and sat.

He still looked like he could serve as a department-store Santa with the addition of a red suit and snowy beard. At the very least, he fit the picture of everybody's favorite uncle.

The waiter appeared.

"A large Bordeaux, my good man," Padre Dom said. "And thank you."

The waiter nodded and scurried off. I must have looked at the padre in a funny way.

"The Bordeaux?" he said with a cherubic smile. "I still give Communion, you know. I don't want to get out of practice."

I couldn't help but chuckle.

"But you?" he said. "What is it you don't want to get out of practice for?" He nodded at the whiskeys.

I didn't respond to his question, at least vocally. Instead, I just shrugged.

He remained silent for a bit, then said, keeping his voice soft, "Your nurse friend? I'm sorry, I forget her name."

"Eve," I said. "Her name is Eve."

Again, Dom remained quiet.

I decided it was up to me to break the silence. "Yeah. Eve. I'm drowning my sorrows."

"Wanna talk about it?"

"You sure you wanna listen?"

"Gotta earn my keep." He tapped the brim of his wineglass with his forefinger. "Besides, I view myself as kind of a Saint Valentine for you two."

So I told him. Told him how after our Calcutta reunion, Eve had disappeared. Told him how I'd searched for and found her. And told him how she'd then given me a swift kick in the ass and blasted me for not recognizing we'd merely had a wartime fling and that it was now DOA.

"I see," Dom said after I'd finished. He lifted his glass and took a long swill of his Bordeaux.

I waited.

Dom wiped his lips with the back of his hand and asked, "She didn't even want to discuss with you why the 'Dear John' brush-off? Just gave you the old heave-ho? No real explanation other than 'wartime fling'?"

"That's about it, Padre." I polished off my first glass of Beam. Dom seemed lost in thought. I listened to the band as they belted out "Tuxedo Junction." In my current mood, the piece seemed both haunting and melancholy.

Dom leaned toward me. "I've been in this padre-ing business awhile, Major Shepherd—"

"Rod," I interrupted.

"I've been in this business awhile, Rod. I've learned how to discriminate between genuine joy and delight-on-demand. What I saw in your friend Eve back there in Calcutta was bona fide joy. Happiness. When you two came together, she was on cloud nine."

I chuckled softly.

Dom cocked his head at me. "Did I say something funny?"

"No. And I don't mean to interrupt your counseling. But the term you used, cloud nine. Highly appropriate to a man in my profession."

"Weather?"

I nodded. "That expression comes from, believe it or not, the original edition of the *International Cloud Atlas*. Cloud types were given numbers. Number nine was a cumulonimbus, a big, billowing bugger—often a thunderstorm. So if you were on top of a cloud like that, you'd be on top of the world, so to speak. On cloud nine."

"Unadulterated euphoria," Padre Dom added.

"Yes."

"And that's what I saw in your lady."

"So what happened?" I eyed my remaining glass of whiskey.

"In my opinion, and please understand it's only my viewpoint, I think she was trying to give you a warning—"

"About what?"

"Well, I'm not Sherlock Holmes. I was just going to say, 'but I don't know about what.'"

Our turbaned Indian friend reappeared, but I waved him off. I thought I caught a glimmer of a smile from the padre.

We concluded our evening with small talk. I asked what brought Dom to Hastings.

"On my way to Assam," he said. "I guess there's something big a-brewing with the Twentieth. I've been told to try to catch a ride to Chengtu—to where you just came from—and prepare to do my chaplain thing."

I had a pretty good idea what was "a-brewing"—B-29 strikes launched from China—but decided that was still close hold, so didn't try to enlighten Dom.

We chatted for a while longer before he excused himself, saying he had to meet some fellow chaplains for dinner. He wished me well and gave me his blessings, then left me alone with my whiskey and my thoughts.

I recalled how I'd felt when I discovered Eve had departed from New Delhi almost a month ago without so much as even having left me a message. *If I stopped believing in love, I'd stop believing in life.* I knew what I needed to do next. Pay another visit to that pompous ass, General Leonard Stone, the guy who'd told me the army had no records of a Captain Genevieve Johannsen. That stunk like a dead fish in a well-fertilized rice paddy.

I bid my full glass of Jim Beam farewell, rose from my chair, and headed toward the dining room. I maneuvered my way across the smoky dance floor, trying not to collide with any of the couples who'd crowded onto it, while the band—and a vocalist doing a poor imitation of Ray Eberle—moved into "I Don't Want to Walk Without You."

∽

I arrived in Colonel Ellsworth's office early Monday. Despite the backbreaking responsibilities I knew he bore, he'd managed to maintain his youthful appearance. And I could spot nary a gray strand in his thick mane of black hair. From behind his desk, he smiled and motioned for me to take a seat.

"Well, you look chipper and ready to take on the world," he said.

I think that was code for, "Well, you stayed sober and didn't try to climb into anybody else's bunk this weekend."

"I got caught up on my sleep, sir."

"How's the leg?"

"Most of the time I don't even think about it. But it flares up every once in a while, and I start stumbling around like Peg Leg Pete."

"Well, I'll try to keep you future assignments less arduous. I know you just got back from a little side adventure to Chengtu, China, but I'd like you to go back."

That caught my attention. Eve. But I kept any mention of her out of our conversation and said instead, "Just so long as I don't have to go there via a C-109, sir."

He nodded his understanding. "I think we can get you there on something else."

"What's happening in Chengtu?" I had a pretty good idea but decided I'd let the colonel answer.

"The Twentieth is about to launch B-29 raids from its bases around there. The first is scheduled to go out today. A big one against rail yards in Bangkok the Japs have taken over. The next one, the one I want you there for so you can debrief the pilots, will be against Japan proper."

"Wow. That'll be our first strike against the Japs in their homeland since Doolittle's, right?"

"It will. We'll be going after steelworks in a place called Yawata. It's located about five hundred fifty miles west-southwest of Tokyo."

At last, I thought, we'll be bringing the war home to the slant-eyed little bastards. It's hard to get excited about war, but I felt a frisson of elation.

"That's great news, Colonel."

"But in terms of weather, we'll be going in blind. We got nothing between Chengtu and Yawata. That's sixteen hundred miles without any weather observations, including six hundred over the East China Sea. All in all, it'll be like traveling halfway across the US with zippo meteorological data."

I let out a low whistle.

Ellsworth went on. "I need you there, at the Twentieth's forward headquarters in Hsinching, to talk to the pilots and crews when they return from Japan. At the very least we need to know what kind of weather problems they encountered. Visibility. Cloud cover. Winds. As an experienced pilot who's flown in the worst conditions on earth—over the Hump—you'll be able to relate to them. Based on what you learn, I hope we'll be able to come up with some ideas on how best we can take care of them."

The colonel and I continued to discuss the challenges we, the Tenth Weather Squadron, faced as a weather support unit for another half hour. As we wrapped up our talk, he got on the phone and got me manifested on a C-54 going out of Hastings to Chabua tomorrow.

Since I had the remainder of the day open, I decided I'd head over to Eastern Air Command and pay my ol' buddy, General Lenny Stone, a "courtesy call." I waited for a break in the incessant parade of showers that seemed to douse us every few hours, the southwest monsoon in full swing, then darted over to the headquarters building through clouds of misty steam rising from the ground as the sun made a cameo appearance.

As before, I was greeted at the entrance to the building by a corporal in a sweat-soaked uniform.

"I'm here to see General Leonard Stone," I announced.

"General Stone?"

"Twentieth Air Force."

The corporal shook his head. "Sorry, sir, General Stone returned to his headquarters a couple of weeks ago."

Damn. "And that's located in Kharagpur, right?"

"Yes, sir."

About seventy miles from Hastings. That General Stone went back to the Twentieth's home base made sense. With the B-29 raids kicking off, I assumed there remained no reason for him to remain detached at Hastings.

But maybe he'd show up at one of the forward bases around Chengtu, where I was headed.

11

Hsinching, Sichuan, China
US Army Air Forces Base
June 10, 1944

I reached Hsinching five days before the launch of the first raid on the Japanese mainland since Doolittle's visit in 1942. Thus, it came as no surprise to me that army brass had swarmed the base. Many of the colonels and generals had arrived from Washington, DC, and I'd heard they were expected to report back directly to the Joint Chiefs of Staff. That seemed strange to me, but then someone mentioned that the Twentieth fell under the direct command of the JCS. That's unusual, but I assumed it was because of the critical importance Washington had placed on at last taking the war straight to the Japs' front doorstep.

Brigadier General Kenneth B. Wolfe, who had been key in the development of the B-29, stood as the commander of the Twentieth, so he also was prowling around Hsinching. I kept an eye out for General Stone, too, but didn't spot him. Maybe later. I wondered if I should confront Eve again, but decided I wasn't quite ready for another stinging rebuke from her. At least not yet.

On my first evening at Hsinching, a Lieutenant Colonel Bradley Smithfield, from the Twentieth's intelligence staff, cornered me at the mess facility and asked if he could join me for dinner.

"Sure," I said, actually glad for some company.

"I appreciate that," he said. "I heard you're the ops guy for the Tenth Weather Squadron."

"Guilty," I mumbled, as I pushed the rice that had been heaped on my plate to one side.

"Don't like it, the rice?" Smithfield asked, nodding at the pile I'd shoved aside.

"I know how it's fertilized."

The colonel, an older bald man, let out a loud guffaw. "I figure if you can eat that stuff and survive, you'll become immune to any disease known to man."

That drew a laugh from me, too. I noticed he gobbled up his rice supply pretty rapidly. Between bites, he said, "I figure if I can eat army food, I can stomach homegrown Chinese rice." After he'd swept his plate clean he went on. "Look, since you're the weather contact here, I wanted to let you know how our first mission went."

"The one to Bangkok?"

He nodded. "We flew it directly out of India, not from the airstrips around here, since it's a shorter route to Bangkok from Kharagpur than from Chengtu. But we had to fly over the Bay of Bengal."

His tone caught my attention. "And?"

"And the returning crews ran into some rough weather. Two Superforts had to ditch in the bay, two others made emergency landings at RAF bases in India. Mind, I'm not blaming you weather guys, because I know how little data you've got to work with, but I wanted to make you aware of what we encountered."

"Yes, we need to know. We gotta work harder at gathering all the weather info we can. Beyond that, what can you tell me about the raid in general?"

He cleared his throat and looked around to make sure no one was close enough to overhear, although the din in the mess hall probably precluded that anyhow. "We learned, unfortunately, but maybe not surprisingly, that the B-29 is still a work in progress. One crashed on takeoff, one had to abort takeoff because of maintenance problems, and eighteen out of the ninety-eight that made it into the air were forced to return to base because of mechanical failures."

"So only eighty birds made it to the target?"

"Yes. And all but two dropped their bombs. The good news is we didn't suffer any losses over Bangkok because we caught the Nips napping. The bad news is only eighteen bombs nailed their targets. Heavy cloud cover made precision work impossible."

"Not exactly a glowing success."

"We caused only minimal damage to the rail yards, but General Wolfe saw it as a great rehearsal for what's coming—going after the steelworks in Yawata."

We finished our dinners—me except for the rice, of course—and agreed to keep in touch over the next few days, mainly because of the JCS spotlight focused on the upcoming raid.

During the next two or three days, the B-29s began arriving from the airstrips around Kharagpur, India. They landed at the four forward staging bases near Chengtu. Superfortresses from the Fortieth Bombardment Group settled into Hsinching, where I was. I had to admit, those beasts seemed magnificent. Bigger, faster, higher flying, and more lethal than any heavy bomber in the world.

As they swooped in for their landings, I imagined they must have seemed like giant pterodactyls to the coolies lining the runway. Well, not that they would have known what a pterodactyl was. But I bet they were thinking, *Boy, that baby could really take care of my bad-luck dragon.*

The terrible truth was that the Superforts, with their massive bombloads, whether high explosive or incendiary, were going to be delivering bad luck, really bad luck, to an awful lot of Japs. As I recalled, the B-24—the emasculated version of which, the C-One-Oh-Boom, I'd flown in—carried a max bombload of eight thousand pounds. The B-29 could tote more than twice that much, twenty thousand pounds or ten tons, of death and destruction. God help anyone on the receiving end of that kind of savagery.

But I knew such brutality was likely the only way we were going to defeat the Japs. The Allied landings in France a few days ago, and the arrival of the B-29s in the Pacific Theater, had given rise to what I felt to be misplaced rumors of optimism—that the war could be over by Christmas. Maybe in Europe, if things went well. But I knew the effort to take down the Japanese Empire would be protracted and bloody. We'd all heard that the Japs had vowed to resist an Allied invasion of their homeland to the last man, woman, and child. That they'd fight us with pitchforks, scythes, and axes if they had to. I could see the war in the Pacific stretching out for another two or three miserable years.

Lieutenant Colonel Smithfield looked me up again two days before the mission was due to launch. "Found out something interesting," he said. "About a dozen members of the press and broadcast media, including correspondents from the *New York Times* and *Newsweek* and *Time* magazines, are going to be tagging along on the raid. Biggest deal since Doolittle poked a stick in the Japs' eyes, I guess. So, I thought if you'd really like to dance cheek-to-cheek with the weather . . ."

He let his words trail off. But I knew what was coming. Another offer to take a stroll in the buff through a cannibal village. Well, why not? Maybe if I tell them I'd consumed Chinese rice, they'd leave me alone. Even before I knew what I was saying, I opened my mouth. "I'd like to ride along," I said, "as long as it's a roundtrip."

"Can't guarantee that. But there's a pre-briefing tomorrow morning for officers and the press. Kind of an overview of the mission, I guess. Eleven hundred hours in base ops."

And here I'd thought after I'd lost my pilot's wings I'd be able to stay out of dicey situations.

The briefing room turned out to be small, stifling, and packed—standing room only. The briefer, a tall full-bird colonel, strode into the room and pulled a canvas cover off a large map tacked to the wall.

"Gentlemen," he said, "tomorrow we are going to pay a surprise visit to our friends in Japan on the island of Kyushu. Specifically, we'll be dropping by the Imperial Iron and Steel Works in a city called Yawata, the Pittsburgh of Japan. That place cranks out about a quarter of the Japs' annual steel production."

Hushed murmurs coursed through the briefing's attendees.

The colonel continued. "As a host gift, we'll be sending them sixty-eight

B-29s, each battle-loaded with two tons of high-explosive, general purpose, five-hundred-pound bombs. A direct hit by one on a coke oven will blow it to kingdom come, or wherever Jap things go after they explode into bits and pieces."

Subdued cheers and chuckles rippled through the crowd of airmen.

"Our scheduled departure is sixteen hundred tomorrow. That will put us over the target around midnight. We'll fly in a column formation and drop our gifts from staggered altitudes, between eight and eighteen thousand feet."

The briefing concluded with a discussion of the equipment the press and observers (me) would be issued and to which aircraft we'd be assigned.

I left the briefing and stepped outside into bright sunshine—rare for Chengtu—and a breeze that swept tiny troupes of whirling dust devils across the base from where the coolies labored on the runway. Their work seemed endless, and I supposed it was, keeping the PSP well supported and smooth for the sixty-ton Superforts. As I limped toward the mess facility, I spotted, of all people, General Stone flanked by two lower-ranking officers.

"General Stone, sir," I called out, and upped my impaired gait to catch him.

He stopped, turned, and waited while I approached. His eyes seemed to narrow in recognition. "Well, damned if it isn't Major Gimp from Hastings. Don't tell me you're still looking for a nurse."

I saluted, proper military protocol, though I really didn't feel like doing so. "Well, no, sir. The thing is, I actually found her. Right here at Hsinching." Stone and one of his sidekicks, a lieutenant colonel, traded a quick, almost imperceptible glance. "Only she's using a different name now."

"I see," he said. He paused, giving me a "don't-forget-I'm-a-flag-officer" stare. "And this relates to me how?" His words came out clipped and sharp.

"Well, sir, you told me you had no records or orders pertaining to her when we met at Hastings."

"Why *would* I—why would the army—if she changed her name?"

"Wouldn't there be record of that?"

"Look, I think I told you this before. At Hastings. You wouldn't be the first Joe an army nurse might be trying to ditch." He stepped closer to me. "One thing I won't tolerate in this command, Major, is harassment of our nurses. I want you—no, goddamnit—*order* you to have no further contact with that nurse, whoever she is."

"Sir—"

"You got that, Major Shepherd? No more harassment of the nurse."

"I wasn't—"

"I asked if you got that?" he growled.

"Sir." I saluted and performed a quick about-face. *Rat fucker*, I thought, but somehow managed not to verbalize it. I wanted to get away from the SOB.

"Hold it, Major," he snapped. "I'll tell you when you're dismissed."

I stopped, pivoted, and stood at attention in front of him.

"You know, Shepherd, I'll be damned if I understand why you're still in the service," he hissed. "You hobble around like Long John Silver, you got your ass booted off flying status—maybe because, according to army records, you've lost two aircraft—and there's been a rumor floating around that maybe you know more than you've let on about someone who fired a flare gun in a *basha* at Chabua and burned it down—"

"It didn't burn down, sir, a hole got burned in the—"

"Can it, Shepherd. I'll tell you when you can speak."

The bastard was dredging up ancient history now. Yeah, months ago, before I got wounded, I had a little too much to drink one night and accidentally triggered a flare gun in my *basha* that set fire to the thatched roof. Like I said, ancient history. Nothing was ever proved.

Stone edged closer to me, something malevolent in his gaze. His jaw flexed, and he seemed to chew on his words before spitting them out. "Just what is it that you do, Major? I mean, what redeeming value do you possess that's actually helping the army now?"

I guessed it was my turn to speak now. "I'm the operations officer for the Tenth Weather Squadron."

"Well, whoop-de-fuckin'-do. A weather guesser. You guys are about as worthless as gunsights on a Gibson Girl." He spoke to the lieutenant colonel at his side. "See if you can find our meteorological major here a beanie with a propeller on it. Something he could wear with pride. Then see about getting him shipped back to the States where he could, I don't know, sell war bonds or something useful. Not hang around here. Good lord, next thing I know he'll be trying to peek through knotholes at nurses."

I remained at rigid attention, thinking of every foul word I could to describe General Stone-ass. He continued to focus a frosty gaze on me. I suppose he meant it to seem intimidating, but I thought it made him look constipated. I willed myself not to snicker and managed to hold a straight face.

Finally he said, "Okay, *now* you're dismissed, Major Propeller Beanie." He turned and walked away from me. Well, not exactly walked. He mimicked my short-legged limp for several steps, which drew a laugh from his accompanying acolytes.

All things being equal, I have a great deal of respect for general officers. By and large they are smart, capable, and fair. You don't get to pin on stars by being a jerk. But I seemed to have encountered a shining exception in Stone. It appeared he had gone out of his way to develop a mental dossier of "crimes against humanity" on me. But why me? What had I ever done to him? I couldn't quite come to grips with his animosity. I needed to speak with Eve again. There might not be a connection between her and Stone, but I sure as hell wanted to find out. His sudden concern about the harassment of nurses and getting me a swift kick in the rear back to the States had more than ignited my curiosity. I was pretty sure Stone-ass couldn't override Colonel Ellsworth and the weather squadron in issuing orders. But, on the other hand, he *was* from the Joint Chiefs of Staff . . .

I decided the heck with lunch, the heck with generals, and the heck with the JCS, and headed toward the hospital to see if Eve was on duty. I wouldn't exactly be disobeying Stone's order, since he commanded me not to *harass* the nurse "whoever she is." But in my mind, I had no intention of harassing her. All I wanted was a civil conversation. Of course, I realized that *civil conversation* could be an oxymoron with Eve when she was on her broom.

I entered the hospital and found a med tech, a private who looked like he should have been in grade school, on duty at the check-in desk. At least it wasn't Nurse "if-you-ever-need-a-friend" Lucy.

"I'd like to see Captain Eve . . . Captain Darlene Ackerman," I said.

"I believe she's with a patient, sir."

I pulled myself as erect as I could on my shortened leg and tried to look and sound like an imposing army major. "Tell her she's got another one waiting," I said crisply.

"Uh . . . I don't think . . . it's—"

"Now, Private."

"Y-yes, sir." He scurried down a connecting hall.

He returned and ushered me into an exam room. "She'll see you shortly, sir."

The exam room appeared primitive with a gurney, a single metal chair, a small cabinet with limited medical supplies, and on the wall a framed set of instructions behind glass of what to do in case of an air raid. I sat for quite a while before Eve knocked and stepped in.

"Oh, Jesus," she said.

"Nope. Just me. Rod."

"Funny."

"Nice to see you dressed. You know, not just stepping out of a shower dripping wet."

"Also funny."

She placed her hands on her hips and locked me in an arctic stare. She was really good at that. And looked gorgeous doing it. "What is it about a brush-off you don't understand?"

"It's not that I don't understand, Eve, it's that I don't believe it."

She drew a deep breath and rolled her eyes. "What would make you believe it?"

I stepped toward her.

The blow came so fast and unexpectedly I never saw her hand move. She popped me on my left cheek with the flat of her right hand, and I staggered back, struggling to keep my balance.

"That?" she yelled. "Does that make you believe it?"

"Eve, what the hell? What in God's name happened to you?" I held my hand against the side of my face.

"Nothing happened. No, plenty happened. So why can't you get it through that thick Idaho potato head of yours that I just don't want to be seen with you?" Her words came out like poison-tipped arrows.

"Why won't you talk to me, Eve?" I mumbled through a swelling upper lip.

"Get. Out."

"Just tell me—"

"Leave now. Or I'll have the orderly call the MPs." She opened the door of the exam room.

I nodded and moved toward the door. "Okay. Let me finish one sentence, if I may."

"Whatever."

"I love you, Eve. I thought—"

"You said *one* sentence."

"Fuck it. I just wanted to say I love you, because I'm going on the raid to Yawata. Just in case things get FUBAR, I wanted you to know that for sure." I stepped into the hallway.

She held me in her patented death gaze for a second or two. I thought I saw a tear cling to the corner of her left eye. "Damn you," she whispered hoarsely. She slammed the door. Hard. I heard the framed air raid instructions crash and shatter on the floor.

That night, I lay on my lumpy bunk rehashing the recent encounters I'd had with General Stone and Eve. Only the occasional bellow of a B-29 engine—testing for the raid tomorrow, I presumed—interrupted my thoughts.

I wondered why Stone's animosity toward me seemed to have been there from the get-go. Or was he that way with everyone? And how had he come up with my name so readily in our verbal exchange this afternoon? On reflection, it seemed almost as if he had it filed away on some special "watchlist" he held within himself.

And Eve. Why wouldn't she talk to me, explain what had happened between us, what was going on? Padre Dom's words from our discussion at Hastings echoed in my mind—"What I saw in your friend Eve back there in Calcutta was bona fide joy. Happiness. When you two came together, she was on cloud nine."

Yet suddenly I'd become a reviled anathema to her? Jack the Ripper or something? Today she'd said "damn you"—with a tear in her eye—and slammed a door in my face. *Damn you* because I'd found her, or *damn you* because I was going back into combat? I guess like most men, I'd never fully understand women.

Something else she'd said also bothered me—"I don't want to be seen with you." An odd choice of words, I thought. Not, "I don't want to see you ever again," or "I want you out of my life forever," but "I don't want to be seen with you." It seemed to me a phrase she'd chosen deliberately.

And that's when something else Padre Dom had mentioned wormed its way into my musings. He'd said it was only his opinion, but he thought Eve might be trying to give me a *warning*. I wondered, after having found General Stone here, if it might have something to do with him. But I had only vague suspicions, fantasies, and speculations relative to that, nothing concrete I could confront him with, especially since Eve had given me no reason whatsoever to support such notions. My deliberations ended there, crashing and burning after flying into the side of a cliff.

Frustrated, I cast my reveries about her and Stone aside and thought about tomorrow. An amalgam of excitement and apprehension had coiled itself around me. Excitement because I'd be flying into combat in the most advanced weapons system the world had ever seen, the B-29 heavy bomber, the Superfortress. Apprehension because I'd be flying into combat in an exotic aircraft that hadn't yet been fully flight tested or, for that matter, fully battle tested.

But that held true for any aircraft built and rushed into service during wartime. There would be problems that would come to light only as the bird accumulated more and more flying hours, or only during the confusion and carnage of battle. Our enemy wouldn't be only the Japs, but all of the weaknesses that came with youth . . . in this case, the youth of an airplane. I had no doubt the B-29 would become the most fearsome weapon of the war, but there would be a high cost in men and material to get it there.

I just hoped I wouldn't become part of the down payment on that cost tomorrow, on the Army Air Forces inaugural jaunt to Japan.

I closed my eyes and listened to the soft chirp of crickets fill the quiet void between the thunderous roar of Superfort engines being run up. I thought back to a time in my life, not that many years ago, when all I had to worry about was whether I'd be able to yank a twenty-pound steelhead trout out of the swift waters of the Wilson River in Oregon.

12

Hsinching, Sichuan, China
US Army Air Forces Base
June 15, 1944

I walked to the flight line in the early morning light beneath a blanket of clouds spread over the base like a thick, ragged quilt. After I arrived, I watched the B-29s being readied for battle. They matched the dullness of the morning, painted as they were in army olive drab.

Still, they appeared magnificent in a terrifying way. I guessed that the sausage-shaped fuselage, tapered toward the rear, would have extended for about a third of the length of a football field. The wingspan would have reached out over the benches of the opposing teams on either side of the field.

Four massive Wright Cyclone turbocharged engines, two on each wing, powered the behemoth. Each engine, as I recalled, cranked out twenty-two hundred horsepower. So the four engines on the bomber would put out more than twice the power of the C-46 cargo carrier I'd flown, and would lift the bird into the lower reaches of the stratosphere.

Thick bulletproof glass encased most of the rounded nose of the Superfortress—where the pilot, copilot, and bombardier plied their trade—giving it the appearance of a greenhouse.

I counted five gun turrets—two on top, two in the belly, one in the tail. Someone told me each turret supported twin fifty-caliber machine guns. In addition, the tail also boasted a twenty-millimeter cannon.

The ground crews busied themselves pumping thousands of gallons of fuel into each B-29 scheduled for the raid on Japland, drawing on the avgas supplies that had been relentlessly ferried into the airstrips around Chengtu from India over the past weeks. Hundreds of trips over the Hump had been carried out by C-46s, the new C-54s, the notorious C-One-Oh-Booms, and even some B-29s that had been stripped of armament and essentially converted to tankers. I'd seen one dubbed the *Esso Express* land at Hsinching several times.

After watching the ground pounders do their thing for the better part of an hour, I headed off for an early lunch with the combat crews. I sat with the guys from the Superfort I'd been assigned to, tail number 42-6489. I'd seen it parked on the ramp. The name *Seventh Seal* had been painted on its nose in large scarlet letters. The name, I presumed—though I'm not a biblical scholar—came from the book of Revelation in the New Testament and had something to do with the final judgment of the wicked. *Japs*, I thought, *take notice.*

At lunch, I found myself seated between the pilot of the *Seventh Seal*, Nestor Woods, and the copilot, Matt Duwamish. Captain Woods, from Middletown, Connecticut, had flown B-17s in Europe but wanted to jockey the new B-29. So he had volunteered for training at Smoky Hill Army Airfield in Kansas, which was where he met his copilot, Second Lieutenant Duwamish. Duwamish, from Sandy, Utah, seemed eager to go into battle, although he mentioned the mission to Yawata would be his baptism under fire.

Nestor introduced me to the rest of the crew, but I couldn't keep track of their names. Too many. Four gunners. The bombardier, the navigator, engineer, radioman, and radar operator. I asked Nestor if radar helped them better identify bombing targets.

"We haven't been trained on that aspect of employing radar, so for the time being, it's mainly a nav aid. And that'll come in handy on this mission, since we'll be over the target at night. We'll use it for ground mapping—for instance, to identify the Kyushu coastline when we get there. Oh, and another thing, it should help us to keep from bumping into each other."

After lunch, we geared up. I got issued a leather helmet, Mae West, parachute, oxygen mask, electrically heated flying suit, knife, hip holster for my newly issued .45, and a quart of water.

"Flak vests are already in the aircraft, Major," the corporal handing out the flight equipment told me.

I had understood the Superfort to be pressurized and heated, so I asked Nestor about the need for oxygen masks and the heated "bunny suits."

"The compartments forward and aft of the two bomb bays are pressurized and heated," he said. "They're connected by a crawlway above the bomb bays. But if we suffer combat damage and sudden depressurization, you'll be glad for the mask and bunny suit. Also, above ten thousand feet, at least one man in each compartment wears an oxygen mask. If the oxygen supply system isn't functioning properly, hypoxia—oxygen deprivation—can sneak up on you. You can black out before you realize what's happening. You don't want that to occur when you're saddled up on two tons of high explosives."

I concurred.

At fifteen hundred hours, I lugged my gear out to *Seventh Seal*. I climbed into the bird through a hatch in the nose wheel well while several of the crew, including Nestor and Matt, completed the walk-around inspection of the plane. As with any aircraft, they'd be checking the wheels, struts, brake lines, engine cowlings, wing seams, ailerons, trim tabs, guns and gun cameras, and dozens of other items.

After completing the inspection, the rest of the crew scrambled into the plane. I watched through the greenhouse glass as the ground pounders pulled each propeller through four three-hundred-sixty-degree turns to get rid of any oil that might have accumulated in the lower cylinders. That would preclude hydraulic lock on start-up.

The crew in the forward compartment got settled in—the pilot and copilot in the upper portion of the cockpit, the flight engineer behind the copilot facing aft, and the radio operator and navigator in the rear of the compartment. The bombardier would be positioned in the lower portion of the nose, but not until after we got airborne. I would sit on a hatch cover next to the engineer.

"Your tush might get cold once we're airborne," the engineer cautioned me. "We'll be tickling the bottom off the stratosphere going out over China, you know, so you might want to cushion your bum with your flight suit."

Seemed like a reasonable idea.

Nestor and Matt ran through the checklist for engine start, then cranked up the eighteen-cylinder monsters one by one. Each bellowed to life, spitting a stream of gray-white smoke from its exhaust port into the shattered stillness of the afternoon. The coolies lined the edges of the runway and watched in wide-eyed amazement as sixteen other Superforts did the same.

I assumed a similar number of bombers at the three other bases surrounding Chengtu were cranking up their engines, too. I wondered how many of them would actually get airborne. As fearsome as the B-29s were, they were still works in progress. Mechanical failures were not uncommon.

Shortly after sixteen hundred hours, we taxied onto the runway, Nestor steering with the engines. He set the bird perpendicular to the runway, ran up the engines one more time, then turned the B-29 into the wind and shoved the throttles forward. We thundered down the runway and, with only a tiny wobble, lifted off into a thick stratus overcast. We quickly burst into bright sunshine above that, on our way to the heart of the Imperial Japanese Empire, a fortress I was sure our implacable enemy thought impregnable.

We continued to climb steadily out over occupied China, bound for the East China Sea.

I called Nestor on the interphone. "Observer to pilot," I said, "I presume the reason we're still climbing is to gain enough altitude so Jap fighters won't bother us."

"They may not even spot us at thirty or thirty-one thousand feet. And if they did, they'd be unlikely to catch us. We're cruising at two hundred thirty-five knots and could goose it up to over three hundred if somebody got hot on our tail. Then, even if somebody could overtake us, I doubt they'd stand much of a chance against the defensive armament we carry."

We joined up with other Superforts in a loose formation, skimming along at the base of the stratosphere as we soared eastward, far above any unsuspecting Japs almost six miles beneath us. It had turned dark by the time we hit the Chinese coastline and winged out over the East China Sea. Only a sliver of a banana moon hung in a black velvet sky, offering virtually no illumination. There seemed very little chance we'd been spotted.

Matt, the copilot, had donned his oxygen mask, but the rest of us remained in pressurized comfort.

Nestor contacted the crew. "Well, I'm told our attack force lost one bird on takeoff and that four others have had to turn back because of mechanical problems. So there will be sixty-three of us making a courtesy call on the Jap homeland. We're about three hours from our target, although the lead bombers will hit it shortly before we do. I'll give you updates as we near Kyushu."

I asked Nestor for permission to crawl through the pressurized passageway to the aft compartment where the radar operator sat. I wanted to see what this modern detection device provided in the way of imagery.

The passageway, a tunnel about a yard in diameter, felt claustrophobic to me, so I closed my eyes and wriggled through it as rapidly as I could. The radar observer, a Master Sergeant Gransden, sat at the rear of the compartment facing the port side of the aircraft.

"On the early model Superforts," he said, "this used to be where folddown bunks for crew rest were located. Now it's home to a cathode-ray tube . . . the radar scope. Here, take a look."

I fit my face against a rubberized viewing mask. "All I see are range rings and a bunch of white dots."

"Other aircraft. There'll be a lot more to see when we get closer to land. The radar beam picks out coastlines for us."

"Where's the radar antenna located?"

"Between the two bomb bays."

"Can you bomb using radar?"

"Theoretically. We haven't been trained to do that yet. But someday, if we get enough information on a target to be able to ID it on a radarscope, yeah, we should be able to use it to aim bombs. Especially at night. But for now, it's more of a navigation aid. Like tonight, it'll help us identify the assembly point, the departure point, and the initial point . . . where we begin our bomb run."

I sat back from the viewing mask. "You work closely with the navigator, I take it?"

"Very."

I thanked Sergeant Gransden and wriggled back through the crawlway to the forward compartment. The engines sounded great—powerful, solid, and noisy. The B-29 growled through the darkness with only occasional jiggles. Because of the lack of moonlight, I couldn't make out if there were any clouds below us, but there was certainly none at flight level. All in all, things seemed to be going well. But I'd had enough mission experience that I remained a strong believer in what a crusty old colonel had once told me as a cadet: "If things seem to be going well, there's obviously a flaw in your plans."

We reached the assembly point, a couple of small islands south of Kyushu, and the birds fell into column formation. We donned our flak vests and helmets as we approached the combat zone—the island of Kyushu itself—and began our descent to bombing altitude. For us, that would be ten thousand feet. Other Superforts would unload their five-hundred-pounders from above and below that altitude. We couldn't maintain our thirty-thousand-foot level to do our bombs-away bit, because dropping from that high would greatly diminish our precision, not that there would be a lot of exactness anyhow if we couldn't ID our targets quickly.

We continued north along the west coast of Kyushu until we reached the departure point and banked to a north-northeast course. That would lead us directly to the Imperial Iron and Steel Works. We settled into our assigned bombing altitude of ten thousand feet.

I sensed the crew members in the forward compartment growing tenser. The flight engineer, whom I sat next to, leaned closer to his instrument panel with its dozens of gauges and dials and seemed to fixate on them. Engine RPMs, fuel pressures, oil pressures, cylinder head temperatures. He focused on engine performance, which allowed the pilots to focus on flying. Nifty idea, I thought.

Interphone exchanges between the nav and pilots became terse—clipped and sharp. My ticker tocked up, and beads of sweat formed beneath my flak helmet. Yes, I'd been in combat before, but never on a bombing run over the Jap homeland.

We hit the initial point and commenced our bomb run. The bombardier and nav took control of guiding the plane. "Ready, guys?" Nestor asked. Rhetorical question. "Here we go."

Up ahead, brilliant white-and-orange flashes erupted from the ground as the lead bombers unloaded on the steel works. But our arrival obviously had not surprised the Japs. Scores of searchlight beams knifed through the darkness. Red bursts of antiaircraft shells filled the night. We clearly had not flown over occupied China undetected.

Nestor ordered the bomb bay doors opened. He talked to the bombardier. "Daryl, you see the target?"

"No, goddamnit. The lights are blinding me. And there's smoke and clouds and shit all over the place."

"Find it, Daryl, find it."

"Yeah, yeah. Gimme time."

The Superfort seemed to be pointed directly into the glare of half a dozen converging search beams—and the heaviest concentration of ack-ack. The airborne explosions rocked the plane in fierce concussion waves and rolling thunder. Despite the hell being unleashed around us, the pilots held the plane on a steady course.

"Daryl, Daryl, you got it?" Nestor screamed into the interphone.

"No. Everything looks the same."

"Shit."

"Wait, wait. Think I see it."

Seventh Seal seemed to hang suspended in a nova of searchlights, a tubular coffin clutched in the claws of a fire-breathing dragon.

"Now or never, Daryl," Nestor yelled.

An enemy shell erupted immediately beneath the starboard wing. The bomber pitched to the port, righted itself.

"Okay," Daryl shouted. "Okay. Bombs away."

Nestor nosed the B-29 down as *Seventh Seal* unloaded two tons of high explosives on the steel plant below.

Freed of its burden, the B-29 bobbed up, and Nestor rolled it to the port. I spotted another B-29 above us, offset, a second one below, each on its bomb run. Dozens of fires—like giant, angry fireflies—blossomed from the city beneath us. Layers of clouds made it difficult to capture a sweeping panorama, but the results of our visit dotted the Jap landscape in brilliant, blazing pinpricks of light.

"Tail to pilot," I heard on the interphone. "Two bandits five o'clock low."

A pair of Jap fighters were apparently coming after us, climbing toward us from the rear.

Nestor responded, "Tail, ventral, open fire when within range. I'll keep climbing."

Within seconds, the tail gunner and ventral gunner opened up. Short, rattling bursts from four fifty-caliber machine guns echoed through *Seventh Seal*, their reverberations ringing like fierce jackhammers. I understood that, except for the tail gun, the B-29's defensive weaponry was remotely controlled by the gunners, and that something called a computer helped them in targeting. I didn't understand it all, but it must have been pretty damn effective. No sooner had the firing begun than the tail gunner called out, "Bandits breaking off."

"Woo-hoo," Nestor yelled. "Guess it helps to have a five-hundred-yard advantage in firing range."

We climbed away from Kyushu and headed back to China. But I noticed the engineer staring intently at his instrument panel and constantly tapping a couple of the dials.

"Something wrong?" I hollered at him, not wanting to use the interphone.

He shrugged and leaned toward me. "Maybe. We're losing oil pressure on number four, and the cylinder head temps are climbing."

The airburst we'd taken immediately under the starboard wing just before we dropped our bombs must have done some damage.

We cruised back over the Chinese coast shortly before dawn. But as the first rays of the morning sun burst over us, one of the gunners said, almost too calmly, I thought, "Black smoke coming out of number four engine."

If things seem to be going well, there's obviously a flaw in your plans.

13

Over China
Seventh Seal returning from raid on Yawata
June 16, 1944

Nestor issued a rapid-fire succession of succinct commands. In less than a minute, the smoke ceased, the engine had been shut down, and the prop, feathered.

"Nav," Nestor said, "give me our position. As soon as we get out of occupied territory, locate some emergency landing fields for us."

"Roger that," came the response.

"Engineer," Nestor next said, "give me our fuel consumption every fifteen minutes."

"Yes, sir."

"Radio, as soon as you get the word we're over Free China, broadcast our position and an emergency landing signal."

Click, click. The informal interphone signal that the radioman understood Nestor's request and would comply.

I realized we'd stumbled into a bit of trouble. The huge plane now flew on three engines instead of four. That meant the engines still running would be sucking up gas like a teenager swilling soda pop on a blistering day. The odds of us making it back to one of the airstrips around Chengtu had dropped significantly.

"Radio here," came a call over the interphone. "Small problem. Our radio is kaput. I can't broadcast our position. But I'm gonna crawl back to the racks and see if I can find a burnt-out tube or something."

"Get on it, Johnny."

"Yes, sir."

Then came a call to Nestor. "Engineer to pilot. Fuel consumption is way up. We got maybe two hours left to fly."

Nestor called the nav. "How far to Chengtu?"

"We're probably four hours out, sir."

"How long before we're out of Jap territory?"

"I'd guess one and a half, maybe two hours. But it's hard to know for sure, 'cuz we don't know exactly where the front lines are."

"Got it."

Nestor gripped the yoke with a stranglehold. He appeared to stare straight ahead, perhaps processing our options. I knew there weren't many. Unless we could find a friendly airfield, which seemed doubtful, we seemed destined to crash-land or be forced to bail out. And whether that would be over enemy territory or someplace controlled by the Chinese, we had no way of knowing with any certainty.

Nestor turned to look in my direction, then motioned me forward. I stepped into the cockpit and put my head next to his.

"You ever crash-landed, sir?" he said, raising his voice and not using his mike.

I snorted a derisive chuckle to myself. "I dead-sticked a C-46 into Kunming about nine months ago. No landing gear, so I dumped it into a rice paddy."

"Nice. A good landing, then?"

"Absolutely. We walked away from it. Well, waded away."

"The plane had a full load?"

"Stuffed with fifty-five-gallon drums of avgas."

"No fire?"

"Not in a rice paddy."

"Whaddaya think, then? Set *Seal* down in a paddy? Or try for an open field?"

Good question. I pondered the variables. "In a field, you never know what the surface will be like. Smooth? Rough? Rocky? Trenches? Ditches? In a paddy, you know exactly. It'll be watery but shallow. That should help prevent any fires."

"I guess paddy it is, then."

"You know the bird could still break up?"

He looked away from me, then turned his head back. "Recommendations?"

"Don't put the landing gear down, obviously. Try to hold the nose up and let the tail down first. Gently. If you come in too steep, the fuselage will crack. Especially on a bird this long." I prattled on like I knew what the hell I was talking about. I suppose, as the senior officer on board, everyone thought that to be the case. Total bullshit, of course. I was about to crap my pants, but damned if I'd show it.

I wondered if Eve would care if I didn't make it back. But I suppose I wouldn't know one way or the other, so what difference would it make? I guess it was just my ego at work, hoping someone might shed a tear when taps sounded at my burial in this godforsaken land in this godforsaken war. On the other hand, I seemed adept at dodging death. Kind of a Harry Houdini of the Army Air Forces—escaping violent storms over the Hump, dead-stick landings, and Jap attacks both in the air and on the ground. But even Harry hadn't been able to do it forever.

Nestor spoke to the crew. "Here's the situation, boys. We aren't gonna make it back to Chengtu. We'll be running on fumes shortly. So, if we can't ID a friendly airfield, I'm gonna try to put us down in a rice paddy. I can't guarantee that will be in Free China, though. So a crash landing may be just the beginning of our problems. Sorry our Cook's Tour of the Land of the Rising Sun has to end in a Chinaman's garden, but I'll see about getting you all a full refund."

At least Nestor seemed to be holding it together. So maybe we had a chance.

"Nav," Nestor called, "any idea if there's an airfield ahead of us that could handle a twenty-nine?"

"Nothing until we near Chengtu. And we ain't gonna make it that far."

"Okay, everyone," Nestor said, "we'll fly until the gauges indicate 'empty,' then I'll put her down. Engineer, let me know when we've got about thirty minutes of fuel left, and we'll start looking for a nice soft paddy. Hopefully with no Japs lurking in the weeds."

"Roger, sir."

We cruised on until the navigator called, "About thirty minutes to empty, sir."

"Keep your eyes peeled, gents," Nestor said. "See if we can't find a paddy big enough to handle us."

After another five minutes, Matt, the copilot, spoke. "Looks like a big paddy off to the starboard, about two miles."

Nestor turned his head to inspect what Matt had seen. "Let's take a gander." He banked the B-29 toward it. We roared over it at about five thousand feet. A dozen or so laborers—Chinese, I hoped—in straw hats stared up at us.

"Looks good," Nestor said. He called over the interphone. "We've picked a spot. But if anyone wants to bail out, I'll hold us aloft until you can. Takers?"

No one responded. Not surprising, since we still didn't know if we were out of Jap-held territory or not.

The paddy appeared longer east-west than north-south, so Nestor circled around to approach the landing—well, crash landing—from the east.

"Let's cut number one," he said to Matt. "We'll make the approach with just the two inboard engines. That'll make it easier to control."

"Roger that, sir." Nestor's calm professionalism seemed to put his younger copilot at ease.

"Everyone, take your crash positions," Nestor announced. "Flak vests and parachutes off. You can leave your boots on since we aren't going into the ocean." Several crew members from the aft compartment scrambled through the crawlway into the forward section.

"Okay, Matt," Nestor said, "we'll come in at about eighty-five knots. That should keep us from stalling. Nose five degrees up. Engineer, shut down two and three when I sound the alarm."

Nestor got us lined up for the approach. He and Matt held *Seventh Seal* steady as it settled toward the Chinese earth—rice and water, too, I guess.

"Prepare to crash land," Nestor announced.

Seconds later, he sounded the bail-out bell—the alarm—six short ranges. Those of us sitting assumed our crash positions. Facing aft, we pulled our knees up, lowered our heads, and locked our hands behind our necks.

The engines fell silent. The only sounds now—the rush of the wind, the rattle of the plane.

"Brace for impact!"

One second. Two.

A thudding, ripping, prolonged splashing sound rippled through the fuselage. The bomber decelerated. Abruptly, rapidly. I pitched backward from my sitting position on the hatch cover. My head slammed against the steel deck. Things went black and purple. Blinking red dots filled my vision. Or what I assumed was my vision. I think I might have lost consciousness.

I sensed myself ascending. Perhaps I'd lost more than consciousness. Did angels have me, lifting me toward heaven? Or wherever my fate might lie?

"Come on, Major, out we go," said a sandpaper voice. "Shit, you're heavier than ya look." This followed by a series of grunts. Apparently not an angel.

"Come on," the voice rasped again, "gotta get ya outta this stinkin' water."

I could feel myself being dragged, hands beneath my armpits tugging me through a shallow lake of some sort. I heard other voices, too, yelling, giving commands, barking orders. I tried to open my eyes but couldn't focus on anything. The sky, the water, human figures, spinning, wavering, rippling. I closed my eyes and lapsed back into a cool, moist blackness.

Some time later—five minutes? five hours?—I opened them again. I looked into the face of . . . I couldn't remember who. Somebody I'd known.

"Good morning, Major Shepherd. Nice of you to join us again."

I blinked. "Uhhh," was the only word I could croak out.

"How ya feeling?"

"Uhhh."

"Right. You got a nasty blow to the back of your head when we went into the paddy."

"Uhhh. Wha'?"

"B-29. Japan. Lost an engine. Crash-landed in a Chinese rice swamp."

"V-29? Uhhh . . . you're pilot, right?"

"Not much of one, apparently. There's my airplane."

He pointed at something. From where I lay on my back, I lifted by head and looked. A big airplane, smoke drifting from one of its engines, the left wing cocked at an impossible angle to the fuselage, sat mired in mud and plowed-up green shoots of some sort. I put my head back down. "Hurts," I said.

"You got whacked pretty hard. Might have a concussion. If it helps, I'm Captain Nestor Woods, the pilot of a B-29 you were an observer in. We bombed a steel mill in Japan. Took an ack-ack hit. Lost an engine. Crash-landed in China. But we aren't sure if we're in Free China or occupied China."

"Ah," I said, beginning to remember. "Somebody lifted me out of the bird."

"Sergeant Gransden, the radar operator."

"Anyblody . . . anybody else hurt?"

"Nothing critical. Cuts, bruises, maybe a broken bone or two."

"Good landing, then, Claptain . . . Captain. We walked away from it. 'Cept for me. How long was I out?"

"Maybe twenty minutes."

I lifted my head again and looked around. We appeared to be on the edge of the paddy, on a bank sloping down from a dirt road. The rest of the crew lay prone on the bank, weapons at the ready.

"Bad guys nearby?" I asked.

Nestor shrugged. "Dunno. Like I said, we don't know exactly where we are. There were some Chinese farmers around when we splattered in, but they beat feet. They likely didn't know if *we* were bad guys or good guys."

I checked to see if I still had my .45. Yes. Not that I could be a straight shooter in a gun fight—if we got into one—in my condition. And not that we could put up much of a fight anyhow. It would be handguns against a well-armed Jap infantry outfit. I sure as hell hoped we'd landed in Free China.

Except for birds chattering as they swooped across a cloud-flecked sky, all remained silent for another ten or fifteen minutes.

Then Matt, the copilot, spotted a column of soldiers moving toward us on the road. They appeared to be walking at a brisk pace and weren't making an effort to conceal themselves.

"Friendlies, I hope," I said. My mouth seemed to be working properly again—at least for simple words and noncomplex sentences—but my head throbbed like somebody was using it for a handball court. Give me a good ol' hangover anytime.

We held our positions, prepared to fire our weapons.

The column halted about three hundred yards from us. A single man detached himself from the unit and, bearing a white flag, proceeded in our direction.

Nestor looked at me.

"Well," I said, "either that's a Jap platoon surrendering to us, or it's a Chinese army unit signaling they come in peace."

The man approaching us wore a raggedy blue-gray uniform and a cap that resembled a short-billed baseball hat. The troops that had halted behind him appeared decked out in a variety of military garb, nothing standard.

"My guess," I said, "Chinamen."

"In this part of China," Nestor said, "probably Commies."

"An enemy of my enemy is my friend." I decided to shut up. Talking made the handball players in my noggin even more vigorous.

The man with the flag halted about ten yards from us.

"Amerisuns?" he called out.

Nestor looked at me. "You're the senior officer here."

The little guys in my head continued to hammer away, but Nestor was correct. As a major, I held seniority in the group. I stood. "Yes, Americans," I yelled back. I kept my hand poised near my .45, just in case.

"Ts'ina soldier," the flagman responded. He lowered the flag and stepped cautiously toward me.

I climbed up onto road.

The "China soldier" approached me and saluted. I had no idea what rank he was, but saluted back. He wore shoulder insignia with two gold triangles on a gold background bordered by a broad red stripe. His face, thin and acne scarred, carried only wisps of whiskers. He appeared quite young, but his eyes shone with maturity . . . and genuine concern.

"I am Ling, Ts'ina officer, Eight Route Army," he said. "We 'elp you."

Not quite knowing what else to do, I bowed and said, "Thank you."

He bowed back. "Jap nearby, we must 'urry."

"How near?"

He pointed east, the opposite direction from which he had arrived. "Eight kilometer, maybe."

Close enough for concern. "Wait," I said, and scrambled back down the embankment to Nestor and the rest. I told them what Ling had told me.

"You think these guys can be trusted?" Nestor asked.

"They aren't Japs. And if they had any ideas other than trying to help us, we probably wouldn't be standing here talking about it. I suggest we get our asses in gear and get out of here."

"We can't leave the bomber in one piece for the Japs to get ahold of," Nestor said. "We need to destroy it."

A distant roar caught my ear. Ling yelled something, then scrambled down the embankment to join us.

"Jap fighters," he said, breathless.

The soldiers that had accompanied Ling dove into nearby ditches and paddies. Ling himself flattened his body against the embankment. The rest of us did, too.

A pair of fighters—Rising Suns emblazoned on their wings—made a recon pass over the wounded *Seventh Seal*. They disappeared behind a low ridge, climbed, then rolled back toward the downed B-29. I had a pretty good idea what they were going to do. They executed a steep dive and came thundering in on a strafing run. Their machine guns kicked up great geysers of water and ripped *Seventh Seal* from nose to tail, leaving it looking like a tube-shaped colander.

We held our positions, wondering if the Jap planes would return for a second pass.

They didn't.

"Must 'urry," Ling commanded. "Japs return with bombers."

"Don't think you'll have to worry about destroying *Seal*," I said to Nestor. "The Japs will do it themselves."

"Dummies," he snapped. "Let's go."

We followed Ling toward the awaiting cadre of Chinese soldiers, apparently a unit of what was known as the Eighth Route Army.

Hsinching, Sichuan, China
US Army Air Forces Base
June 21, 1944

It took five days, but the Chinese troops led us back to Hsinching, where we'd launched from on

June 15. The journey proved arduous—in ox-drawn carts; occasionally in wheezing, coughing trucks; even some short stretches on horseback; but mostly on foot. We traveled primarily at night so Jap aircraft wouldn't spot us. And we stunk to high heaven—dried mud, rice paddy residue, and body funk. Bloodhounds might have fled from us in disgust.

The first order of business after we got back to Hsinching—following extended showers and cremation of our flight suits—was a visit to the hospital. The flight surgeon who checked me out determined I'd sustained a concussion—big surprise—and ordered me to stand down from any flying or combat duties for a month.

"Wait here," he said, after he'd finished. "A nurse will be in to formally release you, give you a couple of prescriptions, and some follow-up instructions."

After five minutes, a sharp rap sounded on the door to the exam room. A nurse entered. She halted at arm's length and handed me two amber pill bottles. "Take as directed."

Even though my heart issued a gentle butterfly flutter, I cocked my head at her and tried to appear unflustered. "I thought you didn't want to see me anymore."

"This is official business, you dope," Eve snapped.

"You dope, *Major*," I corrected.

She rolled her eyes.

We held each other's gaze for several seconds.

"You've got a concussion," Eve said.

"So the flight surgeon tells me."

"Second one."

My first had come when I'd dead-sticked the C-46 into a rice paddy in Kunming. "Yes," I said. "One of my unique talents."

"Explains a lot." Her words came out like icicles.

"Meaning?"

She stepped closer to me, her Arctic-blue eyes focused on mine, but her gaze lacking malice or even disdain. I sensed her body heat radiating outward in a silent, slow-motion explosion. "Meaning it helps me understand why when I say I don't want to see you anymore, it apparently falls on deaf ears . . . or a concussed brain."

"*You* knocked on *my* door."

"I'm not talking about just now, you idiot—"

"You idiot, *sir*."

"Why can't you take this seriously?" she said. Her words seemed to have lost their brusqueness, and she backed away from me, her gaze at her feet.

"Because I don't believe you. I don't believe your words."

"Believe me," she whispered, "because this is how real-life romances end. It's how I want ours to end. Please, please, please, stay away from me, Rod."

"We were in love, Eve," I blurted without thinking.

She didn't respond.

I continued. "Remember me, the guy who came looking for you after we bailed out over Burma? The guy who took care of you in the jungle? Who hugged you when you poured out your heart about what had happened to you in the wake of Pearl Harbor? Who found a way to get you out of the clutches of a covetous headhunter?"

She stared at me, her eyes moist and tinged with red. She remained mute.

"Aren't you the woman who said 'I do' when I asked her if she wanted to be 'my gal' in a hospital in Calcutta after we'd both been shot to shit?"

"I never wanted to hurt you," she whispered. "Never."

"But you fell *out* of love with me?" The question came out in such a raspy croak it embarrassed me.

She stepped close to me again and this time caressed my cheek. She shook her head. "No," she murmured, her voice barely audible. "But, as you did for me in Burma, now it's my turn to take care of you. Understand?"

Tears sliding silently down her face, she whirled and darted from the room before I could react. I stood there stunned. *Take care of me? How? Why?*

And no, I certainly didn't understand. Did it have something to do with that jerk general, Stone? Or was I reading too much into him being an A-1 asshole and his presence at Hsinching? And if it were him, why wouldn't Eve just tell me? I knew I couldn't confront a flag officer with mere suspicions, because I'd be on a slow boat to San Francisco or Long Beach before I could say "hut-sut Rawlson on the rillerah." And then I'd never be able to help Eve, which I damn well now was more determined than ever to do. If only I knew *what* to do.

For the time being, I decided to accede to Eve's demands—I assumed she had a good reason for them—and stay away from her. At least the feeling of having been gut punched by her rejection disappeared, and I could stop worrying about barfing on my shoes every time I thought of her.

I slipped the prescription pills into my pocket and headed to base ops, where Lieutenant Colonel Smithfield, the intel officer from the Twentieth Bomber Command, said he'd like to meet with me to discuss my observations of the raid on Yawata.

I found the colonel seated in an otherwise vacant flight planning room. He greeted me heartily and thanked me for going on the raid.

"I'm glad to hear you and the crew of *Seventh Seal* survived," he said. "I understand it got a bit dicey for a while."

"We had some moments that increased our pucker factors. But in the end, I walked away with only a low-grade concussion. I guess that doesn't matter much, however, since I wasn't on flying status to begin with. I want you to know Captain Woods did a great job in getting the bird down in one piece. Well, two pieces."

Smithfield chuckled. "So noted."

"But tell me, how did the raid go?"

Smithfield shifted in his chair, seemingly a bit uncomfortable with having to answer. "I suppose that depends on one's perspective."

"Okay, let's say one's perspective is that of the Twentieth Bomber Command's."

Smithfield drew a deep breath before responding. "An utter failure," he growled.

"What? I saw bombs hitting the target."

"You saw bombs hitting *near* the target. Do you know how many bombs actually hit the target?"

I didn't venture a guess since it was a rhetorical question.

"One," he snapped. "One goddamn five-hundred-pounder actually nailed its assigned mark."

"Come on." To say I was stunned didn't describe my gut reaction.

"Yes. Of the sixty-three planes that made it to Yawata, only forty-seven unloaded their bombs—one hundred seven tons of explosives. Eleven bombs struck the target *area*, but only one could be described as being on target. One. And we lost seventy-seven airmen and seven multimillion-dollar B-29s in the process. The raid will be used by encyclopedias to exemplify the definition of failure."

"Jesus," I muttered. "But explain something. You said we lost seven aircraft. But the Jap fighters over the target seemed ineffective, and the anti-aircraft fire, yeah, it was dense, but didn't seem particularly accurate."

"You're right, only one bird got blasted by a Jap fighter, and the other six went down due to mechanical problems or because they ran out of gas. So overall, the Jap defenses were pretty shabby. But we need to figure out why virtually no one could nail the target. That's where I was hoping your observations might help."

I closed my eyes and tried to recapture in my mind the terrifying moments during which we seemed to *hang* over the target. I spoke slowly. "The night was thick with ack-ack fire. While not effective, I suppose it made it a challenge for some guys to hold their bombers on a steady course. Especially if they hadn't flown in combat before. Then there were several layers of clouds below us—not expected, as I recall—and that in conjunction with searchlights blinding the bombardiers made it difficult to pick out the targets. And we really had no clue what the winds were like from eighteen thousand feet on down. If the bombsights don't have the correct velocity inputs, the bombs aren't going to go where they're supposed to."

I opened my eyes. Smithfield was writing furiously on a notepad. Finished, he looked up. "Any thoughts?"

"Yeah. Obvious stuff. We need better weather forecasts, much better forecasts—clouds, winds, visibilities. And we need to be able to use that radar thing to help pick out targets. The operator on board *Seventh Seal* told me they hadn't been trained in radar bombing."

"Right, right. We're already on that. I'll leave the meteorological aspects to you."

That I knew. But I also knew the only way we were going to improve forecasts was by getting more observations—well, any at all—from the target areas and along the routes to and from them. A bit of a challenge when the targets all lay in Jap hands.

And the winds. They worried me in particular. Someplace in the deep, rarely visited caverns of my memory, there lurked a story of a Japanese researcher who, years ago, had discovered fierce, high-altitude winds that howled over the island nation. I needed to find out more about that. How fierce? And at what altitude? I suppose my concussion-induced "downtime" would allow me to do that.

Smithfield and I wrapped up our debrief. As we were about to go our separate ways, I remembered something.

"Oh," I said, "you mentioned earlier that the characterization of the raid's results depended on one's perspective. There are other perspectives than the army's, I presume."

Smithfield nodded. He cleared his throat. "I suspect the American public was given an image of the raid as seen through. . . well, shall we say . . . rather heavily tinted rose-colored glasses. Back home, the operation was viewed as an amazing success. It gave everyone a huge emotional boost. And for that matter, we've gotten word that the Japs were pissing in their pants when they realized American heavy bombers could reach their homeland."

14

Headquarters Tenth Weather Squadron
Hastings Air Base
June 26, 1944

It took a while, but I finally caught a hop out of Hsinching on a B-29 (converted to a tanker) deadheading back to Kharagpur Airfield, India. And from there I thumbed a ride on a Gooney Bird bound for Hastings Air Base.

Now, once again I sat in Colonel Ellsworth's office at Tenth Weather Squadron headquarters.

"I've heard about the raid," he said, pushing a pile of paperwork off to one side of his desk. "I gather we've got a long way to go in terms of getting the Twentieth the quality weather support they need."

"Somehow, someway, we've got to expand our observational network. I know we can't do that in Japan or over the East China Sea, but there must be some way we could accomplish that in parts of China."

"I've been thinking about that," Ellsworth said. He stood and walked to a map tacked to a wall. "If we could get some observations from Mongolia or even out of far northwest China"—he gestured toward Sinkiang Province —"that would be a tremendous help."

"It would be. For one thing, we'd be getting information from spots near the birthplace of the Siberian High in winter. I believe the strength of that thing can't help but influence the strength of the westerly winds aloft . . . especially in the wintertime."

"So, if we knew more about that high pressure area, we'd be better able to predict the winds at bombing altitudes for the B-29s?"

"I think we'd be better at it, sir, but not perfect."

"Okay, let's explore that."

Santokh, the Sikh servant, stuck his head into the office. "Would the good sirs care for some tea?"

Ellsworth returned to his desk, sat, and looked at me. I frowned, remembering the shoe cleaning rag incident.

"Two, please, Santokh," Ellsworth said. "And be so kind as to put some ice in it."

The servant bowed and retreated out the door.

"I think," Ellsworth said, acknowledging my facial response, "we've finally taught him to use different cleaning cloths for shoes and drinking glasses." He paused, smiled. "Although the utensil cleaning rag still gets used to dust the furniture occasionally."

I decided I'd take just a few sips of the tea. Although after wallowing around in a Chinese rice paddy, what the hell difference would drinking tea from a glass wiped down with a dust rag make?

The tea arrived complete with ice, and Ellsworth and I continued our discussion.

"Have you heard of a project called Dixie Mission?" he asked.

"No, sir."

"It's sensitive. But in short, we're dispatching a team of army officers and a State Department representative to Yenan to make contact with the Chinese Communists and their leader, Mao Tse-tung."

"Yenan? Not sure where that is."

Ellsworth rose and stepped to the wall map again. He pointed to the location. "Here, a little over four hundred miles southwest of Peking. Mao and his soldiers control almost as much of Free China as Generalissimo Chiang Kai-shek and his Nationalists do farther south. We're not sure how we'll be received by Mao, since we've been buddied-up with the Generalissimo for quite a while now, and Mao and Chiang are not known to break bread together."

"Well, the Commies seemed pretty friendly when they saved me and the crew of *Seventh Seal* after it crash-landed."

"That's what we're hoping for—that since we have a common enemy, the Japs, the Reds will be more than eager to sign on with us. They've got guerrillas operating in occupied China, so we'd like them to help rescue any of our B-29 guys who might end up there. And here's the real kicker for us—we'd like to train some of their men to take weather observations for us."

"Even behind enemy lines?"

"Especially behind enemy lines. And we plan on asking Mao if he'd let a team of Americans take upper-air observations at Yenan using radiosondes and pilot balloons."

"Dixie Mission, huh? When does all this go down?"

"A C-47 will take the first team in on July 22. If that goes well, another will follow in about two weeks."

Ellsworth returned to his chair. "On a more mundane note," he said, "some general officers have figured out that we weather guys had managed to commandeer the Taj Mahal of Hastings for our headquarters. So in July, we're being relocated to the other side of the Hooghly River to a place called Titagarh."

"And the generals will settle in here?"

"Of course."

"Speaking of generals, do you know anything about that one-star, General Stone, who used to have an office here?"

"Not much. Why?"

"Oh, just curious. I've run into him a couple of times over in Hsinch-ing." I wasn't about to bother my squadron commander with the real reason, of course. I knew him to be dealing with a few thousand other things that would take priority.

"Well, all I've heard is that he's kind of an acerbic guy, a my-way-or-the-highway type, and loves to shoot the messenger when things don't go his way. I think he was some sort of a big-shot Hollywood type before the war.

Probably used to throwing his weight and his money around. Not that money makes any difference in the army."

"Well, your assessment of Stone sure sounds logical from what I've seen."

Ellsworth nodded. "But back to you, Rod. I'd like you to take it easy for a while. Do whatever research you think might help with our weather support, but get your health back, too. I'm working on something else I may need your help with."

"Can you give me a clue, sir?"

"Not really. But just let me say your adventures may not be over."

"You're not dispatching me back to the jungle again, are you?"

Ellsworth smiled. "Not even close."

Another mystery in my life. Just what I needed.

Over the next few weeks I busied myself coming up with ideas about how we might improve weather support to the Twentieth Bomber Command. I also began an effort to track down info on the scientist who, if I remembered correctly, years ago had observed howling, high-level winds over Japan. I wanted to find out a lot more about that phenomenon. If it existed, it would obviously be a significant factor in our bombing missions over the Land of the Rising Sun.

I finally decided the best way to go about digging into that topic would be to fire off a telegram to one of the professors I'd had at Cal Tech, where I'd picked up my master's in meteorology, and ask him if he knew anything about it.

Lord, I'd received my master's in '39. That seemed an eternity away now, given all that had happened in my life since then. Getting my pilot's wings. Suffering the death of my wife, Trish. Flying the Hump—with the most godawful terrain and weather in the world. Losing my best friend, Pete Zimmerman, to the Hump. Getting shot down over Burma. Becoming buddies with headhunters. Rescuing Eve. Falling in love with her. Then getting a swift kick in the ass from her. And finally, riding along on the first American bombing raid on Japan since Doolittle's. It seemed I'd done a lifetime of living in five years. And maybe I had. Perhaps that was the fore-boding message that lay embedded in my cosmic biography.

While I waited for a response from Cal Tech, I continued to build a list of ideas regarding how best to support the B-29s. But in the evenings, I'd tramp over to the club, often through monsoonal downpours that cascaded off the base's thatched roofs and canvas tents like river rapids. The humid heat remained relentless, of course, so once in the club, I'd make a beeline to a seat near a fan. There, I could enjoy my Jim Beam—accompanied by a separate glass of ice—in relative comfort.

And despite my inclination to let my thoughts dwell on Eve and her inexplicable antipathy toward me—as subdued as it now seemed—I learned not to overdo it with the booze. As the old saying goes, moderation in all things, including moderation. So once in a while, I'd kick moderation in the butt and stumble around the dance floor with some of the Hastings nurses, but I don't think I ever made a fool of myself.

About a week after I sent my telegram to Cal Tech, I got a reply:

DISCOVERED RESEARCH PAPER BY WASABURO OOISHI. MUST TRANSLATE. STRANGE LANGUAGE. MAY TAKE TIME. WILL EXPEDITE.

Japanese was a strange language? That was a new one on me. But at least the response indicated the effort would be expedited. So I waited.

Headquarters Tenth Weather Squadron
Titagarh, India
July 24, 1944

In late July, a summary of Wasaburo Ooishi's research arrived. The Jap scientist had indeed discovered powerful high-altitude winds over Japan. I studied the summary for two days, then went to Colonel Ellsworth with my own synopsis of Ooishi's work.

By then the weather squadron headquarters had been moved to Tita-garh on the east bank of the Hooghly. Our new accommodations weren't nearly so princely as what we'd had at Hastings, but at least the army brass was happy to have our old digs—a structure truly more fitting for flag officers.

Our building in Titagarh proved to be pretty spartan. It sported concrete walls, shuttered windows—no glass—and a tile roof. And no Sikh servant. Santokh remained behind to attend to the generals.

The biggest drawback to me was that getting to the officers' club, and most other services and organizations on Hastings, required a ten-minute ferry ride on a wooden junk that wouldn't have passed a navy safety inspection. At least growing up in Coeur d'Alene I'd learned how to swim in the lake. So I figured that if—well, when—the ferry made like the *Titanic*, I'd be able to survive.

Ellsworth lowered his lanky frame into a creaky chair behind his desk and motioned for me to do the same opposite him.

"What have you got, Rod?" Distant thunder rumbled up the Hooghly and echoed through the main hallway of our ascetic structure.

"Something pretty interesting." I laid the report on his desk. "This was originally written in what is called an 'auxiliary' language, not Japanese."

"What on earth is an auxiliary language?" Ellsworth squinted at me in an inquisitive manner.

"In this case something called Esperanto. It was, I learned, developed by a Polish ophthalmologist in the late 1800s. It was intended to be a universal second language used for international communication. It gained some acceptance in Europe and Asia, but never caught on in the US."

Ellsworth nodded.

"It's thought that Ooishi published his findings in Esperanto rather than Japanese because he assumed more people would be familiar with Esperanto than with Japanese."

"So, since no one, or at least not many, used Esperanto in the United States, his work went unnoticed by Americans."

"Yes, sir."

"Interesting. Tell me about it."

"Ooishi established an upper-air observation site in Japan and from 1923 through early 1925 took almost thirteen hundred pilot balloon obs." I positioned a graph on the desk for Ellsworth to examine.

He leaned forward and peered closely at it. I pointed out the key elements.

I ran my index figure along a squiggly line. "This is the average wind profile for the winter season. It shows the mean wind speed over the observation site at thirty-three thousand feet to be one hundred forty knots."

Ellsworth's eyes widened. "You're kidding. That's over one hundred sixty miles per hour."

"And that's the average, Colonel. The *average*."

"So . . . we could be looking at winds of, oh, I don't know, maybe two hundred miles per hour in extreme situations."

"And if our bombers are unloading from thirty thousand feet or higher in the winter—"

"Good grief. Their bombs could end up in Juneau instead of Japan."

An exaggeration, but Ellsworth had a point.

"The problem would be *predicting* such powerful winds," I said. "The Japs sure don't share their observations with us. So basically we're blind, in terms of weather, from eastern China all the way to Japan."

"I guess we could hope those observations from Ooishi are inaccurate, but I doubt it. What reason would he have for exaggerating them, especially in the 1920s?"

"All we can do is give the bomber crews a heads-up, I guess," I muttered. "They'll probably have to find out the hard way if winds that powerful really exist in the upper atmosphere."

Ellsworth templed his hands beneath his chin, held his gaze on me, and didn't speak for a while. I sensed he had something he wanted to tell me but wasn't certain he should.

"Okay," he said, after his silence, obviously having made up his mind, "we can't get observation teams into Mongolia, but I've been working on a deal to get some into far northwest China, in a place called Urumchi. It's in a remote part of the country that juts northward, squeezed in between Mongolia and the Kazakh region of the Soviet Union. It truly is in the middle of nowhere. I want you to spearhead the effort. But I'm still working on the logistics. So it will be a while before we can launch it. In the meantime . . ." He flashed me just the hint of a smile.

"Yes?" I couldn't wait for what might be coming,

"I want you to write a report, something we can hand the Twentieth Bomber Command, about the likely existence of powerful winds aloft over Japan, especially in the winter. *And* I want you to remain on hot standby for another B-29 mission to Yawata. I don't have a date yet, but I know we're going back sometime in August. This time in daylight. I'd like you at Chengtu to debrief the crews when they return." He paused and cleared his throat. "But I'm not expecting you to ride along again. Too much of a risk."

I wondered if I'd told Ellsworth the story about the cannibal village.

15

Hsinching, Sichuan, China
US Army Air Forces Base
August 20, 1944

With the daylight raid on Yawata scheduled for August 20th, I'd arrived back at the forward launch base of Hsinching a couple of days prior. Me and hundreds of others. Ground crews, support personnel, brass. I'd kept my eyes peeled for any sign of Eve or General Stone, but spotted neither.

Now, on the morning of the raid, I arose early with the intent of attending the pre-mission briefing. I'd hooked up with Captain Nestor Woods again and invited myself along on the trip to Yawata. Of course, it wouldn't be on the *Seventh Seal*, which rested shattered and shelled in a rice paddy somewhere many miles east of Hsinching. The captain and most of his original crew now had a brand-spanking-new bird, not even named yet, fresh from the Boeing production line in Wichita, Kansas.

I stepped from my quarters into the humid, predawn darkness. I swear, if I'd cupped my hands together and squeezed, I could have wrung droplets of moisture from the oppressive air. From the flight line came the bellow of a Wright Cyclone engine being tested prior to takeoff, still six hours away.

Layers of fog, like diaphanous bricks, drifted across the denuded landscape that marked the base. I moved slowly, picking my way carefully along a graveled walkway.

"It's not like you *have* to go." A voice, Eve's, startled me. I jumped.

"Jesus, Eve."

She emerged from the mists like a wraith from the moors in an English folktale. I could discern only her silhouette, but still sensed the physical beauty she radiated.

"You weren't ordered to go," she repeated. "I checked."

"I wasn't ordered not to."

"So why?"

The roar of the B-29 engine ceased, and a thick silence enveloped the darkness.

"I guess for the same reason you couldn't determine the vital signs of a patient over a telephone. You'd have to meet him, or her, face-to-face. You know, take their blood pressure, temperature, pulse."

"I don't want you to go."

Wow. Talk about doing a one-eighty. First she never wants to see me again, now she doesn't want me to risk my life by riding along on a bombing mission.

"Well, it's not like I have a gal waiting for me if I do go," I snapped, perhaps a bit too harshly. But it wasn't like I knew how to deal with this woman.

She looked away from me. Didn't respond.

"Do I?" I said, resolve in my voice.

"I'm trying to save you," she retorted. Softly.

"From what?"

"Why do you have to make things so damn difficult?" she whispered.

"Me? Me make things difficult?" I hope she detected the exasperation in my voice. Then my emotions jumped beyond exasperation, and I exploded. My voice kicked up several decibels. "I thought things were pretty simple, Eve. I loved you. You loved me."

"Shhh. People will hear us."

"There aren't any other people out here, Eve. Just frogs and nightbirds."

"Well, anyhow, things are never really simple, are they?"

"No shit," I hissed. "Well, I'll make them really simple, then. Do you love me?" No point in beating around the bush anymore. Lay it on the line. Naked bluntness.

She shook her head, then broke down in a cascade of barely audible, heaving sobs. "Just come back," she gasped, her voice choked and muffled as if belonging to someone issuing a deathbed plea. As quickly as she had appeared, she pivoted and walked away, allowing the fog to swallow her.

I remained in place, rooted to the ground, enveloped in the murk of the wee hours, and understanding nothing more than I had before. Even less. I failed completely to understand this woman I'd fallen for. My God, I never knew whether I'd encounter the original Nurse Nasty I'd met a year earlier, or the woman I'd come to love passionately after our jungle adventure, or a young teenager I'd never known before, smothered and confused by adolescent hormones.

I eventually broke loose from where I stood and headed for the mess hall and a too-early breakfast I could scarcely get down. After that, I made my way to the briefing facility.

The makeshift briefing room—space commandeered from an aircraft hangar—turned out to be crammed with aircrews and high-ranking officers. The mood seemed somber, not the rah-rah, happy-go-lucky attitude that sometimes prevailed for less daunting airstrikes, say into Manchuria or Thailand. This raid would be aimed at a place we'd already visited . . . and failed at. Yawata. Only this time we'd be bombing in daylight, not under cover of darkness.

The briefing opened with the base weather officer. He presented a series of huge charts depicting the expected winds, visibilities, and cloud covers. Most everyone understood the limitations of the data the meteorologists had to work with. So they accepted without comment or question the theory that the weak high pressure center that had trundled over eastern China three days ago would be sitting over our target today. That meant good bombing conditions and relatively light winds—even at our assigned bombing altitude of twenty-six thousand feet.

Of course, good conditions for us meant good conditions for the Japs, too. Their fighter pilots and antiaircraft gun crews would have an easy time spotting us and superb opportunities to blow us from the sky.

So, ironically, the following segment of the briefing concentrated on rescue procedures for the various areas over which we'd be flying. For once I hoped I wouldn't end my mission in a rice paddy. I'd done that twice already and wasn't convinced I could pull it off a third time. On the other hand, three's a charm, right?

Next, an intel officer spoke about the topology and layout of our primary target, the Imperial Iron and Steel Works of Yawata. He clearly delineated the bombers' assembly point, departure point, and initial point, or IP, that is, the point from which bomb runs commence. He pointed out the secondary target, the Jap-occupied Haizhou Bay naval installations on the Chinese coast bordering the Yellow Sea. Lastly, he illuminated the third alternate, a railroad marshaling yard in Henan province, also held by the Japs. No one wanted to have to unload their weapons on an alternate, of course. They all wanted to hit the Japs in the mouth and obliterate their damn steelworks.

Following the intel officer came a bit of a surprise. Brigadier General LaVerne Saunders, known as "Blondie"—an ironic take on his thinning coal-black hair—stepped to the podium. Saunders, the interim commander of the Twentieth, announced he'd be leading the strike.

"Gentlemen," he said, "we've got to do better work. We've got to hit our aiming points. Pilots, you've got to get in there at the altitude set, and you've got to keep your speed steady." Easier said than done, I thought, if you happen to be challenging hundred-knot winds. But probably not today.

Saunders went on. "How do you expect your bombardier to do his work if you're flubbing all around with the aircraft? This raid is going to be rough, but goddamnit, it's a rough war and you're flying a good bird, better than anything we've ever dreamed of having. Yeah, you'll have to fight your way to the target, but you're better than the Japs are."

The general completed his message to a few "amens" and soft "hoorahs," and gave way to a Catholic chaplain who concluded the briefing by reciting the Lord's Prayer and a blessing, "In Nomine Patris, et Filii, et Spiritus Sancti," which the assembled airmen mumbled after him.

They understood that not all of them would be returning to Hsinching at the end of the day.

After the briefing, on my way out of the hangar to pick up my gear, Captain Woods fell in beside me. "Gonna be a tough one," he said.

"They all are."

"Blondie's a good man, though, he'll get us there. He was General Wolfe's deputy."

I knew about Wolfe. Rumor had it that General "Hap" Arnold, the Army Air Forces chief, had grown impatient with Wolfe's lack of progress in China as the leader of the Twentieth, and was replacing him with a young hotshot flag officer. The new commander hadn't yet arrived in-theater, but was due any day.

"Do you know who Wolfe's replacement is?" I asked.

"The scuttlebutt is he's a fast-burner from the Eighth Air Force in Europe by the name of LeMay. Four years ago he was a captain. Now he's a major general."

"From two bars to two stars in forty-eight months? That's crazy."

"I hear he's a bulldog."

"Ya think?"

We lifted off from Hsinching on schedule just before eleven hundred hours. General Saunders, copiloting a B-29 christened *Postville Express*, led the way with twenty-one birds in trail. From the three other bases around Chengtu, an additional sixty-four Superforts were scheduled to fall in behind us. The fog had burned off, and we climbed through scattered cumulus—cotton balls floating in an inverted azure sea—and settled in to our cruising altitude of twenty-eight thousand feet. No Jap fighters from occupied China rose to challenge us.

Once we'd cleared mainland China, Captain Woods, Nestor, called me forward from my ad hoc seat on a hatch cover adjacent to the flight engineer.

"Just got word from the lead pilot," he said. "The eighth bird taking off from Qionglai airfield crashed and blocked the runway. So only seven made it into the sky."

"That means how many on the raid now?"

Nestor did a quick calculation in his head. "Seventy-one. A good force, but not the eighty-four we were counting on."

I scanned the sky through the expansive greenhouse glass that encompassed the cockpit. "At least it looks like good bombing weather." We darted in and out of wispy cirrus, while below us, only patches of altocumulus rode the air currents twisting their way toward Japan over the East China Sea.

Nestor gave me a thumbs-up. The big Wright Cyclone engines sounded healthy, too, and filled the aluminum fuselage of the Superfort with a comforting mechanical growl and gentle vibrations. The faint but ever-present odors of fuel and lubricants drifting through the pressurized forward crew compartment added to the reassurance that our virgin warbird would bear us faithfully into battle. Of course, the Japs would have different ideas regarding us *returning* from combat.

We reached Kyushu, the Japanese island on which the Yawata steel-works sat, in the late afternoon and turned northward at the assembly point on the south side of the island. We roared over southwest Kyushu, racing toward the departure point. The Japs certainly had to know we were on our way.

At the departure point, we banked toward the north-northeast and dropped down to our bombing altitude of twenty-six thousand feet. We hit the initial point right on schedule and began our bombing run with Nestor handing over navigational control of the bird to the bombardier and radar operator. Captain Woods had one duty now—hold the B-29 at a steady speed. We thundered toward the steelworks.

The weather remained good. Ahead of us, I spotted our target. And the first bursts of flak. Jap fighters began rising from surrounding airfields to hunt us down. The lead plane, General Saunders's craft, let go with its bombload. Five-hundred-pounders, wriggling like salmon fighting their way upstream in a swift river, plunged earthward.

Pinpricks of light blossomed from the ground as the bombs struck. Additional strings of high explosives tumbled from the Superfortresses following Saunders's *Postville Express*. The bomb bay doors of our bird groaned open.

Black balls of smoke dotted the sky as antiaircraft shells burst all around us, but none close. I figured the Japs had trouble judging the speed of our planes. One lucky shot did bounce our bird hard, but did no damage.

"Hold 'er steady, hold 'er steady," the bombardier growled over the interphone. "I got the target in my crosshairs."

No one spoke for the next sixty seconds. Then, "Bombs away!"

Freed of its bombload, the B-29 jumped, then rolled away from Yawata and climbed. I turned to look back at the steelworks and the fleet of bombers still unloading on it. A beautiful sight. Pillars of black-and-white smoke billowed skyward. We'd obviously done a hell of a lot better job in putting our weapons on-target this time than we had in our first effort over a month ago.

But now the Jap ack-ack gunners had zeroed in on the speed and altitude of our planes. I saw a couple of them take hits. I watched as chunks of one Superfort tore away from its fuselage, but it kept flying. I hoped it would make it back to China. But I had my doubts.

Another bird took a blast in its right outboard engine and began trailing smoke and losing altitude.

"Poor bastards," Second Lieutenant Duwamish, the copilot, muttered. "They'll either bailout and get captured, or crash-land and get captured."

We all knew getting taken prisoner by the Japs was tantamount to a death sentence.

"Hey, hey, hey," a voice sang out over the interphone, "bandits on our tail, seven o'clock low."

I strained to see. Two Jap fighters, Kawasaki Ki-45s, called "Nicks" by the Allies, came at us from below. Designated heavy fighters, they sported two engines and two seats, but had the reputation of not being particularly agile.

The ripping chatter of the fifty-caliber machine guns in the tail and rear ventral turrets echoed through the Superfort as the fighters came at us. The fifty-cals were aided and abetted by the twenty-millimeter cannon in the tail position. Too much for the Nicks. They broke off, deciding not to challenge our armament, speed, and altitude.

Then we witnessed something that none of us had ever heard of or even dreamed about.

"Dear God," Nestor screamed.

We watched dumbfounded and shocked as a Jap fighter over Yawata barreled directly into the side of a Superfort. A deliberate strike. A suicide mission. The B-29 split apart, chunks of it spewing in all directions as it erupted in a ball of fire.

The plane immediately behind the targeted bomber flew straight into the roiling swirl of debris hanging in its wake. It, too, suffered catastrophic damage and spiraled into a steep dive. Three or four good 'chutes appeared, but no more.

We headed for home. A stunned silence settled over the interphone. No one felt like talking. Each of us trying to process, attempting to absorb, failing to understand what had happened. *How many more ways can death come calling in war?* I wondered.

After an hour or so, I squatted down beside the navigator. "How're the winds?" I asked.

He nodded and smiled. "Pretty good. About as forecast. We've got a headwind component of about forty knots."

"So we aren't gonna run out of gas over occupied China?"

He shook his head. "Nope. We won't land with much of a reserve, but unless we spring a leak, we shouldn't have to hoof it home."

Great. Maybe I can avoid the rice-paddy syndrome for a change. Of course, this was summer with relatively light winds aloft. I wondered about the winter, and if those observations taken by Wasaburo Ooishi so many years ago were correct. If so, the B-29s wouldn't be dealing with forty-knot head-wind components. They'd be fighting *a-hundred*-and-forty-knot winds on the nose. There's no way we could run bombing raids on Japan in condi-tions like that, not toting a full load of bombs. The planes would have to exchange bombs for extra fuel to stand any chance at all of getting home.

We landed back at Hsinching in the late evening. Dead tired, we tumbled out of the plane, debriefed, grabbed a bite to eat, then crashed in our bunks. I'd caught a glimpse of Eve as we deplaned. She'd been standing in a dimly lit area near base operations. She nodded at me, said nothing, then disappeared into the haze. I'd been too exhausted to pursue her.

At a late breakfast the next morning, Lieutenant Colonel Smithfield, the intel officer, asked if he could join me.

"Please," I said, "I'd like to hear about the results of the raid."

He sat. "Better than the first."

I studied his face. Didn't see joy in it. "But?" I said, between bites of a semi-fried egg. I knew there was a "but" coming.

"But out of seventy-one planes, only fourteen were able to hit the primary target."

Good grief, I thought. *And that was in good weather without unimaginably powerful winds at bombing altitude.*

"Still," Smithfield went on, "our boys managed to dump a hundred tons of high explosives on the steelworks and obliterate two coke ovens. A few planes unloaded on secondary targets around Yawata, Sasebo, and Nagasaki. Bottom line—all seventy-one Superforts dropped their bombs."

He paused and cleared his throat. The odors of burnt coffee, over-cooked bacon, and cigarette smoke drifted through the mess facility.

"The bad news is we lost almost twenty percent of the birds that went on the raid. That's intolerable. Four got blasted out of the sky over the target. I think you saw the two that got taken out by a suicide pilot. A third B-29 got hit by flak, a fourth, shot down by a Jap fighter. But the greatest losses were on the return trip over China. Ten planes crashed or crash-landed due to mechanical problems or battle damage. Unfortunately, the Superfortress is still undergoing growing pains. All of the kinks haven't been ironed out. There are way too many engine failures."

"Crew losses?" The human toll stuck foremost in my mind.

Smithfield shook his head slowly. "More than anybody likes to think about," he whispered. "Preliminary counts are sixty-five KIA, maybe nineteen or twenty taken prisoner by the Japs from the planes that went down near Yawata."

"And people back home think the only air war is over Europe," I muttered.

"Yeah, and the logistics for the raids here are insane. Having to ferry all that fuel for the bombers into China from India, then having the bombers themselves fly from India into Chengtu and stage from there to the targets."

"What about the Ledo Road?" I thought about Captain Wendell Washington, the man-mountain I'd met in Burma, and the road he and his men were hacking out through the jungle there. "Have you heard how it's coming? Once the Ledo links up with the old Burma Road, won't that open up the opportunity for tanker convoys to supplement the fuel getting into China from India?"

"Probably. I've heard that Stilwell's forces have just recaptured the airfield at Myitkyina in Burma from the Japs. So that should clear the way for road construction to move faster, but I think even then it may be several months—maybe not until early next year—before we're able to get truck caravans moving again from India to China."

We concluded our brief conversation on that somber note and bid our adieus. I would have liked to have hung around Hsinching for a while to see if I could figure out what was going on with Eve, but I'd come to the conclusion that was a fool's errand. Besides, I wanted to get back to Tenth Weather Squadron headquarters and see if Colonel Ellsworth had any more details on that mission he wanted me to spearhead to get weather observation teams into the "middle of nowhere," as he'd so eloquently phrased it—that remote area of China jammed in between Mongolia and Russia.

16

Colonel Ellsworth seemed genuinely pleased to see me again, and greeted me warmly in his ascetic headquarters office. But for some reason, he didn't ask me to sit. So, puzzled, I remained standing while he fumbled through his desk drawers searching for something.

Even though the shutters to his glassless window stood wide open, a dreary morning darkness pervaded the little room. Outside, drenching rain thundered down from thick, death-shroud-gray clouds. That, and the colonel's failure to ask me to be seated sent a ripple of unease through me. Needlessly.

"Ah, here they are," he said. He pulled a couple of small items from a drawer, rose from his chair, and strode around his desk to a position directly in front me. "Rodger Shepherd, by the direction of the President it is my distinct pleasure to inform you that you have been promoted to the grade of lieutenant colonel in the United States Army Air Forces effective 20 August 1944."

I allowed a big shit-eating grin to spread over my face, pulled myself to attention—listing slightly as usual because of my bum leg—and muttered a hoarse "Thank you, sir."

"Help me take off those old oak leaves," Ellsworth said, "and I'll pin these brand spanking new silver ones on you."

"Golly, that's . . . that's swell, Colonel. I'm damned surprised." I probably sounded like a babbling school kid.

"Don't be surprised, Lieutenant Colonel Shepherd. You've more than earned a promotion. Besides, if you're going to be flying a general around, you'd better have a little rank."

"Sir? Flying a general? I don't even have—"

Ellsworth held up his hand to cut me off. "Wings. I know. But apparently that doesn't matter to the new commander of the Twentieth Bomber Command. He told me, 'I want this guy Shepherd flying me over the Hump the first time. He's been around the block more than once and obviously knows what the hell he's doing. Get him lined up for me. I'll furnish the Gooney Bird.' Well, you don't say no to a flag officer, especially a two-star. And since he asked for you by name, be assured he's done his research."

I stood there speechless. Within a matter of a few minutes, I'd been promoted *and* apparently been returned to flying status. I decided then and there that gloomy, rain-drenched days might always be my favorites.

I finally managed to come up with a few words. "I'm sorry, Colonel. Someone mentioned the new commander's name to me in Hsinching, but I can't remember it." Since the new boss knew my name, I decided I'd damn sure better know his.

"Major General Curtis LeMay, from the Eighth Air Force in Europe, where he was the commander of the Third Bombardment Division. I understand he made quite a name for himself. Earned the nicknames 'Old Iron Pants' and 'Iron Ass'—not that you would ever utter those monikers in front of him."

"Not a chance." But I had to wonder what it would be like working for a guy called Iron Ass.

"Take a seat," Ellsworth said. "There's something else I want to go over with you."

The day seemed full of surprises. I sat. The colonel did, too, returning to the abused-looking wooden chair behind his desk.

"Remember," he said, "last time you were here I mentioned I wanted you to take the point on a trip into far northwest China to a place called Urumchi and see if we could get a weather team in there."

"The middle of nowhere, you said."

Ellsworth nodded. "The ends of the earth. But it's probably as close as we'll ever get to the genesis of a lot of the weather systems that are likely to affect our bombers. In fact, I'm hoping we'll be able to pick up some early warning clues about those high-speed winds that howl over Japan in the winter."

"One thing, sir, I gotta wonder how am I going to get to Urumchi if I'm ferrying this General LeMay around?"

"It's one and done with LeMay. He just wants you to fly him over the Himalayas on his first journey into China. Once he's there, at Hsinching, where the Twentieth's forward headquarters is, that's it. You're back under my command. So my plan is to launch the mission to Urumchi from there. I expect to have a team pulled together by mid-September."

I glanced outside. The torrential rain continued, draining off the tile roof of the building in cascading sheets. The landscape began to take on the appearance of a shallow lake.

"Okay, I'd like to hear about this team, if you don't mind."

"You'll be in charge, of course. And Tex—you've met him, the pilot of *Betsy*—will fly you guys there. I've asked two majors to accompany you, Spilly Spilhaus and Doug Mackiernan. I want Mackiernan to take command of the weather station in Urumchi if the Chinese agree. His specialty is cryptoanalysis, so one of his primary duties will be to break Russian codes to get weather data that our Russki 'friends' seem a bit reluctant to share. I'll also be sending along a couple of senior NCOs to help out with things."

"Any Chinese speakers among the group?"

"Don't think so."

"Then I have a special request."

"Name it."

"The Negro captain, Wendell Washington, the guy I met on the Ledo Road, speaks a little bit of Chinese—Mandarin, as I recall. I don't know if that will help where we're going, but it might. Besides, he'd be a great . . . well, I guess the best way to say it is, intimidator . . . if we need one."

Ellsworth flashed a fleeting grin, shrugged his shoulders, and said, "I'll see what I can do." He stood and walked to a paper map of the CBI theater tacked to a wall. The map had succumbed to the steam-bath humidity of the season. Saggy and baggy, it reminded me of my grandma's skin before she passed. Ellsworth smoothed out the chart and re-tacked it.

"After you get General LeMay to Hsinching, you'll launch the mission from there. Urumchi is about thirteen hundred miles northwest, so you're looking at about a seven- or eight-hour flight. Most of it will be over pretty stark landscape. Urumchi itself sits in the shadow of the Tian Shan mountains, but it's really surrounded by deserts—a small one to the north, a big one to the south." He used his finger to point out locations.

"So at least it won't be humid," I interjected, "at least not like some places I know." I plucked at my shirt that clung to my body like wallpaper paste.

"Anything but. We don't have much climo data from the region, but from what we do know, they get maybe eleven or twelve inches of precipitation a year. The ground is snow-covered all winter. And the temperature in January is often below zero. Cold enough to freeze your cojones off."

"But at least it's not humid, right?"

Ellsworth laughed.

"Summer temperatures?" I asked.

"Daytimes are usually in the eighties, but readings well over a hundred aren't uncommon."

"Sounds like it'll be a tourist mecca after the war."

"Long shot. But look, the sooner you can get the Chinese to agree on letting us set up business there, the sooner you can get out."

"You know how to establish incentives, boss."

"But first, let's get you going with General LeMay."

I wasn't sure I was excited about that. But I knew I'd better salute smartly and march off. I spent the next couple of days brushing up on C-47 manuals and directives.

Headquarters XX Bomber Command
Kharagpur, India
September 1, 1944

"General LeMay will see you now," the general's aide, a young captain, said and ushered me into LeMay's office.

The general, writing something on a pad at his desk, didn't look up when I entered. I came to attention—tilted slightly to the right as usual—and saluted. "Lieutenant Colonel Shepherd reporting as ordered, sir."

LeMay flicked a casual salute back at me, but continued writing. "Sit," he said.

I did and gazed quickly around the room, taking it in. Clean, neat, and austere. Behind LeMay, two flags flanked him on either side—the US flag and the bomber command's. Photographs of President Roosevelt and Secretary of War Stimson hung on the right-hand wall. A single picture—that I assumed to be of his wife and young daughter—sat on the general's desk. In a back corner of the office, a small electric fan struggled to move the air around but wasn't quite up to the job.

LeMay stopped writing, lifted his head, and sat back in his chair. The expression on his broad face appeared neither welcoming nor intimidating. "Seriously professional" might be the best description. He held me in an unwavering gaze with olive-colored eyes that sat beneath a shock of thick, black hair. I guessed he probably wasn't much older than I was, despite the fact he wore two stars on each shoulder.

His most distinguishing characteristic, however, was not one that had anything to do with his physical appearance. It was the cigar clenched between his lips. I stared at it as he held it as motionless as his gaze on me.

"Cuban," he said.

"Sir?"

"The cigar." He removed it from his mouth and placed it in an ashtray on his desk. "I've learned about you."

"Yes, sir." I squirmed in my chair.

"Now that I've been given command here, I've been ordered not to fly any more missions."

His sentences seemed non sequiturs, and I couldn't figure out where he was heading.

"I think officers should lead from the front. Not from behind a desk. I should be flying every raid the Twentieth goes on. But I can't. I'm too *valuable*." The last word came out in a derisive tone. "I'll have to beg, borrow, and steal, but I am going to get in at least one mission in-theater before I get chained to a desk."

This time, I didn't respond with a "Yes, sir." I merely waited for LeMay to continue.

His gaze remained fixed on me. "You've come face-to-face with death—Japs, headhunters, crash landings—and then, after serious wounds, instead of heading back to the States to heal and rest up, you climb into B-29s and ride along on bombing missions."

I nodded. Guilty as charged.

"In my mind, you're a leader. In short, the kind of officer I want flying me into China on my first trip over the Hump." He reached into a drawer, withdrew something, and slid a pilot's insignia across his desk toward me. "There are your wings. Meet me on the flight line tomorrow at oh-eight-hundred."

"Yes, sir."

"Dismissed."

I'd completed my preflight inspection of General LeMay's C-47 by the time he arrived on the flight line the following morning. He stepped from the jeep that had transported him to the ramp and strode through a light rain toward the Gooney Bird. Two senior staff officers and his aide followed.

After we exchanged salutes, LeMay said, "Major Lineberry here will be in the right-hand seat. He's well qualified. As long as the air is smooth, I'll be hovering over your shoulder so you can point out the sights to me."

LeMay remained with me on the tarmac as the other officers boarded the plane. He stepped close to me and spoke in an almost convivial tone.

"You know, I've been to South America, North Africa, England, but this"—he swept his arm in an arc to indicate Kharagpur in general—"this is like nothing I've ever seen before. The heat, the smells, the throngs of people . . ." His voice trailed off. He pivoted and entered the plane.

I clambered into the cockpit through the crew entry door. It felt good, like revisiting an old house you'd grown up in as a kid—the well-worn furniture, remembered rooms, familiar smells, and the sense of being embraced by a place where you knew you belonged. Yes, in this case, the home was an aircraft cockpit. But it confirmed I was a pilot again, surgically shortened leg or not.

In short order, Major Lineberry and I had the Gooney Bird airborne and climbing through thick nimbostratus—rain clouds—then bursting out on top into an azure sky and sparkling sunshine north of Calcutta. We continued our ascent, soaring over the fertile plains of Bengal and the great Ganges-Brahmaputra river delta.

I tracked the Brahmaputra River northeast into Assam. I gave the wings a little waggle as we passed over Chabua, the base where I'd been stationed as a Hump pilot.

As I turned the Gooney onto a more east-northeast course to head toward the complex of B-29 bases around Chengtu, China, General LeMay slipped into the cockpit. We conversed through the interphone.

"We'll be flying over northern Burma shortly, General," I told him.

"Memories?"

"Not good ones."

On my initial "visit" to the region, it had seemed a green hell. Of course, the Japs had not turned out to be great tour guides. I carried the remembrance in my leg. My second trip into the jungle, more deliberate, had left me with better memories . . . of the Nagas and the kid Tommy.

"I assume we'll need oxygen soon," LeMay said.

"Yes, sir. I'm going to climb to around fifteen thousand before we reach Fort Hertz. After that, I may have to push it even higher as we approach Li-Chiang. There are some monster peaks off to the north of there. As long as we're VFR, we'll be fine. But if the weather closes in and I can't see the mountains, I'll be testing our service ceiling." That would be over twenty-four thousand feet, but I'd take the bird even higher if I had to.

LeMay grabbed a portable oxygen bottle and strapped on a mask as we passed twelve thousand feet. We resumed talking.

"Do you expect this weather to hold?" he asked.

"It's pretty rare to have conditions this nice at this time of year, sir."

"So your answer is no."

"Early morning flights reported some pretty big buildups just east of the Salween River. So we'll probably experience some real Hump weather in about forty-five minutes or so."

"Rough?"

"If you've got dentures, you'll want to put them in your pocket, sir." Being as young as he was, I assumed he'd take that as a joke.

We hit a few little bumps once we got past Fort Hertz, but the general appeared steady on his feet and unperturbed as he stood behind me. Gradually, we eased out over what seemed to me the most spectacular and, at the same time, deadliest landscape on Earth. A place where towering granite sentinels, some adorned in white helmets, stood silent watch over emerald valleys far below. In them, silvery rivers threaded their way southward from the Himalayas toward tropical seas a thousand miles away.

It seemed easy to forget we were on the Aluminum Trail, an air route marked by the crumpled wreckage of hundreds of Allied aircraft and the mangled bodies of the young men who had flown them. Aircrews who had attempted to cross the Hump one too many times.

The stunning terrain—the massive mountains, the cavernous ravines, the eternal waterways—both welcoming and threatening, offered, I suppose, a metaphor for the yin and yang of the universe. The confusing forces that constantly push and pull on our existence. Certainly mine. Why was I, instead of my best friend, Zimmerman, not part of the Aluminum Trail? Why was I still here, sitting in the cockpit of an aircraft, soaring through the sky and surveying all from above as if I were some sort of demigod. I had no answers.

"So this is what the aircraft—the C-46s, the C-47s, and all the others—carrying fuel, spare parts, bombs to the B-29s in China have to negotiate," LeMay said. More of statement than a question.

I looked back at him. He shook his head, slowly, probably reflecting his amazement. He continued speaking. "That's got to be grueling as hell, summiting this terrain, and at the same time punching through the worst weather on the planet."

"General, you're about to find out just how grueling. Look ahead."

Far in front of us, a massive wall of blackness, a phalanx of billowing thunderheads, obscured a range of snaggletooth peaks that sat astride the Yunnan-Sichuan Province border. Sheets of lightning skipped along the parapets of the clouds, warning that danger lay beyond. I remembered hearing that in medieval times, mapmakers sometimes labeled unexplored waters with "Here Be Dragons." Yes, dragons waited for us. Damn. China and its dragons.

17

Over western China
En route to Chengtu
September 2, 1944

"You've done battle with these monsters before, I gather," LeMay said, looking at the black sky ahead of us.

"Can't say I always came out the victor," I answered.

"Find a way to this time," LeMay growled. He returned to his canvas seat in the cabin and strapped in. I guess that meant we weren't going to abort the trip.

I glanced over at Lineberry in the copilot's seat. He seemed unperturbed. I ran a quick scan of the gauges. All looked good. The engines sounded healthy, bellowing out a full-throated roar as the Gooney rattled along, happily oblivious to the upcoming battle. I sucked in a deep lungful of oxygen and scanned the dark fortress ahead, looking for a break in the roiling clouds. None, but I did spot a saddle, a narrow valley between two pugnacious-looking thunderstorms.

"We'll aim for that," I said to Lineberry, and pointed.

"Roger," he said. "What happens when we get in the clouds?"

"Pray."

"I was hoping for something a little more technical."

"Hold on to the yoke. Tight. Avoid the temptation to fight the atmospheric rollercoaster we'll be riding. There's no way we can overpower it. So don't put the power on and point the nose down when we're going up. And don't try to pull the bird up and fly out of it when we're caught in a downdraft. Just enjoy the ride."

"Really?"

"Unless you ate a big breakfast. Then you'll probably barf in your oxygen mask."

"Okay. This sounds like fun. Any more advice?"

"Don't trust your senses when we're in the storm. Trust the instruments. Do your best to keep the plane straight and level. Unless the wings fall off, we'll be fine."

"Love your sense of humor, Colonel."

"Who said I was being funny?"

"One can only hope."

The Gooney started to wiggle and shake like a hoochie-coochie dancer as we approached the black wall. We banked the plane toward the slim passageway between the two big bruisers and hummed along at about twenty-four thousand feet. The storms towered over us by another fifteen or twenty thousand. The C-47 would be like a gnat flying through a buffalo herd.

Bouncing around like a pinball, we hit the saddle in the cloud mass. We stayed in clear air only a few seconds before we punched into a churning mass of blackness. I hoped we'd get lucky and be able to remain out of the clutches of the main thunderstorm cells.

Nope. A furious blast of wind slammed into us, hurling us sideways. Lineberry and I fought to control the bird, which we did until an unseen iron fist smashed into us from above and propelled us downward. The Gooney creaked and groaned and rattled like an iron beast in its death throes. I expected to hear rivets popping. Adding to the cacophony, a barrage of hail launched an attack, peppering the fuselage with icy shrapnel.

We lowered the flaps in an attempt to slow the dive. It didn't help much. The altimeter needle spun like a second hand freewheeling counterclockwise on a wristwatch.

"Is this where we die, Colonel?" Lineberry shouted over the interphone.

I couldn't tell if he was scared out of his wits or tossing out black humor.

"Only if we hit a granite cumulonimbus." I couldn't remember exactly how high the tallest peaks were along this leg of the trip, but I seemed to recall around twelve thousand feet. We'd already lost seven thousand, so that didn't leave much of a cushion.

"Should we try to power out of this?" Lineberry yelled over the din of the hail and the clatter of the vibrating Gooney.

"Wouldn't do any good. We should fly out of it in a few seconds." Experience had taught me that the strongest downdrafts, usually brief and localized, occurred near the rear flanks of storms. Of course, our next challenge would be an updraft trying to catapult us on a trajectory toward Pluto.

Then as suddenly as the downburst had caught us, it ceased. Abruptly, the Gooney stopped convulsing. We leveled out.

"Wings are still attached, sir," Lineberry noted.

Yep, black humor. "Good, we're ready for the next test, then."

No sooner had the words left my mouth than the test arrived. The updraft. My stomach plunged toward my ankles as we began rising as rapidly as we had descended.

"Hang on," I hollered. Needless advice. Useless.

The gyro compass and artificial horizon went crazy. Not that I could have focused on them anyway. The bird had begun shuddering like a jackhammer breaking concrete. Shit, I was tired of this. For all I knew, we were going to end up inverted over Tibet. No doubt General LeMay was regretting he'd ever shoved my wings back at me.

"Going up," Lineberry said grimly.

We did. Up and up. But again, with startling suddenness, it all ended. The updraft hurled us out of the top of the clouds into blinding sunlight. I glanced out the cockpit window to my left. Not five hundred yards from us sat a magnificent snow-covered peak, peering down on us like an alabaster watchtower.

Lineberry saw it, too. "Jesus, where'd that come from?"

"It's probably wondering the same thing about us." Five hundred yards. That's how close we'd come to death, to being another broken monument on the Aluminum Trail.

From the main cabin of the airplane came the distinct sounds—audible even over the growl of the engines—of someone heaving his guts up. And probably several other miscellaneous internal organs. I hoped to heck he was barfing into his hat and not his oxygen mask. It's impossible to get the stench out of the masks.

"Believe me, that's not LeMay," Lineberry said. "He flew enough combat missions in Europe that a little turbulence isn't going to bother him."

It took me five or ten minutes to figure out where we were. Off course, for sure, but using an aeronautical chart and matching it to the topography below us—thank God we didn't have an undercast—I got us back on track.

General LeMay reappeared in the cockpit. "Ya know, I flew half a dozen bombing raids with the Eighth and never encountered anything like that. Nice job keeping us in the air."

"I had no choice, sir." I meant it as humor, but LeMay ignored the remark. I decided not to mention to him I'd basically been a passenger. Just like he'd been.

"How much time to Chengtu?" he asked.

"Another couple of hours."

He nodded and headed back into the cabin.

"Quite a talker, isn't he?" Lineberry quipped.

"Only interested in the important stuff, I guess."

Hsinching, Sichuan, China
US Army Air Forces Base

Two hours later, we entered the landing pattern at Hsinching, the air base southwest of Chengtu that would serve as LeMay's forward headquarters.

We got slotted in between a C-54 and C-One-Oh-Boom . . . although I understood a lot fewer of them were going boom these days. I guess my suggestions about configuring and flying the C-109 to make it safer had paid off.

LeMay stepped back into the cockpit to get a good view of our surroundings as we flew our upwind leg. He studied the C-109 and the C-54. "Carrying fuel for the Twentieth's bombers," he noted.

"Probably, sir," I answered.

"What a way to run a war," he grumped. "Crazy logistics." He didn't expound.

We landed without incident and rolled to a stop in front of base ops. A jeep bearing a small red flag sporting two stars waited for LeMay. He stepped off the plane first.

I unhooked my safety harness and tried to stand but crumpled. Lineberry caught me.

"Whoa, there, Colonel, you okay?"

I sat back down and massaged my right hip. "More or less. Damn hip is as stiff as hell. First time I've been in a pilot's seat since the docs made my leg shorter. Guess that's something I'll have to get used to."

"Get you a cane or a wheelchair, sir?"

"You're a funny fellow, Lineberry. Get the hell out of here."

I continued to rub my leg vigorously for another five minutes or so, then managed to scramble down out of the passenger door in the rear of the cabin. LeMay, standing by his jeep, motioned for me. I limped over.

"Old war wounds?" he asked.

I nodded. "It's been a while since I was in a left-hand seat."

"I get it. But you did well. Thank you."

"My pleasure, General."

"Okay, one more thing. My office, oh-nine-hundred tomorrow." He turned to the soldier driving his jeep. "Where is my office, Private?"

The driver, a kid with wavy, blond hair who looked no more than fifteen, snapped to attention like a board had been rammed up his ass and stuttered, "It's . . . it's . . . I . . ."

"Private," LeMay said, "it's a simple question. You don't have to stand there like a telephone pole. Just relax and give me a building number. I'm not going to feed you to the Japs."

The kid, to his credit, recovered. "Building three-oh-nine, sir, on the eastern edge of the base."

LeMay turned to me. "See you tomorrow morning."

"Yes, sir." I saluted, then hobbled off to base ops to file my post-flight paperwork and find out where my overnight quarters would be. General Curtis LeMay would no doubt inform me in the morning that my short status as a reinstated pilot was over. Geez, my leg told me that much.

The following morning I awoke early, made sure my right leg still functioned, and shuffled off to the mess facility. I wouldn't say it was exactly cool, but at least the wet-sponge humidity of Calcutta was absent.

I finished breakfast and relaxed for a bit, sipping almost-potable coffee. The odors that drifted through the mess hall reminded me of home. Bacon, eggs, hot oatmeal, biscuits. All with a whiff of Oriental seasoning. So, not quite home, I guess.

At quarter to nine, I pushed away from the table where I'd been seated and headed toward the exit and my meeting with LeMay.

But before I reached the door, I heard a voice from behind me—a voice I'd never wanted to hear again. "Well, as I live and breathe, if it isn't Major Propeller Beanie."

I stopped but didn't turn around. Talk about ruining a perfectly good breakfast. Brigadier General Leonard Stone.

"Back to ogle the nurses, Major? I hope you haven't forgotten my previous warning."

I heard his footfalls approaching and wheeled to face him. A few of the men eating paused and looked up as the general, flanked by his ke-mo sah-bee lieutenant colonel, halted a foot from my face. "Oh, my mistake," he said. "I see you've been promoted."

He turned to the officer at his side. "Colonel, I thought I asked you to see about getting this man shipped back to the States."

"I did, sir. But he isn't part of the Twentieth. So we have no jurisdiction over him."

"Did you contact his commander?"

"Yes, sir. A Colonel Ellsworth of the Tenth Weather Squadron. But he said Shepherd is much too valuable to be relieved of duty."

"Really?" Stone looked back at me. "So if you aren't a Twentieth asset, what the hell are you doing at their forward operating base?"

I drew a deep breath before answering and tamped down my tendency to want to blurt out a wiseass answer. But you don't do that with flag officers, no matter how big a jerk they might be. So I answered straight up. "I flew General LeMay here, sir," I answered.

"General Curtis LeMay? The Twentieth's new boss?" Stone glanced at his sidekick, who shrugged.

"Yes, sir," I said.

"Jesus, Shepherd." His face reddened, and he clenched his jaw. "How big a fool do you think I am? I wasn't born yesterday, you know. You can't walk a straight line, and you were stripped of your wings, and you want me to believe you piloted General LeMay in here. Well, I sure as shit don't need any more smart-aleck retorts from you. You try that crap again and I'll bring you up on charges, Colonel."

His face had turned the shade of a five-alarm beet. And the mess hall had fallen as silent as a morgue at midnight. The general now had an audience of about fifty men and officers. I decided it was time to mount a counterattack and call this jerk's bluff.

I glanced at my wristwatch. "Tell you what, General Stone. Sir. I have a meeting with General LeMay in about ten minutes. Have you met the incoming commander? If not, it would be my pleasure to have you tag along. I'll introduce you. And LeMay can explain to you why he requested me to fly him here. That might clear up your acute confusion." I knew I had walked out onto thin ice with that response. But I just didn't care anymore. General officers should be respected, of course, but this guy really rubbed me the wrong way.

Stone stood there, merely staring at me. Fuming. Uncertain. I looked closely to see if I could spot any steam issuing from his ears. Nope.

Finally he spoke. "I've got my own staff meeting to attend." He stepped past me and strode out the door, his Sancho Panza in trail.

I scanned the faces of the folks in the mess hall who had witnessed the exchange. More than a few flashed me a smile. I gathered Stone perhaps didn't command widespread respect. I checked my watch again. Thanks to Stone, I would be late for my meeting with General LeMay. I recalled one of his nicknames was Iron Ass. I assumed you didn't want to be tardy for a rendezvous with a guy called Iron Ass. Well, there went another brick onto my pile of dislikes for General Leonard Stone.

18

Hsinching, Sichuan, China
Forward Headquarters, XX Bomber Command
September 3, 1944

I arrived only a couple of minutes late at General LeMay's office. He didn't note my tardiness, merely told me curtly to enter. I did. The general stood with his back to me, looking out a window behind his desk.

"That's the main road to Chengtu," he said, continuing to stare out the window.

I noted a steady stream of coolies pushing wheelbarrows along the road and others pulling large carts outfitted with automobile tires. I guessed the tires proved useless on cars and trucks since there was so little gasoline available. One of the carts held a huge hog with his eyes sewn shut. I'd heard that was because if the hog couldn't see anything, it wouldn't raise a fuss . . . until the moment it began its journey to becoming pork chops.

"You know," the general continued, "these Chinamen constructed the runways here by hand. By hand, by God." He turned to face me, a cigar clamped between his lips.

He motioned me to sit. I did, and he did, too. He continued speaking. "Initially, they were paid by the amount of dirt they moved to level the field.

After that, they carried stones out of a nearby riverbed to the runway site. Big stones first. Then smaller and smaller ones. They pounded them into gravel with hammers and sledgehammers. Once that was finished, they added a slurry made of clay and tung oil. Finally, they flattened everything out using handmade rollers so heavy—ten tons—they took fifty coolies to pull and fifty handling ropes from behind to control the speed." He took a big puff of his Cuban and set it in an ashtray. "I'm told it took half a million men to build all four main bases around Chengtu in addition to half a dozen auxiliary airfields. Half a million. Laborers, cooks, managers. They did it in nine months."

I could read the awe reflected in LeMay's eyes—his amazement at what had been accomplished without mechanization and modern technology. It also explained his unusual loquaciousness.

"So," he continued, changing the subject, "how's the leg?"

"Achy, sir. I guess I have to get used to driving an airplane again."

"Yes. Well, what I called you in here for wasn't to talk about flying. I want to discuss weather support."

So maybe he wasn't going to snatch my wings after all. "Yes, sir."

"I know from Europe how important weather is to bombing. I realize you know that, too. And I want you to understand I know how limited your resources are here compared to what we had on the continent."

He placed the cigar back between his lips. It oscillated up and down while he continued to talk. "For obvious reasons, we receive no weather info out of Japan. The Russians refuse to give us any reports. We get a few obs from Mao Tse-tung's troops, guys your squadron trained to work in northeast China. And we receive a smattering of reports from an outfit the navy has plopped down in the Gobi Desert. Why on earth the navy is in the Gobi is beyond me, but they are."

I already knew everything LeMay was telling me, of course. But it was refreshing to hear a general officer acknowledge the restraints under which we worked, not spouting off nonsensical dictums such as "there is no weather on the Hump," as I'd heard another senior officer pronounce.

LeMay went on. "So I understand what a strain it is to forecast conditions over an area seventeen hundred miles away with no information for thousands of miles to the west where the weather originates. So to help out,

I'm going to try to get a recon bird in the air over Japan prior to each bombing raid."

"That would be a tremendous help, General."

LeMay nodded. "And I'm also going to request your meteorologists give me a degree of reliability, on a scale of one to ten, for each mission forecast. I'll toss that into the pot along with all the other factors I have to consider before making go-no-go decisions. I hope that'll take some of the pressure off your boys."

I had to admit, Curtis LeMay seemed to be an exceptionally insightful officer. I could see why he'd become a two-star at such a young age.

"It will, sir," I answered. "And it will be greatly appreciated. Also, there's another thing in the works I think will help."

He took a puff of his cigar and leaned forward, peering at me with curiosity. I related to him Colonel Ellsworth's plans to get some observer teams deployed into Urumchi, that remote place in far northwest China . . . "at the ends of the earth."

"All well and good." He blew a smoke ring. "Now, there's something else I want to ask you about, this report you wrote for the Twentieth. The one about the winds over Japan."

He was referencing the paper I'd written summarizing the work of Wasaburo Ooishi and his discovery of the awesomely powerful wintertime winds in the upper atmosphere over Japan.

"Yes, sir."

"Go over that for me in a bit more detail, if you would. I want to make sure I clearly understand everything about it."

I did, and after I'd finished, he leaned back in his chair and moved the cigar clamped in his mouth in small circles. "We had strong winds aloft over Europe, too, you know. Sometimes one-thirty, maybe one-forty knots. But you're telling me that was the *average* observed over Japan? And that they could peak out at maybe one hundred eighty or more? Why so much stronger?"

A reasonable question. "I think because Japan sits at the crossroads of great airmass collisions in the wintertime—bitter cold Arctic air streaming off the Asian continent from Siberia and Mongolia, and warm tropical air flowing northward from the South China and Philippine Seas. The result is—"

"Winds almost as fast as the cruising speed of a B-17. Unbelievable." He didn't speak for a while, seeming to stare into an empty middle distance. Maybe deep in thought. I didn't know.

I looked past him, over his shoulder, out the window onto the road where a steady stream of wheelbarrows and wooden carts continued to kick up dust—the morning rush hour in Chengtu, China.

LeMay abruptly stood, slammed his cigar back into the ashtray, and growled, "Well, that's another nail in the coffin."

"Sir?" I had no idea to what he referred.

"This whole operation, flying bombers out of China to hammer Japan. It's a logistical nightmare. Unsustainable. Only Washington could have dreamed up something like this. Or maybe it's something out of the *Wizard of Oz*." Anger threaded his words, though I knew the anger wasn't directed at me.

He paced back and forth behind his desk. "We're flying seven trips over the Hump with every fuel-hauling aircraft we have just to supply enough gas to fill the tanks of a B-29 so it can fly a single mission against Japan. That limits us to one raid per week. Does that make any sense?"

I knew it was a rhetorical question, but answered anyhow. "No, sir."

"And now you're telling me we could be fighting winds so strong trying to get back home from raids in the winter that our ground speeds could be a hundred knots or less?"

I nodded.

"Wouldn't Jap fighters based in China love that? I mean, assuming our B-29s didn't run out of fuel first and end up as fifty-ton Chinese junks floating in the East China Sea?"

I didn't think B-29s would float, but kept my mouth shut. I fully understood, however, his point. That Superfort bombing operations out of China made absolutely no sense. I hadn't thought about the logistics before, but LeMay had picked up on the problem in a matter of days. That's another reason he wore stars on his shoulders and I probably never would.

I knew the general was venting his frustrations at the operational situation he'd found himself thrust into. I was not necessarily a trusted confidant, but I happened to be there when he felt moved to verbalize his exasperation. And I guess I'd been sort of a catalyst when I'd put together the report about the powerful wintertime winds over Japan.

The general quit pacing, sat down, and reached for his cigar . . . which had gone out. He scowled at it, relit it, and jammed it back in his mouth. I noted he didn't ask me whether I minded if he smoked or not. Of course, why would he? Rank has its privileges. Puffing on Cuban cigars was obviously one of them.

That aside, I was curious about any possible alternatives to mounting the bombing operations from China. It certainly was not my place to ask, since I wasn't a staff officer, but it piqued my interest. I decided to go ahead and pose the question. He could easily enough tell me it was none of my business.

After I tossed out my query, he rolled the cigar around between his lips and gave me a hard stare. I decided I'd overstepped my bounds.

"You ever hear of the Mariana Islands?" he asked.

"That's where Guam is, isn't it?" I knew American forces—mainly marines but some army, too—had recaptured the island from the Japs last month.

"And Saipan and Tinian. Once we get air bases built on those islands, we'll be able to launch airstrikes on Japan from there. We'll be eight hundred miles closer to Tokyo than we are here. And we won't have to make trip after damn trip lugging fuel and munitions over the Himalayas to supply the Superforts. Navy tankers will do the job. All they'll have to do is sail in and we'll say 'fill 'er up.'"

"How long—"

"Construction of facilities is already underway on Saipan and Tinian. I'm sure our Engineer Aviation Battalions and the Navy Seabees will do a great job, but what I wouldn't give for a battalion or two of those Chinese coolies that did the work here."

I thought I saw a faint smile do battle with LeMay's cigar, but wasn't sure.

He glanced at his wall clock. "Well, I've got another meeting coming up. That'll be all, Colonel Shepherd. Unless you've got something else for me."

I'd considered bitching about General Stone, but decided it wouldn't do any good, and more likely would just end up making me look bad. I assumed general officers had their own little club with star-studded membership cards and secret handshakes, and that they watched each other's backs and would never speak ill of a brother flag officer.

But I had another idea.

"No, sir," I said and stood. "Oh, one thing. Do you know a General Stone?"

"Not familiar with the name."

"He's a liaison from the JCS, I believe. Anyhow, if you ever come across him, please thank him for the mature advice and career guidance he's offered me."

LeMay nodded.

"Thank you, sir." I saluted, did an about-face, and limped out of the general's office. If Stone ever got my message, I hoped he'd wonder what and how much I'd really told General LeMay about our back-and-forth and whether or not LeMay was being facetious. If I was lucky, maybe it'd give ol' Lenny a sleepless night or two. Prick.

After I left LeMay's office, I walked to the flight line. I found an upended wheelbarrow, without a wheel, and sat on it. I watched as a parade of aircraft—B-29s, C-109s, C-54s, C-46s—landed on the coolie-built runway and, with engines humming, taxied to the Superfort hardstands where they disgorged their cargos—fuel and munitions for the next raid.

I thought of what the general had told me, about the absurd logistics of the operation, and could see it clearly now as the cargo carriers swarmed around the bombers like worker bees attending to queens.

Captain Nestor Woods, the pilot I'd flown with on the Yawata raids, walked by me.

"Hey, Nestor," I called out. I stood and hobbled after him.

He stopped and pivoted and popped a salute as I approached him.

"As you were," I said. "Good to see you again, Nestor."

"You, too, Major—holy cow. Lieutenant colonel! Congratulations, sir."

"Thank you. Look, I wanted to ask you, since that last raid on Yawata, have there been any others?"

"No, sir. Nothing."

"Nothing in two weeks?"

"Just can't get enough gas and bombs. It's crazy."

Wizard of Oz, I thought.

"Do you know when the next mission is scheduled?" I had to raise my voice as a C-46, smoking and growling, lumbered down the taxiway toward its off-load point.

"I've heard the next raid is scheduled for the eighth, but it won't be targeting Japland."

"Oh?"

"We'll be going after the coke ovens at the Showa Steel Works in Anshan, Manchuria, a place the Japs have occupied since '31."

"Big raid?"

"Ninety-eight planes. And get this, scuttlebutt has it that General LeMay will be flying one of the birds."

"Really." I guess the general had been able to weasel one last mission before he became "chained" to his desk. I thanked Nestor and wished him well. He asked me if I wanted to ride along again, but I decided not to press my luck. Besides, I had my trip to the "ends of the earth" coming up.

I returned to my wheelbarrow perch and thought about Eve. Not that there was anything I could think about her. She remained an absolute, total enigma to me. Before I took off on the Yawata raid, she'd begged me not to go, but wouldn't admit to still being in love with me. She'd shaken her head in the negative when I'd asked, but had never said no, never verbalized if she did or didn't. She'd merely broken into a fit of sobbing. What in the Sam Hill was I supposed to make of that?

I decided not to try to make anything of it. Or try to contact her again. It seemed so fruitless. In all likelihood, we'd end up going our different ways as this damned war wore on, and I'd never find out how she truly felt.

But I knew one thing. I would always cling to the notion I had in New Delhi so many months ago when I first began my search for Eve.

There, I'd decided if I stopped believing in love, I'd stop believing in life.

I arose from the wheelbarrow and walked to base ops to check to see if I had any messages from Colonel Ellsworth regarding my journey to Urumchi.

Life goes on.

19

Hsinching, Sichuan, China
US Army Air Forces Base
September 10, 1944

Colonel Ellsworth contacted me on September 4 and asked me to hang around Hsinching for another week to greet and get to know the men who would be flying to Urumchi with me. I did. And while the temptation was there during that period to contact Eve, I made no effort. If nothing else, I'd learned the futility of attempting to talk to her, to understand her. It seemed the wisest course for me—though it cut deep into my soul—would be to relegate her to memories of a passionate and stirring wartime romance. Memories I could hold dear until my time on this Earth expired. Memories I could regale my grandkids with. If I ever had grandkids.

Anyhow, dismissing Eve allowed me to concentrate on my mission to the middle of nowhere. Launch had been set by Ellsworth for September 11.

Word got around the base about the weather guys planning to schlep off to the ends of the earth. A lot of folks stopped by base ops, where we held our planning sessions, to wish us well, say thanks, and offer encouragement. Even General LeMay dropped by one afternoon to give us an attaboy and shake hands.

"You know how much getting good weather data from that place will mean to me and the Twentieth," he said to me as he prepared to leave, "so let me know when you get things up and running."

"I will, sir. By the way, how did your Manchurian raid go?" I knew I probably shouldn't be asking, but I was curious. I knew the general wanted to fly one final mission before he was relegated to command from behind a desk, and the attack on the Manchurian target was supposed to have been it.

LeMay didn't speak for a moment, eyeing me and wiggling the cigar jammed in his mouth. Then he removed the stogie and said, "Disappointing." He paused, then went on. "I wanted to see how good the Jap fighter pilots really were. But they never mounted a decent counterattack. They were up in force waiting for us, but I think they misjudged the speed of our B-29s. Except for one guy, they never got close enough for us to fire on them."

"But a successful raid?"

"We did a lot of damage. Only lost four birds. Flak."

With that he gave a quick nod, jammed the ever-present cigar back between his teeth, pivoted, and strode off.

"So that was Old Iron Pants?" one of the men I sat with said after the general had departed. "Seems like a nice enough guy."

"Yeah," I answered. "Just don't ever cross him."

We continued with our planning session, and I got to know the key figures assigned to the team better. Major Douglas Mackiernan, selected to head the weather station in Urumchi, seemed a dedicated and serious officer. His knowledge of cryptology appeared immense. If anyone would be able to break Russian codes to snatch weather data, it would be Mackiernan. And since he'd also spent some time at MIT studying physics, he seemed a natural to command the operations in Urumchi.

Major Athelstan Frederick Spilhaus, "Spilly," a native of South Africa, was the other senior weather officer bound for Urumchi. He, like Major Mackiernan, had studied at MIT, where he'd earned degrees in aeronautical engineering and meteorology. He came off as adventurous, fun loving, and inquisitive. I suppose the term "Renaissance man" might also fit him.

I introduced the guys to Captain Washington, the Ledo Road engineer, but saw no need for him to sit in on our planning meetings since he wouldn't be remaining in Urumchi. Instead, he busied himself gathering supplies for our journey.

Major Spilhaus spoke to me as we wrapped up our meeting. "That bodyguard of yours, that Washington fellow, he's an impressive specimen. Smart, too, I noticed. You expecting trouble?"

"He's not my bodyguard, Spilly. And no, I'm not expecting trouble. I just don't know what to expect, how we'll be received. So think of Captain Washington as a contingency force."

"Well, I'm glad he's *our* contingency force," Spilhaus responded.

As the men exited base ops, I reminded them, "We'll meet on the flight line at oh-six-hundred tomorrow and head for the ends of the earth."

Both excited and apprehensive about our upcoming journey, I headed back to my billet. The competing odors of fertile earth and military petroleum filled the air. The intermittent bellow of big airplane engines rolled over the base, blotting out the soft chirping of songbirds, as a steady procession of B-29s, C-54s, and C-109s—transporters of fuel and bombs for the next raid—landed and took off.

Now that September had settled in, the days around Chengtu had turned less oppressive and the rainfall less frequent. A leaden sky hung over the base, but I noticed a glimmer of brightness—a silver streak of clearing—to the west and hoped that augured well for our long flight tomorrow. I'd reached the entrance to my barracks when the barely audible crunch of gravel on the walkway behind me reached my ears. I wondered if perhaps my own personal bad-luck dragon had snuck up on me and was at last about to snare me. Then I heard a voice.

"I want to come with you tomorrow."

Eve. I didn't turn to face her. I had truly grown tired of her unpredictable, indecipherable moods and proclamations. "Eve, I don't think—"

"Please, let me finish what I want to say."

I sighed and turned around. "Yeah, okay."

She stood not four feet from me, in her brown-and-white-striped nurse's uniform, looking . . . a little bit of everything. Tired, sad, confused, maybe even a little frightened. Crimson tinted her face. Her blue-eyed gaze locked on mine. But the iciness it often harbored, and of which I had so often been the target, was absent. In its stead I saw something bordering on pleading. I bore a massive amount of uncertainty about whether I wanted to hear what she would impart, having been so often filleted by her words in the past, but decided to keep my powder dry and listen.

"Let's walk," she said softly.

I moved to her side, and we headed toward a distant wooden fence that marked the edge of the air base.

"I need to get away from this place," she said. She looked at me.

I kept my mouth shut. *We all need to get away from this place*, I thought.

"I know I've been unkind to you, but it's been for a reason."

I would hope so.

"I've been trying to protect you."

She'd said that before. I broke my silence. "From what?"

She fell quiet for a while as a Superfort, probably deadheading back to India, lifted off from the runway and filled the late afternoon with the roar of eighty-eight hundred horsepower at full gallop.

As the bomber became a speck on the horizon in the encroaching twilight, Eve resumed speaking. "From the wrath of a general."

I stopped walking. "Not Leonard Stone?"

"Yes."

"You're too late. As minor as it may have been, I've already incurred his wrath."

"No, you haven't."

"What the hell do you mean, Eve? What have you to do with General Stone? Or vice versa? What are you trying to tell me? Why does Stone have it in for *me*? And why do you need to get away from Hsinching?"

I realized I'd fired too many questions at her all at once. But as usual in my conversations with her, I'd become totally lost. This time, very quickly.

She took my arm—a rather intimate gesture, it seemed, given her recent put-offishness toward me—and we began walking again.

"I love you," she murmured, and leaned against me.

"Could have fooled me," I mumbled in return. But my heart fluttered, and I felt a frisson of happiness rifle through my being. But I also heard, at least metaphorically, a warning buzzer go off somewhere deep within me. I knew by now that Eve was often impossible to decode. Or even post-analyze.

"You're confused, aren't you?" she said quietly.

"Duh."

She issued a soft laugh. "I know. I've been . . . enigmatic. Is that the right word?"

I nodded. "It would fit."

"It was deliberate."

"Okay, start at the beginning."

"I'll start at the end."

Of course you will. "Okay, start at the end."

"I know you've got a mission prepared to launch tomorrow morning. To someplace faraway in northwest China."

"The entire base knows that."

"I want to go with you. As I said, I have to get away from here. And I was thinking, well, hoping, you might need medical support. Remember, I'm a flight nurse."

"I know what you are, Eve. Look, we aren't embarking on a combat mission. It's more of a diplomatic undertaking. We don't expect to take any casualties."

"I understand that. But here's the thing. Maybe it would enhance your diplomatic position if you had someone in your delegation who could offer medical assistance to the indigenous people of wherever you're going. You know, to attend to simple things like cuts or open wounds, maybe even set broken bones and cure upset tummies."

Eve had obviously thought through her pitch to me. But I didn't fully understand her sudden need to escape Hsinching, to get away from General Stone, asshole he might be. We reached the fence and stopped. My leg had begun its usual "gimme a break" routine.

"Eve, you know you can't just come along with us on a whim. You need orders. And I don't have any for you." I gave her my best commanding officer stare. "Tell me what's really going on."

She lowered her gaze from mine and didn't respond.

"Eve, what is it?"

"I've got orders," she said.

"What? To go to Urumchi?"

"No. That's the problem." She reached into a pocket of her uniform and extracted a letter-sized paper. She handed it to me. Military orders.

I read them, a bit stunned by what I saw.

"From the Joint Chiefs of Staff?" I said, after I'd finished. "I thought your orders came from the Army Medical Corps."

"Usually."

"But these came from the JCS assigning you to Hickam Field in Honolulu as medical advisor to the Chief of Personnel for the Twentieth Air Force. The Twentieth Air Force is what the Twentieth Bomber Command here falls under, right?"

"Right."

"I'm missing something, Eve. What is it? I'm not a private gumshoe. Help me out here. Why are you so damned determined to fly away with me to God-knows-where in China rather than settle into a nice cushy assignment in Hawaii? I don't get it."

The night peepers inhabiting the fields and paddies surrounding Hsinching began to tune up for their nightly concert as twilight took over, turning the sky a velvety indigo. Eve stared at me, an infinite sadness festering in her eyes.

"You do know who the Chief of Personnel for the Twentieth Air Force is, don't you?"

I didn't. But then I did. It hit me like an anvil plummeting from a Superfort and nailing me square on the head. It didn't flatten me, but it figuratively knocked the wind out of me, and I couldn't speak.

"Yeah," Eve said. "Brigadier General Leonard Stone, United States Army Air Forces."

I managed a few hoarse gasps but no words.

"And he doesn't want me as a medical advisor," she whispered. "He wants me as his personal concubine." In the dimming light, I saw tears brimming in her eyes.

I managed at last to suck in a deep gulp of air and speak again. My words came out quietly but wrapped in a low, sharp growl. "And he was the one who raped you after you lost your fiancé in the Pearl Harbor attack?"

Eve nodded. A muffled sob escaped from her.

"But he came after you again?"

"I thought I'd never see him again after Pearl. He was a colonel then, but when he got promoted to his position of personnel chief for the Twentieth, he discovered I was in India. You know, recovering from my injuries in the hospital in New Delhi. I guess that's when he decided to claim me as 'his own.' Probably figured I couldn't resist a general officer. Especially one who'd been a big-time Hollywood movie producer. He's the one who got me shipped off to this godforsaken base this spring. I guess he figured it would be a good out-of-the-way place to hide me until he could figure out what to do with me next."

I knew now why the general had been unable to uncover any information about Eve for me at Hastings Mill. He knew about Eve and me and wasn't about to let me get close to her again.

"I'll kill that son of a bitch, I swear to God, Eve." Rage like an erupting volcano surged through me. My body tensed as if zapped by an electric shock. "I'll draw and quarter the bastard and leave him for the buzzards."

Eve reached out and laid her hand on my arm. "No, you won't. That's what I've been trying to protect you against. Stone knows about us, our relationship. He said if you ever challenged him or threatened him, he'd ruin your career and your reputation."

"Jesus, Eve, I don't have a career in the army. There's nothing to ruin, I'm a cripple and can't fly. And when this war is over, I go back to being a civilian."

"Stone understands that. He said he could make your civilian opportunities disappear, too. He'd accuse you . . . us, of lying, being blackmailers, maybe even traitors by falsely accusing a senior army officer of criminal assault and battery. He's got the rank, the power, friends in high places, and even the money from his career in Hollywood to be able to do that. Both of us would end up broke and with shattered reputations."

I knew Eve was right, but my anger grew, reaching unfathomable depths. I realized I'd clenched my fists so tightly that pain shot through my wrists and surged up my forearms. I forced myself to relax. But at least now I understood why Eve had so persistently pushed me away. And why Stone had demonstrated such unbridled animosity toward me and loved to denigrate me every chance he got. Jealousy.

I stood as his rival, but unfortunately—for me—an emasculated rival tilting at windmills. He knew with certainty steeped in tradition and convention that the word of a nurse, a woman, a junior officer would never stand up against a flag officer's. Well, damn him and tradition and convention. Lenny Stone, without knowing it, had thrown down his gauntlet at my feet. I picked it up without hesitation.

Eve's orders stated she was to report to base ops tomorrow for transportation to Hickam. That left me only one option. One that could end up with both of us being court-martialed, but what the hell. I wasn't going to leave the woman I loved, a lady who had been trying to keep *me* out of harm's way, to a cretin who wore stars on his shoulders. To a rapist.

I drew Eve to me. We embraced. And kissed. For quite a long time. For a fleeting instant, all seemed right with the world again, but I knew it wasn't.

"How do you feel about going AWOL?" I asked after we ended our kiss.

"I was hoping you'd come up with a better solution than that," she whispered, still clinging to me. Darkness had settled over us.

"I don't have time to try to get you a new set of orders. Too much bureaucracy involved. But I am going to get you out of the hands of that bastard Stone. Meet me on the tarmac tomorrow morning at oh-six-hundred with your bags packed for a trip to the middle of nowhere."

"You know what," she murmured, "that sounds better than Waikiki."

I didn't know what I was getting us into, but I knew what I was getting her out of.

20

Hsinching, Sichuan, China
US Army Air Forces Base
September 11, 1944

Dawn blossomed over Chengtu in a sunrise explosion of brilliant reds and sunburst oranges. The cloud deck that had hung over Hsinching yesterday had trundled away to the east overnight. In its wake, rare clear skies graced the area. At least our journey would begin in favorable weather.

Betsy, Colonel Ellsworth's C-47, waited on the tarmac for me and my team. I spotted Tex Albaugh, the pilot, doing his preflight walk-around inspection. I gave him a wave. He motioned me over.

"Good to see you again, Colonel." He saluted, and I returned it. "I understand you'll be sitting in the right-hand seat today."

"More than I understood. But if you don't mind having a gimp for a copilot, I'm game."

"Couldn't think of anybody better, sir."

I completed the walk-around with Tex.

Shortly after my arrival, the other members of the team—the two majors, Captain Washington, two senior NCOs, and Eve—showed up. Eve, decked out in her flight nurse fatigues, elicited an incalculable amount of wide-eyed amazement from the men. She tossed her B-4 bag on the tarmac and announced, "There's a small crate of med supplies waiting on the front steps of the hospital. I wonder if one of you gentlemen could pick it up and bring it to the plane?"

One of the NCOs, Ralph Hemming, stepped forward, a big grin smeared across face, and said, "Yes, ma'am. I'll grab a jeep and go get it."

I introduced Eve, Captain Genevieve Johannsen, to the crew and explained the reason for her presence.

"Captain Johannsen will help us out if we suffer any medical problems. But more importantly, she might be able to enhance our negotiating position with the folks in Urumchi if she's able to give medical assistance to any locals who might need it."

My flimsy excuse seemed to be accepted by the group, and Eve was welcomed immediately into the party. It probably helped, too, that she looked like a movie star, even in her flight gear.

Master Sergeant Hemming arrived back at the plane with the medical supplies. We loaded them aboard and buttoned up, ready for a daylong journey to far northwest China.

I asked Eve if asshole Lenny was around, and she told me she hadn't seen him in several days.

"But," she said, "I'm sure he'll be arriving in Hsinching later today to make certain I get safely aboard my transport to Hawaii."

I felt certain he hadn't learned of her "change of plans," but still, as we taxied into takeoff position, I scanned the flight line for any sign of a staff car or MP jeep in hot pursuit of *Betsy*. None.

We received clearance for takeoff from the tower, roared down the runway—scattering a few Chinese early-bird laborers—and lifted off into a pristine sky bound for a place less than two hundred miles from the border of Outer Mongolia. The ends of the earth.

We climbed northwestward out of Chengtu, threading our way through the Bayan Kara mountains. The clear weather allowed us to track through river valleys and keep our distance from nearby snow-covered peaks that jutted skyward like vertical daggers.

"These mountains," Tex said over the interphone, "I hear separate the drainage areas of the Yellow and Yangtze Rivers. The source of the Yellow is supposed to be somewhere in the northern reaches of this range."

"Brutal-looking terrain," I responded.

"Well, let's try to keep ol' *Betsy* up in the air, then."

Gradually, the coniferous forests of the mountain valleys gave way to alpine shrubs and meadows as we continued to drone northwestward, soaring out over the flatter steppe land of a plateau. Below us, herds of deer, antelope, and sheep trotted across sprawling grasslands. Wild and free. No humans in sight.

I went back and sat by Eve for a while in the canvas seats that lined both sides of the Gooney Bird.

"You doing okay?" I asked.

"For an AWOL army nurse, yeah."

We had to raise our voices to be heard over the throaty roar of the plane's engines. But with nobody else seated near us, we weren't worried about being overheard.

"It's a long flight," I said.

"How much longer?"

"We're about halfway through it. If you get hungry, there are some C rats in a box in the rear of the plane. Help yourself."

She smiled at me. "Remember Burma? How hungry we got before the headhunters found us?"

"I'm glad *they* weren't hungry." I gave her hand a surreptitious pat and stood to go back to the cockpit. "Oh. If you get bored, and I know you will, come up front and visit for a while. The views are great."

Again she smiled. It felt good to see her that way. I wondered if I'd be able to help her maintain that relative happiness.

In another hour or so, we winged out over the eastern edges of the Takla Makan Desert, a vast basin of sand dunes that extended over six hundred miles to the west. Eve had come forward to gaze out the cockpit windows.

"Talk about barren," she said.

"I told you we were headed for the middle of nowhere," I responded.

"This doesn't look like the middle of anywhere," she said, her words coated with disappointment.

"The fabled Silk Road," Tex interjected. "Imagine camel caravans strung out far below us."

"There's a road down there?" Eve asked.

"Once upon a time. Well, it wasn't a single road from what I've read, but a network of trade routes. Kind of like the Oregon Trail wasn't one trail but a bunch of different ones. The old Silk Road was over a thousand miles in length. It extended from China through Persia to southern Europe and eastern Africa. And it was in existence for over fifteen hundred years."

"Fifteen hundred years?" I said.

Tex nodded. "From just before the time of Christ to the fifteenth century."

"Then what happened?" Eve asked.

Tex seemed to have a pretty good historical handle on the wasteland over which we flew.

"Oh, several things. The Black Death from Europe, the fragmentation of the Mongol empire, regional wars."

"Are the trade routes still used?" I asked. I sure as hell hoped we wouldn't need to make an emergency landing in an area where we'd have to wait for our rescuers to show up on camels.

Tex shrugged. "Probably not. There may be a few nomadic tribes down there. But most commercial trade these days is by sea."

"So if we had to crash-land . . ."

"Let's hope it's someplace other than here."

But my fears of going down in an Asian Sahara never materialized. *Betsy* remained strong with her engines throbbing almost melodically. At least they provided music to *my* ears. Another hour of flying brought us to Urumchi.

"Nice to see trees again," Tex said.

Urumchi, though boxed in by deserts, sat at the base of the snowcapped Tian Shan mountains. I supposed runoff from glaciers and snowmelt provided the town with enough water for scattered stands of pines to thrive, and near riverbeds, willows and poplars.

We contacted the control tower at the airstrip on the radio frequency we'd been given. The response came in Chinese. I called Captain Washington forward and asked him if he understood what the controller was saying.

The captain listened but shook his head. "Not well enough I'd want to try to give you landing instructions."

We made a couple of low, slow passes along the length of the runway and waggled our wings, hoping to show our intent to land. A man in a military uniform stepped from the ground level of the two-story thatched-roof control tower and waved at us, then beckoned us to land. Apparently, we'd been expected.

"Looks like a couple of birds didn't have such good luck setting down here," Tex noted. At one end of the runway rested the carcass of a burned-out Gooney Bird. At the other, the skeleton of some sort of old Russian transport.

"I'll do better than that," Tex promised.

He did, putting *Betsy* down in a smooth landing pilots would term "a grease job." We taxied toward the tower.

"What in the hell is that?" I exclaimed.

Rolling toward us, belching black exhaust, came an early 1930s vintage Packard.

"Must be the local Welcome Wagon," Tex said.

"Yeah, running on coal instead of gasoline." I assumed the engine had been converted to run on coal since gasoline would have been for military vehicles only.

We rolled to a stop in front of the tower and shut down the engines. Tex suggested I, as senior officer, disembark first and take Captain Washington along as my interpreter.

Fortunately, the Chinese had a set of rolling stairs they pushed up to the cargo door, and I was able to get out of *Betsy* with a modicum of grace on my by now very stiff leg. Two Chinese gentlemen, one wearing a tailcoat and an honest-to-God silk top hat strode toward us. The second man, outfitted in a more traditional American-style business suit, greeted us. He said his name in Chinese, but I didn't quite get it. I turned to Washington for help.

"Did you catch his name?" I said.

"I think he said it was—"

"Bob," the Chinese man said, "just call me Bob." He spoke in almost perfect English, Chinese accented to be sure, but tinted with a flat Midwestern dialect.

Washington and I stared wide-eyed at him.

"I know," he said, "a Chink speaking English. Bit of a surprise, no? To explain, I attended Northwestern University and am now the chief banker in Urumchi. This gentleman"—he turned to the person accompanying him —"is the town's mayor. He likes the name Edward—very English sounding, I suppose—so you may call him that." Edward, with a pockmarked round face and several missing teeth, smiled a lot and seemed a friendly enough guy

We all shook hands, grinned, and bowed awkwardly to each other. By then, the others were filing off the aircraft, so I introduced them, too. Bob seemed keenly interested in Eve, especially when I told him she was a nurse who could perhaps lend some medical care to anyone who had relatively minor problems.

"That would be jake," Bob said, using American slang. "We have medical doctors here, but most are not up to date on modern practices and lack the latest medicines."

He guided us to the Packard. I noticed it had a left front fender fashioned out of wood. And in place of the original headlight on that side of the auto, it sported a kerosene lantern.

"Had a crash," Bob said, as he noticed me inspecting the crude repair. "And we cannot get replacement parts here, so we do the best with what we have."

"Do you have a lot of car crashes here?"

"We do not have a lot of cars. The Packard hit a camel."

"Oh." *Of course it did.* I didn't know what else to say. The way Bob said it, it sounded like a not unusual occurrence.

Bob ushered me and the two majors into the rear seat of the Packard, the mayor sat in the front passenger seat, and Bob took the wheel. He slipped the car into gear, and we took off with a wheeze and a clatter and giant puff of black exhaust. The rest of the cadre, seated in the rear of a canvas-covered military truck, followed.

"In case you were wondering," Bob said as we jounced along a rutted, rough road, "I bought the car when I was in Evanston and had it shipped to Urumchi after I finished school. It has become the town's 'official' car for important visitors."

I noticed the truck followed us at a great distance, probably because the Packard persisted in belching out exhaust like a navy destroyer laying down a smoke screen in combat.

"You mentioned you were the town's banker," I said to Bob. "What brought you to Urumchi?"

Bob chuckled. "I know, this place looks like a backwater burgh, right? Why would a guy with an American college degree come here? Well, first of all, family. Second, Urumchi will not always be a remote dump. I think with its proximity to mountains and a decent water supply, and the likelihood of air travel exploding after the war, this place could become a thriving metropolis."

"Money to be made?"

"I think lots."

Bob was no dummy, and probably had more vision than most, but I knew he'd have to be prepared to hang around for the long haul. As far as I was concerned, we truly had reached the middle of nowhere . . . and our arrival in the "city center" confirmed that.

21

Urumchi, Sinkiang Province, China
September 11, 1944

Urumchi boasted just a single main street. Along one side of the street ran a stream that had been fashioned into sort of a canal. The canal, as I quickly discovered, served as both a source of "fresh" water and a sewer. I had rolled down the rear window of the Packard, but quickly rolled it back up. I hoped Eve had laid in plenty of medicine for dysentery.

Cross planking on the canal served as footbridges for the public. The public, it seemed to me, consisted of a cosmopolitan blend of what I assumed to be primarily nomads. They ranged from dark-haired, dark-skinned Mongolians to a scattering of blond Caucasians whom I guessed to be Russians, or of Russian descent. Lots of Chinese, too, of course.

As Bob had told me, very few automobiles or trucks plied the street. The vehicular traffic comprised ox-drawn carts, hand-pulled wooden wagons, some fierce-looking warrior types on horseback—maybe Mongols or Kazakhs—and yes, even a few camels. My team and I were a long way from home.

We pulled up and stopped in front of what I assumed to be a hotel, a three-story affair built of wood and what I guessed to be adobe. Bob and Edward scrambled from the car and opened the back doors for us.

"Not quite The Drake," Bob said, referring to a hotel in Chicago, "but the best Urumchi has to offer. It has steam heat, the rooms are clean and have heavy down comforters, and the windows can be opened." I didn't view that as a plus, however, given the malodorous bouquet I'd detected wafting from the city's "water system." I will admit, the weather seemed quite pleasant—clear skies, warm, and dry—so perhaps an open window might prove welcome . . . depending on the wind direction.

Bob went on. "Each floor has a community bathroom, so you will have to work out visits with your female officer. You Americans will at least have the floor to yourselves, though. We assumed you would be tired after your long journey and would rather hit the sack, I think the expression is, than partake in a big dinner. So we have placed some snacks—fruits and breads —in each room and will have a large lunch tomorrow where we can celebrate your arrival and begin to discuss matters."

Several Chinese porters rushed from the hotel to grab our B-4 bags and usher us to our rooms. Edward waved, smiled, and tried to say goodbye in English—*goobli*—and Bob wished us a good night's sleep and said he would pick us up just before noon tomorrow.

I slept well that night, my aching muscles and tired bones enjoying a respite from sitting in the cockpit of the Gooney for almost eight hours. Interestingly, the mattresses turned out to be filled with rice chaff. They were comfortable enough, but whenever I rolled from one side to another, the soft crackle reminded me of crunching through fresh snow in northern Idaho.

Bob picked us up the following day in the late morning and carted us off to a restaurant. He seated us at a large table approximating the size of the landing deck on an aircraft carrier. Many local dignitaries, including the mayor, joined us, though I had no idea what all their various functions were.

They proved to be gracious hosts, however, and served a great deal of rich food and unmixed alcohol. I wasn't apprised of the provenance of all the various liquors, but there seemed an abundance of Russian vodka and high-test brandy.

Eve sat on one side of me, and a Chinese, whom I gathered might have been a meteorologist, sat on the other. Even though the gentleman spoke no English and I spoke no Chinese, with the assistance of the vodka, we eventually became involved in an animated conversation about weather, flying, and food.

Eve kept a close watch on me and carefully monitored my alcohol consumption, making sure I didn't embarrass myself. Or her.

At one point I whispered to her, "I think this booze has aphrodisiac qualities. I'm getting horny."

She surreptitiously kicked me in the ankle. "Behave yourself, Colonel," she hissed. "You're the senior officer here. Besides, I'm spoken for, in case you've forgotten."

I hadn't forgotten. She was AWOL. And I probably would be brought up on charges by a certain general officer for aiding and abetting her when we got back to Hsinching. I hadn't embarked on this venture, however, without thinking it through. I did have an ambush and counterattack planned for my buddy, Lenny, if he remained determined to challenge me. But my more immediate concerns lay here in Urumchi.

The luncheon dragged on for several hours, and I truly had to meter my intake of both food and booze. But overall, things went well. Bob told me after the gathering wrapped up that local officials seemed amenable to the idea of having an American weather station established in Urumchi. He said follow-up meetings could be held over the next several days in which we could discuss the details involved in getting our operation up and running. "Anything," he snapped, "to help us rid China of those damn Jap dwarfs."

He also said he'd try to make himself available as much as he could to facilitate translations. "But someone from the American consulate will also be there to help out," he added.

"There's an American consulate here?"

"And a Russian and an English one."

The meetings got underway the following day. A young man, a Chinese-American, James Shih, from the consulate, joined us. It turned out he spoke fluent English and Mandarin Chinese, plus something called

Uyghur, which I'd never heard of before. But apparently a lot of folks in this part of China used it.

Before the meeting kicked off, Shih handed me a cable the consulate had received, addressed to me, from the air base at Hsinching. The message proved to be short, clear, and blunt.

TO: LTC RODGER SHEPHERD, USAAF/10WS
FROM: BG LEONARD STONE, JCS/20AF
SUBJ: CPT GENEVIEVE JOHANNSEN
MESSAGE: RETURN CPT JOHANNSEN, USANC, TO HSINCHING
USAAFB IMMEDIATELY TO AVOID AWOL/DESERTION CHARGES

To say the message pissed me off would have been like saying the Brits were miffed by the German Blitz. Evidently Shih saw the expression on my face. He asked, "Would you care to send a response, sir?"

I read the cable again. It didn't ask for a return message, only an action. But I had a response in mind. One that would get ol' Lenny's knickers in a twist as much as he had mine.

"Yes," I said to Shih. "I'll draft one. But there's no rush on transmitting it. Late today would be fine."

I sat down at a table and penned the following:

TO: BG LEONARD STONE, JCS/20AF
FROM: LTC RODGER SHEPHERD, USAAF/10WS
SUBJ: CPT GENEVIEVE JOHANNSEN
MESSAGE: SUBJ OF 13 SEP MSG UNKNOWN. A CPT DARLENE
ACKERMAN, USANC, ACCOMPANIED ME TO URUMCHI

I figured by using the name Darlene Ackerman, the name General Stone had stashed Eve under at the hospital in Hsinching, he'd stay busy for the next couple of days trying to figure out his next move. I also hoped he might catch a glimpse of the first little thread of the scheme he'd knitted together to keep Eve for himself beginning to unravel.

I left Major Mackiernan, who would eventually be in charge of the Urumchi operation, to chair the meeting and went in search of Eve. I found her at the far end of town working under a canvas canopy supported by wooden poles. Outside the makeshift shelter, someone had erected a large Red Cross sign. A long line of what looked to be primarily nomads, and a few Chinese, waited patiently to be seen by the "golden-haired army doctor."

Several blocks away, three rough-looking men on horseback—they could have been Mongol warriors, I suppose—sat quietly, apparently keeping an eye on things. They didn't seem like troublemakers, so I dismissed them as any kind of threat to our presence. Or Eve's.

The day had turned out to be comfortable with temperatures holding in the seventies, I guessed, and only a scattering of cotton-ball clouds dotting the sky. That made the wait in line less than arduous. Soft breaths of wind carried the aroma of the "Main Street Canal" away from the makeshift clinic.

Eve spotted me, finished with a patient she'd been working with, signaled for the next in line to wait a moment, and walked over to me.

"Looks like your little field hospital is a big hit," I said. "Great idea. I think we've worked our way into the good graces of the locals." I wanted to hug her, but maintained military decorum.

She brushed a strand of hair from her eyes. "Yeah, it's mostly cuts and sores and sprains. A few minor burns. Easy enough to deal with. The real challenge is dysentery. A lot of that."

"Can't image why."

"Not much I can do for that kind of sickness. If they've got fever or pain, I hand out some APCs. If I had that new medicine called penicillin, that might work. But most of that went to the troops in Europe."

"What's penicillin?"

"It's an antibiotic. It attacks bacteria. So if this is the kind of dysentery caused by bacteria, it would be great. But I don't have any penicillin, so it's a moot point."

"Can you do anything?"

"Not beyond trying to educate them. There's an old Chinese lady here who speaks a little English, so I tell her to tell the people they must boil the water before they use it, use it for anything. To drink, to bathe, to wash vegetables. I explained to her there are invisible bugs in it, bacteria, that cause the sickness. I tell her that boiling the water kills the bugs and makes it safe to consume. And then I say that once the water has been boiled, the sick people must drink a lot of it."

"Because of dehydration?"

"They lose way too many bodily fluids from the diarrhea caused by dysentery. So all I can tell them is to rest, drink lots of water—sanitized— and to wash their hands."

"What about giving them some halazone tablets?" Halazone tablets were included in our C rations for water purification.

"Halazone tabs degrade too rapidly after a bottle is opened. I could use them in an emergency, I suppose. But better to teach the people here a simple procedure like boiling water."

I had to agree with that. I looked up and spotted a large hawk hitch-hiking on a thermal, keeping its eyes peeled for a late breakfast or lunch far below. At least it wasn't a buzzard soaring into the blue. That would have been a bad sign. But the thought of a buzzard triggered another image.

"I heard from our friend Lenny today," I said.

Eve's eyes widened.

"He ordered us to return to Hsinching immediately." I told her about the cable and about my response to it.

"Rod, you're going to get us in trouble," she exclaimed.

"In case you hadn't noticed, I think we crossed that Rubicon when we flew the coop in Hsinching." I glimpsed a few of the people waiting in line beginning to shuffle impatiently. "I think the natives are growing restless. Better get back to your Clara Barton duties."

Eve gave my hand a quick, hidden bump with her fist and returned to the shelter.

She ended up working until just before sunset, then joined the rest of us for another dinner with an overgenerous supply of booze. I wondered about replacing the water supply with vodka, but didn't think this would be the right time to bring it up.

The evening cooled off rapidly with a hint of frost hovering in the air. We returned to our hotel rooms where I, and I assumed everyone else, collapsed into bed exhausted from meetings, doctoring, too much food, and sipping high-octane liquor that could have powered the Wright Cyclone engines on B-29s.

Sometime in the wee hours, I awoke, having to pee. The steam heat had been turned off for the night, so after I tossed aside the bed's down comforter—that really did provide a great deal of warmth—I found myself shivering. I didn't feel like traipsing down the hall to the community lavatory in my skivvies, so I pulled on my pants, jacket, and shoes and shuffled off through the darkness toward a glimmer of light that marked the restroom.

Mission accomplished, I stepped back into the unlit hallway.

From the darkness, an arm wrapped around my neck and snapped me backward.

"*Uns-ca?*" a foreign voice rasped. It sounded like sandpaper scraping across cement. *What the hell?*

The arm tightened its hold on me. I struggled to breathe. *Jesus.*

"*Uns-ca?*" the voice repeated.

All I could do was grunt in response. I felt the cold metal of the barrel of a pistol press into my temple. I sensed the presence of several others besides my captor in the blackness. I smelled horses, sweat, earth. Were these the guys I'd seen on horseback earlier in the day?

Another voice growled something like "kellensder," and we were off. I got frog-marched down the inky passage toward the stairs. Then down the stairs, across the vacated hotel lobby, and into the deserted street.

Dim illumination from a distant streetlamp allowed me to see my new "friends." The boss turned out to be a big, swarthy guy with a bald head and a thick, black mustache that drooped over the sides of his mouth. He reminded me of a Mexican bandido, at least the ones I'd seen in movies.

He wore a long, fur-lined leather coat that had seen better days. But what really caught my eye was an elaborately woven belt of colorful fabric that secured a broadsword the size of Rhode Island to his hip. I hoped he wasn't a distant relative of the headhunters I'd encountered in Burma. He didn't brandish the sword, but kept a small-caliber pistol, maybe Russian, pointed at my head.

I sure as shit didn't know who they were or what they wanted. To kill me, kidnap me, dismember me? My breathing became shallow and rapid. I wished I'd taken a dump when I'd visited the lavatory.

The other two men accompanying Mr. Broadsword looked equally as fierce with brown skin and dark eyes. Like Broadsword, they wore long, fur-edged coats, like raggedy dusters from the 1920s. But unlike their leader, they sported big furry hats with earflaps, similar to those I'd seen Russians wearing in photos. *Ushankas*, I think they're called. But they sure didn't look like Russians. One of them, in fact, bore a short, braided beard like I'd seen on some Chinese men.

They urged me toward where their horses waited, snorting and pawing the ground and issuing great clouds of steam into the cold when they exhaled. I noticed they'd tethered four instead of three. One for me? I didn't like this. I began shivering again, probably as much from fear as from the chilliness, which I wasn't dressed for. I sure as hell didn't want to go anywhere with these guys, whoever they were, but they hadn't offered me any other options.

I decided to holler and raise a ruckus, attract some attention.

"Hey, you guys," I bellowed, "I'm not goin' anywhere with you. Help! Help!"

Bad idea.

"Tinis," or something like that, Broadsword screamed and whacked me on the skull with the butt of his pistol. Stars blossomed in my vision, but not those of the night sky. I felt myself being dragged, then hoisted onto the back of a horse and draped over the saddle like a sack of flour.

Geez, all I wanted to do in the first place was take a pee.

22

Urumchi, Sinkiang Province, China
September 14, 1944

The guys who snatched me took off down a dark street with me on my stomach draped over a horse. I jounced around as if I were in a Gooney Bird challenging a thunderstorm. My head throbbed, my guts spasmed, and I felt as alone as I'd ever been.

"Hold on there, partners," a voice boomed out of the blackness. The horses stopped. My captors muttered to one another in a language I didn't understand. I lifted my head, trying to determine the source of the voice. Couldn't see a thing.

I heard Broadsword issue a command. The horses began moving again. A shot exploded through the chilly stillness of the night. Sounded like a .45. My ears rang. The horses halted, whinnying and neighing and stomping in place.

The deep voice spoke again. This time in halting Chinese. I recognized it. Captain Washington. Broadsword responded, also in broken Chinese. Captain Washington, hands raised, emerged from where he'd been hiding into a dim shaft of light.

I heard one of the captors gasp. I guessed they'd never seen a Negro, certainly not one who stood higher than their horses' heads.

"Captain," I said, struggling to get my words out, "good to see you."

"Going for a little midnight ride, sir?"

"Just call me Paul Revere. Not my idea, though."

Keeping his hands above his head, Washington walked toward me. He spoke to Broadsword. Then Washington stepped next to the horse I'd been flung over and helped me down. I tried to stand, but my head spun, and I sank to the ground.

"Better stay there for a few minutes, Colonel. You might have a concussion."

I didn't argue. "How'd you get here?" I mumbled.

"I'd just gotten out of bed to take a whiz, and I heard a commotion in the hallway. Peeked out of my room just in time to see your buddies here dragging you downstairs. Decided I'd better investigate. I threw on some clothes, grabbed my Colt, and got outside where I heard you whooping and hollering. That told me which way to go, and I figured I'd better use my natural camouflage and set a little ambush in the dark before you got your ass ferried out of town."

"Any idea who these guys are?"

"Well, me and the guy with the sword both know a few words of Mandarin. So that helped. I told him we're Americans. And that helped. But I need better translation."

"You think they're Mongols?"

"Maybe. But they don't really look like the ones I've seen."

"So what do you think we should do?"

Washington smiled. Lots of white teeth. "You're the senior officer."

"Who's been bopped on the head with a chunk of steel and had a cannon fired in my ear."

"Forty-five," he corrected.

"Sounded like a cannon."

I tried to stand again. Washington helped me. This time I made it, albeit with my ears ringing and my head throbbing. Broadsword waved his pistol at us and indicated we should keep our hands on top of our heads.

"I guess we're still captives," Washington said.

"I'd rather think of us as detainees."

"Any ideas?"

That's one of the problems with being a senior officer. You're always expected to have the best ideas and make learned decisions. It doesn't always work that way, but I knew I had to come up with something. "I think we need to find someone who can talk to them, whatever language they're babbling, and to us. So I suggest you see if your limited Mandrin can get them to take us to the American consulate. Maybe someone will show up for work early and we can start to figure out who these guys are and what the hell they want."

After an extended exchange using hand gestures and Mandarin words with our "detainers," Washington got us all moving in the direction of the consulate. I noticed he still bore his .45 in his holster, so our captors apparently didn't view him as a major threat. Broadsword kept his handgun trained on us, though, and another of the horsemen held a rifle at the ready. It looked like an old British Lee-Enfield bolt-action piece from the turn of the century. That, of course, didn't mean it wouldn't work.

Captain Washington and I, hands raised, trudged ahead of the horsemen. The first thin slice of silver, the harbinger of dawn, glinted on the eastern horizon. The tips of my ears tingled in the near-freezing temperatures. I wished I'd worn a stocking cap when I'd gotten up to take a pee. Not that I'd known I'd end up being snatched by Mongol warriors, or whoever these guys were.

We reached the consulate, but it remained buttoned up for the night. I had no idea what their normal business hours were, or if they even had such a thing. We had no choice but to wait. I sat again, my back against the front door of the building. My leg ached, my head hurt, and I began shivering.

The trio of horsemen appeared to have relaxed a bit after hearing we were Americans. One of them, who I guessed noticed my shivering, even tossed me a blanket. It smelled of horse and dust, but provided welcome warmth.

I pulled it tight around my shoulders and waited. I thought about our captors and allowed a bizarre notion to creep into my musings. Which seemed normal, since I'd been hammered on the noggin and probably teetered on the threshold of a concussion. Again. Bizarre notions probably go hand-in-hand with that. I leaned close to Washington.

"Ask these guys if Lenny sent them."

"What?"

"Just ask."

"Lenny who?"

"They'll know. He's an army general."

"Are you okay, sir?"

"No. Forget it."

We continued to wait. The sun crept higher in the sky, but didn't do much to goose the temperature. Broadsword asked if we'd like a smoke and offered us some foul-smelling cigarettes. I didn't know where they came from, but I decided if we partook, we'd probably have to be medevaced back to Hsinching. We politely declined.

Finally, just as the warmth of the sun began to kick in, a young Chinese worker showed up at the consulate. Captain Washington explained our dilemma to him, and he took off, apparently promising to return with help.

So once more we waited. But not long. The promised help showed up within ten minutes. The newcomer, the help, looked a lot like Broadsword and his buddies. Wrapped in a fur-edged duster, he sported the same leathery skin, dark eyes, and black hair as our horse-mounted friends. But he clearly had a couple of decades on them.

In surprisingly fluent English, he confirmed who Washington and I were, why we were in Urumchi, and what had happened

Then he exchanged greetings with the horsemen and began a long conversation. Our detainers sometimes laughed as the back-and-forth went on, but they continued to hold us in their piercing gazes and keep their weapons handy. At last, the discussion ended. Broadsword stowed his pistol. The rifleman sheathed his Lee-Enfield. The horsemen smiled. Washington and I didn't.

The older gentleman moved closer to us. I stood. In a soft voice, his breath tinged in garlic and onions, he explained to us what had happened.

"First," he said, "please accept my sincere apologies. These men thought you were someone else."

I nodded. "Accepted. But who are these men?"

"Kazakhs, like myself. We are descended from nomadic tribes that roamed the Eurasian Steppe back in the fifteenth century. But Russians eventually colonized us. We now live in the Kazakh Soviet Socialist Republic. And the Russians, as they battle the Germans, are attempting to change us from an agricultural society into an industrial one. Not only that, they have built labor camps—gulags—here for their enemies, and have taken to pillaging our mineral wealth. They are not welcomed, not liked. Kazakh warrior groups, like you see here, have taken a stand against them."

Continuing to hold the smelly blanket tight around my upper body, I asked, "But what does that have to do with us?"

The old Kazakh gave an uncomfortable shuffle with his feet, looked away from me briefly, then brought his gaze back to me. "These warriors"—he gestured at the horsemen—"thought you and your compatriots might be Russians. You know, coming to curry favor with our Chinese friends, then using any toehold you might establish to spread even more unwanted Soviet influence."

"I understand, but what on earth made them think we were Russians?"

As the sun continued to climb into a cloudless sky, more and more people, and Urumchi's eclectic traffic, began to fill the street. The Kazakh warriors, the old man, and Washington and I attracted little attention as we continued to discuss things in front of the American consulate.

"I think perhaps the warriors thought of you as Russian," our translator said, "because of your military uniforms and the blonde doctor who set up shop here."

I explained that the "blonde doctor," Eve, was not a doctor but a nurse. And that she'd come to help the locals. Deciding to try to score any political points I could with our Kazakh warrior friends, I added that if they had any minor medical needs, our "blonde doctor" would be glad to address them.

The message was passed to them. They conferred among themselves. There appeared to be a lot of head nodding as they talked. Then they spoke to the elderly Kazakh, glanced at Washington and me, then galloped off.

"They said they will return," the translator said to me, "later today."

By the time we'd finished our meeting, Eve and the two majors had shown up, all looking concerned and confused, and all asking questions at the same time. I got them quieted down, then explained what had happened.

Eve, ever the nurse, wasn't buying my proclamation that I was fine, hustled me back to my hotel room, and began running through the examination protocols for a concussion. I had to admit I still felt woozy.

Finished, she told me to lie down on my bed. I did, and she placed a cool, damp washrag on my head and said, "I don't think you have a concussion, but I want you to rest and try to get some sleep the rest of the morning. I'm going to go get you some APCs. I'll be right back."

I grabbed her hand before she could leave. "Hey, we could fool around, you know. Everybody's off to breakfast now."

She snatched her hand away. "My God, you're incorrigible."

"I think that was the name of a British battleship," I mumbled. By the time Eve returned, I was half asleep. The APCs finished me off, and I sawed logs through noon.

A soft rapping on my door awakened me. "Sir, sir, it's James Shih from the consulate."

"What time is it?"

"Three in the afternoon. I have another cable for you. It arrived early this morning."

"Okay, hold on while I pry my eyes open." I had a pretty good idea who the cable might be from and a pretty good idea how I was going to reply to it . . . thanks to the Kazakh warriors.

I wobbled to the door with Gene Krupa still whacking out a drum solo in my head. I hoped Eve had left me some extra APCs. I opened the door and invited Shih in. He handed me the cable. The message, as I suspected, had been dispatched by good ol' Lenny.

TO: LTC RODGER SHEPHERD, USAAF/10WS
FROM: BG LEONARD STONE, JCS/20AF
SUBJ: CPT GENEVIEVE JOHANNSEN
MESSAGE: MANIFEST FOR USAAF AIRCRAFT TAIL NUMBER 8325
INDICATES CPT GENEVIEVE JOHANNSEN A PASSENGER; RETURN

CPT JOHANNSEN TO HSINCHING BY END OF DAY TODAY TO AVOID COURT-MARTIAL

Tail number 8325 was *Betsy*, the C-47 we'd flown into Urumchi on. "Got something to write with?" I asked Shih.

"Yes, sir."

"Please respond to General Stone's cable."

Shih nodded.

"Say this: 'Lieutenant Colonel Rodger Shepherd taken prisoner by Kazakh warrior group this morning. Released, but currently under medical care.'"

Shih looked up. "That's all?"

"Send it out under the name of a senior staff member in the consulate." No point in providing Stone with additional details or elaboration. Let him stew awhile longer. I loved pulling the bastard's chain. Of course, I might be just digging a deeper grave for me and Eve, but I didn't think so.

Shih departed with the message. I tidied myself up, found a couple more APCs, and limped off to see how Eve and her ad hoc clinic were doing.

I found the line of patients waiting to see Eve had shortened considerably compared to yesterday. She appeared to be in the process of wrapping up with a tiny, wizened Chinese lady as I approached.

"She okay?" I said softly when I reached her.

"More or less. Not much I can do for her. She's just old. Lots of aches and pains."

"How old?"

Eve shrugged. "She looks like she's a hundred. But in this environment, lacking the conveniences and care we're used to, she's probably more like seventy-five or eighty."

"So a handful of APCs?"

"That's about it."

"Seen anything of our Kazakh friends?"

"No." She motioned for the next person in line to step forward.

"Good. That'll give me a chance to round up a translator before they show up. I'm going to head over to the consulate and see if I can retrieve the guy who helped out this morning."

By the time I returned to Eve's clinic with the old Kazakh who had translated for us earlier in the day in tow, the wild-looking nomadic horsemen had indeed returned. But this time they had an extra rider, a young male who looked to be in his late teens. A heavy bandage encased his right forearm.

While Eve worked with the last few patients of the day, I explained, through the translator, I'd like to take a look at the boy's arm. He dismounted, and I unwrapped the bandage carefully. As I did, the elderly man explained to me the boy had fallen off his horse a few days ago and hit a rock with his arm. The Kazakh warriors had tried to repair the damage— a large open gash—but apparently had made it worse. I got the bandage off and found the kid's forearm had swollen to the size of a cantaloupe.

I touched it gently. The boy yelped. The bulge was red and warm. I put my hand on the kid's forehead. He seemed to be burning up with fever. Not good. I wasn't sure if this would be something Eve could handle. And I wasn't at all certain how Broadsword and his henchmen would react if we couldn't help their kinsman. Or, God forbid, made him worse.

The sun had begun to sink toward the western horizon, and the town's buildings surrounding our little field hospital cast us into deep shadow. I hoped Eve would be able to work quickly before dusk set in. I also hoped she'd be able to help the kid.

I explained to Eve before I brought the boy to her what I'd seen.

"Sounds like a bad infection," she responded. "Bring him over."

I did, and Eve carefully examined his swollen arm. "Not good. I'll do what I can."

The Kazakh warriors hovered nearby, keeping a close watch on us. They looked neither threatening nor accepting, but I sure didn't want the boy to start yelping and screaming when Eve went to work on him. I figured Broadsword probably had more than a few notches in that huge weapon he carried.

The only anesthetic Eve had were some morphine syrettes, so she jabbed a couple of those into the young man's arm. The kid remained stoic as the needles went in. While she waited for the morphine to take effect, she bathed his arm in warm water (boiled) and soap.

Once the boy seemed off in woozyville, Eve fished a small surgical knife out of her kit. She sterilized the blade with iodine, then asked me to hold the lad.

"You mean restrain him?"

She nodded.

"This is gonna hurt?"

"Yeah, even with the morphine."

I quickly asked the translator to explain to the horsemen that the kid was likely to holler, but that no permanent damage would be done to him.

Eve ran her hand over the swelling, likely trying to determine the best place to make her incision. Then she cut. The kid screamed. I held him tightly. Blood poured from his arm. The Kazakhs muttered. I said a little prayer. Eve dug deeper with her knife.

More blood. More moaning. Then a flow of yellow pus. The Kazakhs muttered again. The boy relaxed.

"That's good," Eve said. "I want to make sure I get as much crap as I can out of that wound." She continued squeezing. More pus.

"Is he going to be okay?" I asked.

"I did the best I could." She sprinkled some crystalline sulfanilamide over the incision she'd made, then placed a couple of gauze bandages over it. I helped her secure the bandages with surgical adhesive.

"Thank you, nurse," she said to me.

"Ya done good, doc," I told her.

The boy appeared relaxed, and the warriors seemed pleased. At least I spotted a twinkle in Broadsword's eyes. I think. Maybe we'd made a pal for life.

But things can never go well forever, right?

Just as I ushered the young man back to the horsemen and gave them a few rudimentary care instructions, James Shih, from the consulate, appeared again.

"Another cable, James?" I forced a smile.

"No. Some visitors."

I cocked my head at him.

"Two soldiers. They say they're military policemen from the air base at Hsinching. They're looking for the captain." He nodded at Eve.

23

Urumchi, Sinkiang Province, China
September 14, 1944

"What?" Eve exclaimed. "Military police?" Her eyes widened. She gripped my arm with remarkable intensity. I could sense fear in her grasp.

"Yeah," I said. "And you damn well know who sent them. The bastard sees this as his chance to separate us. To get you alone."

"Rod—"

"It ain't gonna happen. Give me a minute. I want to see our Kazakh friends off." I walked back to the translator and spoke briefly to him. He talked to the warriors, we waved our goodbyes, and the horsemen took off at a gallop with their hopefully healed compadre. I returned to Eve.

"Okay, let's go find our MP arrivals."

We found them at the consulate. A lanky corporal and a fireplug sergeant. They saluted us and introduced themselves. Bill Matthews, staff sergeant, and Art Barzee, corporal.

"We are here under orders to take a Captain Genevieve Johannsen into custody and return her to Hsinching Army Air Forces Base," Matthews growled, trying to sound authoritative.

"Whose orders?" I snapped back. I already knew, of course, but wanted confirmation.

"Brigadier General Leonard Stone's."

"What's the charge?"

"AWOL," Matthews barked.

"Does she look AWOL, Sergeant?"

"Not my decision, sir. I'm just here to escort her back to Hsinching. Following orders, you understand."

I did, and didn't want to give the MPs a hard time. As the sergeant had pointed out, they were merely doing their job. But I wasn't about to just hand Eve over to them.

"What's the plan?" I asked.

"We'll hold her until tomorrow morning, then fly her back to Hsinching."

"Fly her how?"

"On the general's C-46. We're to have it back to him by tomorrow evening."

*What a damn waste of army resource*s, I thought. *The general dispatches his personal aircraft to retrieve his concubine. Correction: would-be concubine.*

"And where do you plan on holding Captain Johannsen until tomorrow morning?"

"Here at the consulate."

"There are no sleeping or messing facilities here, Sergeant."

"We've got sleeping bags and C rats, Colonel."

"We aren't in a combat zone, gentlemen. There's no sense in making the lady uncomfortable. I propose that you be our guests in the local hotel tonight, allow Captain Johannsen to remain in her room, and I will personally escort her to the general's plane tomorrow morning. You have my word as an officer of the United States Army Air Forces."

I sensed Eve glaring at me. I hoped she didn't believe I was really going to turn her over to these guys.

Sergeant Matthews seemed uncertain, too. "I don't know, sir . . ." He shuffled his feet and looked around, as if searching for some sort of hidden threat. "It seems highly irregular."

So is using a general's C-46 to snatch an army nurse. "Again, you have my word I'll get her to the plane early tomorrow. And, if it will make you more comfortable, you and Corporal Barzee may take turns standing guard outside the captain's room tonight."

"Ma'am," Matthews said, "may I have your word, too, no funny stuff?" He cast a hard glare at her. I caught the sense he'd been a policeman in civilian life before the war.

"Sure," she snapped, obviously miffed I hadn't made more of an effort to keep her out of the clutches of the guys dispatched to turn her over to General Stone.

As we walked to the hotel, she sidled up next to me, the MPs following a few yards behind. "Tell me you've got something up your sleeve," she hissed. "That you aren't just going to toss me to the Big Bad Wolf."

"You don't really think I'm going to back down from that SOB, do you?" I whispered.

We walked on for several steps before she said, "No," in such a low voice I could barely hear her. "But what's up?"

"Shhh. Try to act surprised when it happens."

"When what happens?"

"Please, ma'am, sir," Matthews rasped. "I'd appreciate it if you didn't whisper. It makes me uncomfortable."

"Sorry, Sergeant," I said, "it won't happen again." I needed to build trust with the guy. To his credit, he made sure he kept Eve and me separated for the remainder of the evening.

I arose early the next morning, well before dawn, and hobbled down the hallway to Eve's room. The MP corporal sat outside her door, his chair tipped back against the wall, his chin resting on his chest. I thought he might be lost in a dream of scantily clad women, American beer, or perhaps the St. Louis Browns making it to the World Series. Maybe all three.

I kicked his feet. His chair thudded down. His chin came up. He looked around wildly, trying to figure out where the hell he was.

"She still in there, Corporal Barzee?" I snapped.

"I . . . I . . . I don't know—"

"Good thing you weren't guarding a Jap POW." I tried to speak in an officer's firm voice.

"I'm sorry, sir, I—"

I decided to extend the kid's misery, teach him a lesson. I knocked softly on the door. No response.

"Well, she probably climbed out the window," I said.

"Should we break it down, Colonel?"

"Break what down?"

"The door?" The poor guy was about to pee in his pants.

"Why don't we try knocking again?"

"Yeah, yeah. Good idea."

I rapped on the door more firmly this time.

This time Eve's sleepy voice came back. "Hold on, hold on. Good grief. What time is it?"

"I guess she didn't slither out the window, Corporal. You can relax." Then I called to Eve. "It's time to get up and grab breakfast. You've got a long journey ahead of you. Meet you in the dining room in half an hour."

I patted Corporal Barzee on his shoulder. "Don't worry. This'll stay between you and me. Sarge doesn't have to know about it."

"Thank you, sir." He cleared his throat. "If you don't mind, I'll wait out here and escort the captain to the dining room when she comes out."

After breakfast, we stepped outside into the half-light of a cold sunrise. The Packard, belching opaque clouds of black exhaust into the still air, waited for us. Bob the Banker sat behind the wheel. I clambered into the front passenger seat, Eve squeezed into the rear between the two MPs.

We took off toward the airfield, the once stately automobile bouncing like a Western buckboard.

"You ever think about getting new shocks for this thing?" I asked Bob, trying to get my sentence out without severing my tongue.

"Yes, but you can't get them here. Maybe after the war."

We continued lurching toward the airport. The barren steppe, tinted in an early season frost, glinted as if encrusted by a thin film of tiny diamonds as the sun crept upward into a deep blue sky.

When we reached the airstrip, I thanked Bob and told him I'd be back shortly if he didn't mind waiting. Eve and the MPs slid from the back seat, and we began walking toward the tower. The C-46 sat on the ramp with the pilots doing their walk-around.

The two MPs had managed to keep Eve and me apart since our whispered exchange on the way to the hotel yesterday, so she had no idea of what was about to happen. To be honest, I didn't either. Not for sure. I'd come up with a seat-of-the-pants plan, and truly didn't know if it would work or not. I just hoped nobody would get hurt.

But I understood why Eve now glared at me with the fierceness she used to before we, I guess you would say, became a couple. Back when I had labeled her "Nurse Nasty." I'd forgotten how those glacial-blue eyes of hers could burn a hole in you with the intensity of an arc welder. I felt the heat on the back of my neck as I walked ahead of her and the MPs.

We reached a tiny anteroom at the base of the control tower. Corporal Barzee strode toward the aircraft, probably to ask the pilots if they were ready to board passengers. Even in the frosty cold, I began to sweat. Time had just about expired. I sensed my half-assed scheme beginning to come apart at the seams, and that Eve was about to be returned to Hsinching and sentenced to sexual servitude by a guy who had no business being a flag officer in the United States Army.

Corporal Barzee motioned from where the aircraft sat for Sergeant Matthews to bring Eve on out. *Shit.*

The first rifle shot pinged off a corner of the tower. The second one zinged off the concrete ramp. Sergeant Matthews shoved Eve to the ground, whipped out his sidearm.

"I thought you said we weren't in a combat zone," he yelled at me.

Near the C-46, the two pilots and the corporal had taken cover behind the landing gear. I ducked behind a wooden bench.

"What the hell's happening?" Matthews growled.

I shrugged. "Dunno." I did, of course, but needed to do some play acting now.

Eve cast a questioning glance at me. The only way I could respond was with a quick nod.

"Where'd those damn shots come from?" the sergeant hissed.

"There," I said, and pointed down the runway. Broadsword and two of his compatriots on horseback trotted toward us.

Matthews went into a combat crouch with his .45 extended in front of him in a two-handed grip. "We got these bastards."

"Hold your fire, Sergeant."

"What? They fired on us, sir." His breathing came in heavy, short bursts.

"If they'd wanted to hit us, we'd be dead. They just wanted our attention. Besides, we're outnumbered."

"There're only three of 'em, sir. We can take 'em out easy."

"Look behind us."

"Oh, Jesus."

A line of mounted warriors, ten, maybe a dozen, cantered up the runway from the opposite direction. They carried a variety of weapons, rifles, swords, pistols. One guy even bore an honest-to-God spear that looked to be about eight feet long.

"Whatta they want?" Matthews croaked.

"I dunno, but we're about to find out. Holster your sidearm."

Eve continued to focus on the three warriors we'd spotted first. "They look like the Kazakhs we helped yesterday."

"Yeah, could be," I said. I knew damn well who they were. They'd shown up a bit later than I would have liked.

Broadsword and his buddies reined up in front of us; the other line of warriors halted about twenty yards away and formed a semicircle around us. It turned into quite a show with the horses snorting great clouds of steam and stamping and pawing the earth. The warriors, looking fierce and wild, also exhaled jets of condensation from their mouths as their chests heaved in exertion, or maybe excitement. It could have been a scene from medieval times on the sprawling steppe of central Asia with nomadic warriors facing down an enemy.

I raised my hand in peaceful greeting to Broadsword. He didn't smile. Great acting on his part. At least I hoped he was acting.

He stood in his stirrups and pointed at Eve, spoke in Kazakh, then motioned her forward.

"What?" I snapped, and stepped forward.

Broadsword extended his arm toward me, palm up. *Stay back.*

I stopped.

He babbled some more, pointing at his forearm. He turned and pointed at the distant horizon, the direction from where he had come. Then he gestured at his forearm again and mimicked being in pain. He placed his hand on his forehead and yanked it away as if he'd been singed by a hot skillet. "Boy," he said in English.

"Ah." I turned to Eve. "I think he wants you to come with them. The boy with the arm wound you treated yesterday, it sounds like he's taken a turn for the worse. I think he's in a great deal of pain, has a fever."

"Lady ain't goin' no place," Matthews growled.

"You really wanna take these guys on, Sarge? They aren't kidnapping her. They asked for help. They'll bring her back."

"How do you know?"

"We forged a bond yesterday. They're fierce and proud. We can trust them." *I think.*

Matthews fell silent, seemingly mulling things over.

Eve appeared apprehensive. I didn't blame her. Maybe I was about to pluck her from the fire and drop her into a frying pan.

"You sure that's what he wants?" Eve asked.

"Pretty sure."

She rolled her eyes. "I'll need my medical kit."

"How long would she be gone?" Matthews asked, perhaps ready to accede to the Kazakhs' demand.

"Beats me. I can ask, not that I'll understand anything."

Matthews nodded.

I turned to Broadsword and enunciated the question clearly and slowly. In English, of course. He stared blankly in return. I repeated the query. This time he responded with a string of Kazakh words. I nodded as he spoke. Didn't understand a damn thing.

I spoke to Matthews. "Head man says two, maybe three days. Their village is far from here."

"No. Absolutely not. General Stone said we hadda be back by the end of today."

"I don't think you have a choice, Sarge. Look, I'll get Captain Johannsen back to Hsinching. I promise. But it won't be for a few days. You're going to have to put your faith in me."

"I can't go back to General Stone without the nurse." I detected a note of panic in the MP's voice.

"The best I can do, Sarge, is give you my word of honor. I'll even write General Stone a note explaining things, how Kazakh warriors showed up and demanded Captain Johannsen come with them to treat a badly injured boy. I'll explain that none of this was your or the corporal's fault. Not when faced with over a dozen armed men."

"I dunno, sir. The general seemed really bent on getting the captain back to Hsinching."

"I'll bet he did. But *I* will get her back. And *you'll* get his plane back on time. He'll understand." *No, he won't. He'll fume and fuss and cuss. But at least he's not going to be able to grab Eve and make a run for it.* And I knew damn well that's what he wanted to do. He could have cared less about her being AWOL.

Matthews stood with his arms folded across his chest. "I just don't know, Colonel. I can't go back to the general empty-handed."

"What are your options, Sergeant? You gonna chase down the Kazakhs and get the captain back? You don't even have a horse. And you wouldn't know where to go anyhow."

"I don't even know how to ride a horse," he mumbled.

"I'll get that message to the general written, then I suggest you and the corporal hop on that C-46 and hightail it back to Hsinching."

Broadsword hollered something in Kazakh. I understood his growing impatience.

"We're outgunned, Sarge. Gotta let her go." I motioned for Broadsword to leave. Eve, with her medical kit, had struggled up onto Broadsword's horse and sat behind him with her arms wrapped around his waist. Once again she shot me a gaze that could have melted steel.

The Kazakhs wheeled their horses around and took off at a gallop down the runway, heading toward the scrublands and the vastness beyond. Wavering runnels of dissipating steam—the only lingering evidence of their recent presence—hung in the icy air as they disappeared into an arroyo beyond the airfield. The second band of warriors thundered off, following the lead bunch.

I'd engineered the whole affair, of course, but now my heart thudded like a jackhammer as I wondered if the Kazakhs could really be trusted. It seemed like a good idea at the time, last evening, when I'd spoken my good-byes to them with the help of the translator and then added my knee-jerk scheme.

I hadn't had time to think it through thoroughly, but the driving force was keeping Eve out of the grasp of General Stone-ass, and I'd had to come up with an idea really quickly. I hoped my words had been translated correctly, and that the Kazakhs understood they were to return Eve—that she wasn't a gift to them—to Urumchi immediately after they saw the plane lift off.

At any rate, I got a note written for Sergeant Matthews to take with him, then bid him and Corporal Barzee adieu—Matthews still fussing and grumbling—and waited while they took off, bound for a rendezvous with who I knew was going to be one highly pissed off general.

My greatest skill, apparently, was pissing people off. First the general, then Eve. Again. I limped back to the Packard. I told Bob what I'd done. He beat his head against the steering wheel in mock dismay. "And I thought the Japs were crazy," he said.

"I asked the Kazakhs to return Eve as soon as the plane left. At least I hope that's what the translator told them."

"Then they should be coming soon."

"What's been your experience with Kazakhs?"

"Most are honorable and trustworthy."

"Most?"

"There's always a black sheep in the family."

Well, crap. That statement boosted my spirits, especially since the Three Musketeers hadn't shown up after we'd waited for them for another half hour. My luck. I guess I'd managed to connect with the black sheep of the family.

"Do you have any idea where these guys hang out?" I asked Bob.

"There are about a dozen villages toward the west, along the China-Soviet border."

I sagged down in my seat, cold, disenchanted, worried, and a little bit angry. Great, now I'd even managed to piss off myself. I wondered if Captain Washington knew how to ride a horse. Or, maybe an ox. A horse might not be big enough to carry him. I'd done a little riding in Idaho, where I'd grown up, but that was years ago. But I guessed if we were going retrieve Eve, it was going to have to be on horseback. Perhaps we could work in tandem with Tex—get him and *Betsy* in the air to fly reconnaissance for us.

A sharp rap on the Packard's window snapped me out of my funk. Eve! I flung open the door.

"You sure know how to win a gal's heart," she said, her words slicing into my soul. "Selling her off to Kazakh warriors."

"I didn't sell you off." I pulled her to me in a bear hug. Very unmilitary.

"I know, I know," she whispered. "Whatever you set up, however you set it up, it worked."

"Yeah, it did. The MPs are on their way back to Hsinching without you. I was getting a bit worried when you didn't show up immediately after take-off, though."

We broke our embrace.

"The guy you call Broadsword wanted me to take a look at a couple of his fellow cowpokes, you know, minor cuts and scrapes. And the kid we fixed up yesterday was there. I changed the dressing on his arm."

"Florence Nightingale."

"Calamity Jane, maybe. I hope you don't mind a bowlegged gal friend. I'm chafed as all get-out."

"Not used to riding a horse?"

"I'm an Army Air Forces flight nurse, remember? I'm supposed to be airborne, not saddle sore."

I opened the rear door of the car, ushered her in, then scuttled in beside her. "Let's get you back into town, cleaned up, and"—I looked closely at her —"rehydrated, I think."

She grasped my hand and grew serious. "We still have to deal with General Stone, don't we?"

I looked away from her. "Yeah," I said softly. "*I* have to deal with him." I paused, giving free rein to my thoughts, then added, "And for one of us, Stone or me, it's going to end badly."

Eve gripped my hand with the ferocity of a mama bear.

24

Urumchi, Sinkiang Province, China
September 17, 1944

We spent the next couple of days wrapping up details with the Urumchi locals regarding establishing an army weather station in their town. We figured we could furnish around-the-clock surface observations, make at least two upper-air runs (with radiosondes) each day, and provide forecasting services eighteen hours per day.

I planned on leaving the two NCOs and Major Mackiernan in Urumchi to prepare facilities at the airport where weather operations could be set up. Meanwhile, I'd return to Hsinching with Eve, Captain Washington, who had to get back to work on the Ledo Road, and Major Spilhaus, who would round up the equipment—radios, theodolites, barometers, sling psychrometers, anemometers, and so on—that would be needed in Urumchi.

Over the two-day period, I received several more blistering cables from General Stone. I ignored them. I figured I couldn't get into any more trouble with him than I already was.

On the morning of the seventeenth, we were ready to wing our way back to Hsinching, and I was prepared to meet my fate. We lifted off into a gray deck of altostratus tinted with colorful streaks of salmon and peach.

Once we reached our cruising altitude, I let Tex take over the controls, and I shuffled back to the cabin, where I plopped into a seat next to Eve.

Captain Washington appeared to be in a deep slumber, sprawled out on top of a sleeping bag in the rear of the cabin. Spilly sat in a seat near the cargo door, checking off items in a manual of some sort. The businesslike roar of *Betsy's* Pratt & Whitneys resonated through the aircraft, both comforting and annoying, annoying at least when it came to trying to carry on a conversation. I put my mouth close to Eve's ear.

"I'm sorry you've had to go through all this," I said.

"This?"

"With General Stone."

She closed her eyes but didn't respond. When she opened them, she said, "I just don't want you to get hurt, Rod. I know you're swimming upstream, a lieutenant colonel taking on a general. That goes against all military tradition."

"General Stone goes against military tradition. I've dealt with more than a few flag officers during my career, Eve. To a man they've been smart, fair, and honorable. They can be harsh, demanding, and intimidating at times, to be sure. But they've always been high principled. Stone is an anomaly. I don't know how he got to where he is. Blinding others with that civilian Hollywood charisma of his? Stroking egos? Being a loudmouthed braggart? I don't know. But we both know he's not an officer and a gentleman. Not in the United States Army I know."

"But he's still a general officer. That's got to count for something. Don't they belong to some kind of protective club or something, or have the ability to hide behind a virtual shield of stars?"

I squirmed in my seat. "Yeah, probably. But I'm not letting him take you back. If I come out of this crucified and bloodied, believe me, he's coming out the same way."

"Rod—"

"Shhh. Nothing more from you. He had his way with you once. It's not going to happen again."

In truth, I knew I'd be putting my career—both military and civilian— on the line by jousting with a general. I thought I held the moral high ground, but sometimes that doesn't make any difference. Sometimes the winner is the most bellicose bastard. But there are some things, some people, worth taking a stand for. If I ended up getting my ass whipped, you know what? I'd feel downright terrific.

Tex motioned me back to the cockpit. I gave Eve a pat on the shoulder and returned to my copilot's position.

"Pretty thick clouds up ahead," Tex said after I got my interphone head-gear on. "We're gonna have to climb. Some of the peaks in the mountains before we reach Chengtu poke up above twenty thousand feet. I'm gonna take us up to our service ceiling to avoid bumping into something. So make sure everyone in the cabin is on oxygen. Then get back here and help me drive. Might get a little rough."

I got Eve and Spilly hooked up to their masks, then woke up Washington and helped get him ready, too.

"Think I liked it better on the Ledo in a six-by-six," he mumbled, although the words came out rumbling like a volcano on the verge of erupting.

We drove into the murk, and the visibility dropped to zippo. *Betsy* started to wiggle and jiggle like a toddler who had to pee. But Tex and I held her on a steady course at twenty-four thousand feet, and the trek over the Bayan Kara mountains proved uneventful.

On our approach into Hsinching, we broke out of the clouds at around five thousand feet and settled into the landing pattern between two B-29s. I assumed they probably carried bombs and fuel in preparation for the next raid on Japan or Manchuria or wherever.

Hsinching, Sichuan, China
US Army Air Forces Base

Tex dropped *Betsy* onto the runway with only a slight bounce, and we taxied toward base ops. "Uh-oh," he said, nodding in the direction of the operations building as we rolled along the taxiway. "What's that all about?"

Two MP jeeps, red lights flashing, and a staff car sat near the entrance to the building.

"It's my welcoming committee," I said. "Well, mine and Captain Johannsen's."

Tex looked askance at me. "Something you want to tell me?"

I shook my head. "Nope. You and Spilly and Captain Washington have nothing to do with this. You're all free to go."

"You sure you wouldn't like us to stick around, Colonel?"

"Thanks for asking, Tex, but it's really more of a personal deal. Between me and a general officer."

"Okay, good luck, sir."

We pulled up to base ops, stopped, and shut down the engines. I told Spilly and Captain Washington to go ahead and disembark, that the MPs were not there for them. Tex and I ran through the post-flight shutdown checklist. Then Tex deplaned, and Eve and I followed.

Two MPs, not the same ones we'd dealt with in Urumchi, approached us. Brigadier General Leonard Stone stood nearby watching the proceedings. I noticed Captain Washington hovering a few yards away from Stone, keeping an eye on him. I didn't know if Washington was just curious, or feeling as if his intimidation duties extended to Hsinching.

One of the MPs stepped up to Eve. "Captain Genevieve Johannsen?" he asked.

She nodded

The other MP, a ruddy-faced, slightly chubby sergeant, stepped in front of me. "Lieutenant Colonel Rodger Shepherd?"

"I am."

"General Stone has asked that we accompany you and Captain Johannsen to his headquarters. Would you please come with us?"

Eve stared at me and blinked. In that brief moment, I caught a glint of deep concern. And the reality hit me like a punch in the gut, that I might fail in my quest to keep her out of harm's way, that I might not be able to keep her from the talons of a moral degenerate.

"Let's go, Eve," I choked out. "We'll get this cleared up in no time and be on our way." *Or I'll be on my way to being court-martialed, and you'll be on your way to being a military courtesan.*

The sergeant, more powerful than his chubbiness would have suggested, gripped my arm in a viselike clench. It bordered on painful.

Captain Washington stepped in front of the MPs. The one escorting Eve, a burly corporal—probably an offensive lineman in high school football—actually took a step backward.

"Hey, boy," General Stone snapped as he moved out of the shadows toward Washington. "This is none of your business. On your way." He gestured with his thumb like a hitchhiker.

Washington glared at him, and I thought I caught a flash of hatred, something almost atavistic.

"Captain," I said in a low voice, "I'll be fine. You've done your duty, and I appreciate it."

He saluted me and about-faced.

"He's not a boy," I barked at Stone. "He's an officer in the United States Army."

"The darkies know their place," he said. "Now, let's go have a little chat in my office while I consider what charges to draft against you and Captain Johannsen."

The sergeant sat in the back of the Plymouth staff car with Eve and me, the other MP drove, while General Stone perched in the front passenger seat. We rolled off, headed toward the general's headquarters.

It turned out to be located in the same two-building complex that housed General LeMay's operations. The buildings didn't seem to be much, temporary one-story wood-and-stucco structures that probably wouldn't last long after the war. Their interior appearances certainly weren't fancy, either, at least in the one that housed Stone. It looked more like a GI barracks than something in which you'd expect a flag officer to be working.

The MPs ushered us down a long, narrow hallway that stank of stale cigarette smoke and burnt coffee. The offices lining either side of the hallway appeared largely unoccupied. I suppose since early evening had settled over the base, most of the guys had probably headed out to dinner or somewhere to grab a few drinks.

After we reached Stone's office, he spoke to the MPs. "That's all, guys, beat it. I'll handle it from here. If I need you, I'll call." He turned to Eve and me. "Sit," he said as if we were hunting hounds. He went behind his desk, opened a drawer, and pulled out a shoulder holster with a .45 jammed into it. Not good. The MPs were gone, and a general who had already run off the rez now possessed the only gun in the room.

"Just a precaution," he said as he strapped the rig around his shoulder. "You guys have already busted army regs, big time."

Pot calling the kettle black, I thought.

It felt good to sit. My leg ached like hell, and my head had begun to follow suit. A quick glance around Stone's workplace suggested he hadn't spent much time here. The walls remained mostly bare. No framed certificates, plaques, or photographs. Not like I'd seen when I'd first visited him in Hastings Mill, India. The only item on the wall: a map of the CBI Theater.

"You know," Stone growled, "for a gimp-legged balloon blower, you got a lotta balls."

He stood over me, glowering down as though he expected a response. But he hadn't asked a question, so I kept my mouth shut.

He went on. "You grab a nurse like she was your personal property and cart her off to some godforsaken Chinese dump."

Still no question. I motioned with my hand for Eve not to speak.

"Without orders," he bellowed, spittle flying from his mouth. I brushed a droplet from my cheek.

"You and Captain Johannsen ignore the orders she had, orders from JCS, I'll note—"

"No," I interjected forcefully, "orders signed by you, not the JCS."

"Under JCS auspices."

"No, you chickenshit. You. I'll bet no one at the JCS even knew about those orders before they were given to the captain."

Stone's face turned the color of a Red Delicious apple. "Chickenshit?" he yelled. "You call me chickenshit? You'll give me the respect I'm due as a general officer, Colonel."

"Respect is something that's earned, not given. Sir."

"Well, I'll tell you something I'll give you . . . *after* we're done with your court-martial. That's a one-way ticket to Leavenworth."

Leavenworth. The United States Disciplinary Barracks—a military maximum-security prison—in Leavenworth, Kansas.

"On what charges?" I snapped.

He laughed, a sneering response. "You mean besides disrespecting a senior officer? Besides ignoring orders given to Captain Johannsen? Besides aiding and abetting her AWOL?"

"She wasn't AWOL. She had orders."

Stone stared. Then laughed again. "You lying sonofabitch. She had orders to Hickam in Honolulu, not Urumchi in Bumfuck Province, China."

"No, she had orders to Urumchi."

"Not before she had orders to Hickam."

"The orders for Urumchi superseded the ones you issued."

"You mean that the JCS issued."

"No. The ones signed by a Brigadier General Leonard Stone."

"And I suppose you think orders signed by a light colonel leading some diddly-shit little journey into the wilds of China would trump that?"

"No. But orders signed by a major general would."

Stone didn't respond immediately, probably trying to decide if I was bluffing or not. I got the same sort of look from Eve. She hadn't known about what I'd done.

"You—you—" Stone stammered. I thought I'd just managed to ambush the bastard. But he recovered and barked, "Let's see 'em."

I reached into my flight jacket and withdrew a set of orders that Major General LeMay had signed the night before our mission to Urumchi had departed, orders stating that, based on military exigencies, Captain Johannsen was to accompany my team. I handed them to Stone.

He studied them. "You trying to tell me you're buddy-buddy with General LeMay? Some little weather-guesser dick like you?"

"I've known Curt for a while." I hoped LeMay would never hear about me referring to him as Curt.

"Bullshit. These, I'll wager, are forgeries." He waved the orders in my face.

"Let's call LeMay's office and see." I reached for a phone sitting on Stone's desk.

He swatted it away from me. "I'll check on their authenticity later. Let's all take a deep breath for now."

All? As far as I could tell, the only one whose pulse was up was his.

"Look," he said, "maybe we can forget about this Urumchi SNAFU." He tossed the orders onto his desk. "For now, let's say I back off on charging you, or her, with anything."

Had I just won the first round with this asshole?

"Tell you what," he said, "why don't we just get Captain Johannsen on her way to Hickam, and then we can forget about the rest of this shit?"

"Let's not," I retorted.

"I won't go," Eve snapped.

We both got Stone's hard-ass stare. "What? What did you say? You're refusing to obey direct orders from the JCS?"

"There you go again," I growled. "I know why you're so damned anxious to get Captain Johannsen to Hawaii, you bastard." I stood. I sensed myself on the edge of losing control. Maybe I *was* destined for Leavenworth. "You want her as your personal concubine," I shouted.

"Careful there, gimp. You're digging your own grave."

"I'm digging yours, General. Yeah, the captain told me what happened in Hawaii after Pearl Harbor. How you forced yourself on her." I stepped closer to Stone. We stood face-to-face. "How you raped her," I hissed.

"Her word against mine," he snapped. "Anything that happened between us—if anything did—was consensual. If she says otherwise, she's a goddamned liar."

"You're the goddamned liar," Eve screamed, out of her chair now, too. "There was never anything consensual. Why do you think I'm trying to get away from you, you bastard?"

"Yeah, and whose word do think would prevail if it ever came to an inquiry?" Stone said, his tone sneering. "A female captain's against a general officer's? You're way outta your league here, you two." He raised his voice to a shout. "You're both teetering on the verge of a court-martial!"

"You think you can intimidate *me*, General?" I yelled back. "I've flown through the worst weather in the world in the deadliest mountains of the world. I've crash-landed twice. I've come face-to-face with headhunters. I've fought the Japs in the jungle and in the air. So your little tin stars don't come close to fazing me."

"Test me," he fired back. "We'll see." The Red Delicious color had returned to his face. I sensed within him there brewed a pyroclastic flow on the verge of eruption. He leaned close to me, a smug smile smeared across his face, and whispered, "And you can't tell me you never got *your* stinger wet in that mouthy nurse's pussy."

My fist moved faster than the restraint synapses in my brain. I nailed the sonofabitch square in the nose. A satisfying crunch. A spurt of blood. He went down like a sack of potatoes falling from a top shelf.

He lay on the floor glaring up at me. My fist hurt. Broken bones? It felt great. "In answer to your question, General—Lenny—I never did. I guess I'm just not the man you are." *Thank God.*

"Well, Colonel, you just ended your fucking career," he slurred, "both military and civilian. An unprovoked assault on a general officer. You stupid bastard." He held his hand to his nose to stanch the bleeding.

I knelt next to him. "You know who else knows about what you did to Captain Johannsen? General Curtis LeMay. I laid it all out to him. I explained why she wanted to accompany me to Urumchi. He didn't want to hear it, naturally. You know, a fellow flag officer and all. Booted me out of his office. Curiously enough, though, without dressing me down. Yeah, the commander of the Twentieth Air Force heard it all. Still want an inquiry?"

He continued to lie on the floor, staring poison darts at me.

I stood and turned back toward Eve. "Gun!" she screamed.

I whirled. Stone had scrambled up, blood streaming from his nose, his face twisted in rage, the .45 in his hand.

"Attack a general officer, will you, you prick? You're dead!" He aimed the pistol at me.

The door burst open. Wendell Washington charged through it. He nailed Stone with an open field tackle from behind just as the general pulled the trigger. The shot went wild, into the ceiling. The .45 clattered to the floor. Stone and Washington hit the floor with coordinated "ooofs."

Washington rolled off him and leapt up. I kicked the handgun away. Stone lay on his side on the floor, breathing heavily, his face and blouse covered in blood from his nose.

"Captain," I blurted, "what are—"

"Just doing my darkie duties, boss. I heard all that was said. I saw the general attempt to murder you." He turned to the general. "You can deny everything, sir. But I'll stand with Colonel Shepherd."

My ears rang from the explosion of the shot in the room, but I made out every word Washington said.

"How on earth—" I started to ask another question, but Washington answered before I could complete it.

"I was just following up on my intimidator tasks, Colonel. I didn't much care for the general's treatment of me, so I got worried about you. I tracked the staff car over here and slipped into the building after the MPs left. Then I put my ear to the door."

I shook my head in dumbfounded amazement.

"Help me get the general up," I said to Washington.

"Leave me alone," Stone burbled. "Don't touch me."

"Sorry about your accident, General," Washington said. He put special emphasis on the word *accident*. "I'll find some paper towels. We gotta get that blood flow stopped."

"Wait," Eve said. "Don't forget, there's a nurse here." She moved to Stone and squatted beside him. "Your nose is a mess, General. Hurt?"

He nodded his head and mumbled something.

"Well, I can make you forget that. I know exactly what you need." She patted his arm, smiled, and stood. Her kick to his testicles lifted him off the floor. He howled in pain like a wounded wolf. Like an animal whose paw had been snared in the jaws of a steel trap.

"Uh, uh, uh," was all he could say.

"Uh, uh, uh."

Tears drained from his eyes. They mixed with the blood smeared across his cheeks. Then he vomited.

"Bet you don't notice the pain in your nose anymore, do you?" Eve said.

"Uh, uh, uh."

"We'll send someone from the hospital to attend to you, General," I said. "We'll tell them you suffered a nasty fall in your office and need help. Okay?"

"Uh, uh, uh."

"The pain will be gone in about an hour, General," Eve added, "but you may not want to 'get your stinger wet' for a while."

Washington accompanied Eve and me as we walked to the hospital.

The night critters had begun clearing their throats for their evening's work. Patches of thin mist hung in the air.

"That was quite a story you told the general, sir," Washington said. "True?"

"Some of it."

He smiled. "I won't ask what was and what wasn't."

"Good idea."

"Just know I'll always be on your side."

"Couldn't ask for a better wingman, Captain. Especially one who's got a shovel for a weapon." I couldn't help but laugh when I recalled the incident with the Jap soldier, the kid, on the Ledo Road.

"Well, gotta get back to Burma," he rumbled as we reached the hospital. We all shook hands and traded salutes, and Captain Wendell Washington, 1883rd Engineer Aviation Battalion, United States Army, disappeared into the growing darkness.

We entered the hospital, and Eve asked that a medic be dispatched to General Stone's office. But added that there was no big rush. Then she said to me, "Let's see that hand."

I extended it to her. "I think it's broken."

She examined it. "Nope. Badly bruised, though. Let's get it bandaged." She led me down the hall to an exam room that harbored a few medical supplies.

While she attended to me, she asked about what I'd really told General LeMay.

"Only that I needed a nurse, you, to accompany me on our trip to Urumchi. He bought my story about helping the locals with medical issues."

"But the bit about me being raped by General Stone?"

"Nope. Never mentioned it. I doubt he ever would have stood for it, a lieutenant colonel ratting on one of his fellow flag officers. Besides, he's got a war to fight."

"But you think General Stone bought it?"

"Maybe. Maybe not. But I don't think he wants to find out for sure."

"You're crazy," she whispered.

"Well, there is one more thing."

"Oh?"

"I can still get you an assignment to an island with palm trees, tropical breezes, and bathtub-warm ocean waters."

"Really?" Her blue eyes glistened.

"General LeMay has offered me a job in such a place. And I asked if he needed nurses, too. He said yes."

"Oh, my, back to Hawaii after all?" She hugged me.

"No, a place called Guam."

"Geez. Where all the fighting's been going on recently?"

"US forces took Guam last month. It's part of the Mariana Islands. Includes places like Saipan and Tinian. LeMay says we'll fly our B-29 raids on Japan out of those islands and win the war."

"Well, you sure know how to sweep a gal off her feet, Colonel." She planted her lips on mine and held them there. A long time.

We ended the kiss, and she whispered, "Yeah, I'll accept an assignment to Guam. As long as I can be with my guy and there's no general named Stone within a thousand miles of us." She leaned her head against my shoulder. "We've been through a hell of a lot, haven't we?"

And it all began in Burma, I thought, '*where the dawn comes up like thunder outer China 'crost the Bay!*'

WHEN HEROES FLEW: BLACK THURSDAY
Book 6 of When Heroes Flew

Late 1943: The fate of the air war in Europe hangs in the balance, and Colonel Matt Barrington carries the weight of thousands of lives on his shoulders.

Colonel Matt Barrington knows the cold calculus of WWII strategic bombing. As one of the masterminds behind the US 8th Air Force's daring raids into Nazi Germany, he's accustomed to making decisions that send men to their deaths. But when a mission goes terribly wrong, resulting in the loss of 60 bombers, the weight of command threatens to crush him.

Seeking solace from his guilt-ridden insomnia, Matt finds unexpected comfort in the arms of Charlotte, an English widow, who understands the true cost of the war. Their budding romance offers a glimmer of hope amidst the chaos of conflict. But as the casualties mount, Matt realizes he can no longer lead from behind a desk. Determined to share in the risks his men face, Matt volunteers for a dangerous bombing raid, returning to the skies alongside the soldiers he sends into battle. But surviving one mission only deepens the weight of his guilt.

Haunted by loss and driven by an unyielding sense of duty, Matt defies direct orders and enters the cockpit once more. In a heart-stopping raid high above occupied Europe, he faces not only the lethal forces of the Luftwaffe and their deadly new weapons but also the demons that have long plagued him—and his last chance at a future with Charlotte. As flak bursts around his B-17 and enemy fighters close in, Matt must confront the ultimate question: In the crucible of war, can one man's actions truly make a difference?

Get your copy today at
severnriverbooks.com

AUTHOR'S NOTE

First of all, let me say that Brigadier General Leonard Stone is a creation of my imagination. He is modeled on no one I have ever known or heard about. Flag officers—generals and admirals—in our military are, and always have been, men and women of exceptional integrity, wisdom, and intelligence. An officer such as General Stone would be an exceptionally rare—or maybe even nonexistent—anomaly. But he sure made for a good story.

The majority of the primary characters in *Where the Dawn Comes Up Like Thunder* are fictional. The exceptions are Colonel Dick Ellsworth, the commander of the Tenth Weather Squadron, Major General Curtis LeMay, commander of the Twentieth Bomber Command, and a few other generals briefly mentioned.

Ellsworth was promoted to brigadier general in 1952, then tragically lost his life in a military plane crash in Newfoundland in 1953. LeMay went on to become a four-star general. He commanded the Strategic Air Command for nearly a decade (1948–1957), and eventually became Chief of Staff of the US Air Force in 1961. He retired from the military in 1965 and passed away in 1990 at the age of 83.

Two other officers mentioned in the novel, Majors Spilly Spilhaus and Doug Mackiernan—who helped the Tenth Weather Squadron establish the weather station in Urumchi—were also real characters. Spilhaus spent the bulk of his post-military career as a professor of meteorology at the University of Minnesota. He also became dean of the university's technology institute. He died in 1998 and is interred in Arlington National Cemetery. Mackiernan became the first CIA officer to lose his life in the line of duty. In 1950, he was shot to death, mistakenly, by a Tibetan guard along the China-Tibet border.

While there was an Army Air Forces weather operation established in Urumchi during the war, I moved the date of that event forward a couple of months in the novel to better fit the flow of the story.

The dates and locations of the other military operations depicted in the book—those dealing with the construction of the Ledo Road, the launches of the first B-29 bombing raids on Japan, and the placement of weather observation teams in northern Burma and northeast China—are all true. Also, the military bases depicted are all factual.

In case you're wondering, the anecdote about the work of Japanese researcher Wasaburo Ooishi and his discovery of powerful wintertime winds aloft (winds that later became known as the "jet stream") over Japan in the 1920s is true. Also true is that a large number of African-American soldiers, almost sixty percent of the military construction force, helped hack out the amazing Ledo Road through the Burmese jungle.

As I have stated before in my Author's Notes in other novels, I am fully aware that terms such as Japs and Nips and Chinks are offensive labels these days. But during WWII, such terms were common and accepted. It was a different time then with different sensibilities.

For this novel, I used several of the same books for research that I did for *When Heroes Flew: The Roof of the World*. Those included *Flying the Hump*, by Jeff Ethel and Don Downie, *Hell Is So Green*, by Lt. William Diebold, and *Thor's Legions*, by John F. Fuller. Additional books employed for this novel were *American Warplanes of World War II*, edited by David Donald, *Curtis LeMay*, by Warren Kodak, *Superfortress*, by General Curtis LeMay and Bill Yenne, and *The Superfortress in China*, by Li Xiaowei. The internet offered up a trove of articles, maps, and graphs about operations in the CBI Theater, too, but I always made an effort to turn up additional supporting references.

As always, my cadre of beta readers kept me on the straight and narrow. Barbara, my wife (and an avid reader), always gets first crack at my manuscript and doesn't hesitate to tell me if I've stepped on my poncho. Gary Schwartz has been with me as a beta reader for over a decade, and like Barbara, always speaks his mind. Tom Rodgers helps make sure I've got the flying stuff right. Lee Clevenger, who is a former author and publisher, is also not afraid to tell me what he thinks of my work. (Even though sometimes I might not want to hear it.) And finally, my brother Rick is a wonderful analytical reader. I love 'em all.

A book doesn't come to life without a great publishing team, of course, and that is something that Severn River Publishing offers. There is Andrew Watts, Founder; Amber Hudock, Publishing Director; Julia Hastings, Associate Publisher; Mo Metlen, Social Media Manager; and Kate Schomaker, a superb editor and proofreader who makes me appear a better writer than I really am. All are great people to work with.

Finally, there are my readers, folks like you. Without you, my novel would be meaningless. So thank you so much for inviting me (and Rod and Eve, et al.) into your life.

ABOUT THE AUTHOR

H. W. "Buzz" Bernard is a bestselling, award-winning novelist. A retired Air Force Colonel and Legion of Merit recipient, he also served as a senior meteorologist at The Weather Channel for thirteen years. He is a past president of the Southeastern Writers Association and member of International Thriller Writers, the Atlanta Writers Club, Military Writers Society of America, Willamette Writers, and Pacific Northwest Writers Association. Buzz and his wife live in Kennewick, Washington, along with their fuzzy, strangely docile Shih-Tzu, Stormy... probably misnamed.

Printed in the United States
by Baker & Taylor Publisher Services